DEMON'S TOUCH

A Reverse Harem Tale

Mountain Magic
Book Two

by

Dakota Brown

DEMON'S TOUCH

A Reverse Harem Tale

Mountain Magic, book 1

ISBN: 978-1-945893-14-8

Published by Untold Press LLC
114 NE Estia Lane
Port St Lucie, FL 34983

www.untoldpress.com

PRODUCED IN THE UNITED STATES OF AMERICA

10 9 8 7 6 5 4 3 2 1

Dedication

To Justinn

Thank you for believing in me.

Acknowledgements

I want to start off by thanking all of my readers for helping to make Becoming such a success. I'm thrilled with how well it has been received, and I hope you like Demon's Touch as much, or more. While I'm thanking readers, I want to single out my moderator, Therese. She's responsible for a great deal of fantastic posts on my readers group and is the best!

This series has been an amazing adventure that I never would have started on without people like Jen, Sean, Lizzy, Justinn, Shoshanah, and so many more that I can't even begin to thank you all. Know that if you've been a part of this journey in any way, I really appreciate it.

Chapter 1

Ed

"Oh gods, I can't believe they stayed a week," Sofia groaned dramatically as she led the way to her magical grove. She had created it a couple of weeks ago when Doc had managed to help her access her powers on purpose.

Ed watched Sofia walk, admiring the confident swing to her hips, the short bob she kept her dark brown hair in, knowing it framed dusky skin, brown eyes that probably flashed with her lavender magic, and an absolutely perfect aquiline nose. She held his older brother, Allan's hand.

A small part of him whispered he should be jealous. That he should claim Sofia as his and only his. The other part of Ed, the much louder and happier part, was thrilled she had accepted his pack as her own and was willing to share herself with all of them–that she wanted all of them. Ed told the tiny part of his mind that couldn't quite wrap around sharing Sofia to take a hike and never come back.

Having Sofia's human parents around had been difficult for everyone. Even Victoria, Sofia's roommate and friend, had nearly snapped at her father a few times. For him and Allan, the hardest part had been to remember to keep their hands off Sofia when the folks were around. They thought she was only dating Doc. Doc had managed to evade talking about what he did for a living, because everyone knew Sofia's father, at least, would lose his mind if he knew Doc was also Sofia's teacher. That was awkward enough without having to involve the parents.

It was bad enough that they thought Doc was a mage. Ed had no idea what her parents thought about him and Allan, and he didn't want to know. It had also become apparent that her father had some deep-seated prejudices about Native people that Sofia hadn't known about. He wasn't exactly friendly toward Doc, who was half Native, but he had stopped glaring by the end of the week.

Ed thought Doc deserved a medal for not strangling Dan Collins sometime during the long week. A few times, he had thought Sofia might try.

They had stuck around so long because they were worried about Sofia. Ed got that, but they could have been a little less invasive of her life while they were here. Doc was the only one who had spent any time with her over the week outside of classes, and Ed didn't envy him at all, though he was glad Doc had been able to support her during the week.

After the run in with Alex and his family, who appeared to be the leaders of the local magical black-market ring, Ed had worried Sofia's parents would take her out of school and move her home. Sofia made an easy target because she was a strong untrained mage. Apparently, they thought they could force her to host a greater demon. Not only would that destroy Sofia, but it would give them so much power that they would be free to do whatever they wanted. Including capture or kill Doc, Ed, and Allan.

Fortunately, she had convinced her parents to let her stay. He wasn't sure how. Maybe Doc had used some of his vampire mind control on Dan and Beth Collins. He doubted Doc would admit to it, if he had, though.

That the guys had managed to rescue her, and Doc's promise to teach her magic, had probably also helped. Of course, Doc didn't actually know how to do more than a few simple spells, and by all rights, shouldn't have even been able to do that much. He would do his best, but they really needed to find someone else to teach Sofia.

That led to other complications, but Ed didn't want to think about those right now. Especially after he followed Doc, Allan, and Sofia into the pine grove, and the trees sealed up behind him.

Sofia took a deep breath, tension draining from her as she relaxed in the safe space.

It was the first time the four of them had been in the pine grove together, and the energy of the place sent pleasant shivers up his arms and down his back.

Allan looked down at Sofia. "So, what did you want us all in here for?"

She gave him a wicked grin, grabbed his arm, and tugged him closer. "Maybe I just wanted my pack all together with me in here." She flipped his hand over and ran her fingers lightly over the three wolf paws tattooed on the inside of his wrist. Ed and Doc both had matching tattoos.

Allan blushed, but stepped into her, sliding one arm around her back and the other behind her neck. She pressed her lips to his.

Ed watched, still expecting jealousy to cloud his emotions. Instead, he felt peace. This was how it was supposed to be, his pack all together. Maybe they would have to see about adding a fourth paw to their marks.

Allan came up for air, a grin on his face. "Is that really the reason, or did you have something you wanted to talk about?"

"No, that really was the reason," Sofia replied, eyes shining. "I needed to recharge after a week with my parents hovering over every move I made, and I wanted you all here with me."

"By recharge, did you mean quiet meditation?" Allan's hand wandered lower, cupping her very fine rear, while he nibbled on her neck.

Ed glanced at Doc, wondering how he was taking this. His pack brother had a faint smile on his face, as if amused but also happy.

"Not exactly, but if that's what you'd rather do..." She leaned back, and Allan growled and pulled her back to him.

She laughed and held out a hand toward Ed and Doc, a clear invitation.

Allan glanced toward them, eyes twinkling happily before turning his attention back to Sofia. She was quickly distracted, eyes shut, mouth open slightly as Allan's hands wandered. He hooked his hands under her shirt, and after a quick check to make sure Sofia was okay with it, he pulled her shirt off over her head.

Ed's breath caught at the sight of her bare back. He curled his fingers, wanting to caress her skin.

They had really caught Doc's interest. He stared intently, unable to take his eyes off of her.

"Go," Ed ordered.

Doc hesitated.

"They invited us. You go. I want to watch." He was surprised that he did want to watch. He'd join them later. "And if you're still worried about them wanting you specifically, you just need to get over that. Or do I need to drag you over there?" Ed smirked.

Doc took a deep breath, and Ed thought that if he did actually touch Doc at that moment, he might get more than he intended from the other man. Ed didn't think Doc was actually into guys so much as he didn't care, especially when blood was involved. Doc had never really expressed any sort of interest before, but he certainly hadn't been upset with Allan or Ash when they had kissed him the previous weekend. Of course, Doc had been so high on Ash's demon blood, it was hard to say how the vampire would have reacted without it.

Sofia had Allan's shirt off now, and she ran her hands over his muscular back. She dragged her hand over the claw scars that traced across his shoulder blades. Ed had a matching set across the back of his thigh. The marks had never gone away after the brothers had been turned to werewolves.

Allan and Sofia noticed that they were still alone, and Allan walked Sofia toward them. They got to Doc, and Sofia snatched his arm and dragged him back to the center of the small tree ring. Allan glanced at Ed, and Ed nodded, saying he was still okay.

Sofia pulled the two guys down to the ground. "Need to do something about the hard ground," she laughed.

Apparently, the tree ring was into Sofia's comfort. No sooner had she spoken then a thick moss that probably wasn't native to Colorado pushed up from the ground underneath all of them. Ed shifted and sank to his knees to keep his balance as the thick carpet grew beneath his feet.

"Nice trick," Doc breathed.

Sofia giggled, then gasped, back curving as Doc's hand slid down her belly.

Ed shifted, pants growing tight, starting to think about joining the fun.

Sofia moved so that Allan lay between her and Doc. She trailed her hand down his stomach. Allan groaned when she undid the top button of his jeans.

"Good?" She checked in with Allan.

He nodded, eyes closed.

Ed caught his breath at the same time Allan did, as she slid her hand down the front of his jeans, sliding his zipper down and stroking.

After a few minutes of watching Allan writhe in pleasure under Sofia's touch, Doc hesitantly ran his hand up Allan's arm, and leaned over, his long hair draping over Allan's chest. Sofia must have disintegrated his hair band again. She liked his hair down. Doc had told him about that little trick of hers.

Doc bit down lightly on Allan's neck.

Ed's breath quickened. He wasn't going to be able to just watch much longer. He shifted his attention to Sofia, relishing the enjoyment on her face as she pleasured Allan.

Allan’s back arched, crying out as Doc sank his fangs into Allan's neck.

Sofia's look of pure satisfaction drew Ed to her. Time to join the fun.

Chapter 2

Sofia

"I was starting to wonder if you were just going to watch," I said as Ed sank down behind me. Strong hands gripped my waist and dragged nails up my back.

Allan lay in front of me, content, breathing heavily, but a sleepy drunk smile curling at his lips.

I groaned as Ed worked his teeth up my back, nipping gently, finding my ear and sucking at my earlobe. His fingers found the clasp to my bra, which somehow hadn't yet found its way to the ground.

"Okay?" he whispered in my ear.

"Please," I replied.

He unhooked the clasp with one hand, wrapped his other arm around my waist, and held my stomach, supporting me while I slid my arms out of the straps.

Allan's gaze turned predatory, and I wasn't prepared for the intensity in Doc's eyes as their gazes roamed over me.

I gasped as Ed fondled one of my breasts, squeezing gently. He pressed himself to my back and sucked at my neck gently. I leaned my head back against his shoulder, giving him access.

Doc and Allan traded spaces, and Doc traced his fingers down my stomach. I moaned.

"Looks like it's your turn," Ed beamed.

"Thought I got to play with you this time?" I gasped as Doc undid my jeans.

"You first," Ed whispered.

I cried out as Doc slid his hand into my pants. I was already soaked from my reaction to getting Allan off, and I tilted my leg to give him better access.

One of them growled softly, and Doc's long hair brushed across my breasts as he leaned down and traced kisses across my collarbone while he rubbed. The pleasure built, tightening under my belly, until I was begging for release.

Doc slid a finger into me, and I cried out as my body responded.

Once I stopped trembling, I looked at Doc, whose lips curled, pleased. Unfortunately, he was still wearing his shirt. Fortunately, it gave me something to grab onto. I yanked him forward, planting my mouth on his, not caring that I could still taste Allan's blood on his lips.

"Guess she liked that," Ed purred as he fondled my breasts.

I grinned against Doc's lips, and he returned my smile.

Before Ed could get away from me, I twisted around in his arms and shoved against his shoulders, pushing him to the ground. I straddled him, leaning on his shoulders while he cupped my breasts. Moaning to let him know I approved, I shifted my hips against him. He let out a breath, hands tightening, then sliding down to my hips, holding me against him.

"Now, if you hold me there, how can I get what I want out of you?" I teased him.

Ed's eyes went wide, and I remembered that, while he was my age, he probably wasn't all that experienced, and he acted a bit shyer than either Allan or Doc. Not that I was super experienced myself, but I wasn't hesitant about exploring. Watching to gauge his reaction, I slid my hand down my stomach. His eyes widened as I slowly went lower. He whimpered when I dragged my fingers across the soaked front of my jeans and trailed further until I was reaching between us where I pressed into his hardness.

"Want me to stop?"

"No," he squeaked.

"Good," I purred, and lifted myself slightly so I could stroke my hand along his length.

He trembled beneath me, arousing me further. I didn't want to push him if he wasn't ready, so I leaned forward and nibbled on his ear, much as he had earlier.

"You want to wait?" I whispered. The others would be able to hear, but I could pretend, for a moment, that they didn't have super hearing. They had moved back, letting me and Ed have this moment together.

"No," Ed replied after a slight hesitation.

I rolled over onto my side, pressed up against him, leg hooked around his, and tracked my hand down his stomach, hesitating at his waistline.

"You sure?"

"Yeah." He sounded more certain, and I pressed my lips to his. He moaned, still kissing me, tongue exploring my mouth, as I undid his jeans. He gasped, pushing against me as I ran my hand along his length. He shuddered, and I gave him a minute to get used to someone else touching him.

"Good?"

"Oh yeah," he breathed.

I purred in pleasure as I stroked him. He clutched my shoulder, thrusting against my hand. I couldn't hold him down by laying on him, like he could me, but I kept my leg twined in his and kissed him until he was gasping.

He grabbed my arm. "I'm…"

"Ed, we're all going to have to take showers anyway, but it's up to you." I nibbled at his ear.

He released my arm, met my eyes, and nodded. It didn't take much before Ed was clutching at me hard enough to bruise my arm as he shuddered in release.

I lay next to him, cuddling him. Doc spooned against my back, breathing against my neck, hand on my shoulder, so as not to intrude on Ed's space.

I propped myself up on my arm, thinking we were done for now, but Doc tightened his grip on my shoulder. "We're not done with you yet," he growled, voice low. His tone did things to me that made me not want to be done, ever.

Twisting around to face him, I smirked. "Bring it."

"I intend to."

Despite everything we'd already done that day, I blushed. Doc chuckled as he brought his lips to mine.

It turned out werewolves recovered awfully fast too, and we were thoroughly worn out by the time I let everyone out of the pine grove, and we headed to the cabin, showers, and food.

Chapter 3

Sofia

"Was that always so beat up?" Allan sat next to me on the couch as I turned over the knife I had taken from Alex's house the night they had kidnapped me.

"No. The handle is all cracked now, and the blade actually looks like it is cracking, too. I blocked a magical attack with it. Before it was pristine. Very sharp."

I tested the edge with my finger. "Still sharp." I winced and sucked on my thumb.

"Can you fix it?" Ed came over and sat down on the other side of me, squeezing me in between them. He nuzzled my hair for a moment.

Doc came out of the bedroom wearing flannel PJ pants and drying his hair with a towel. He leaned against the wall, watching as I fiddled with the blade. I spared a quick moment to eye his lean but muscular frame, especially admiring the way his pants perfectly molded to his hips, before re-focusing on the knife.

"Maybe? Probably not, but I could try." Intrigued by the idea of poking at it with my barely usable magic skills, I pushed a little magic into it.

The blade sucked up my power.

"Huh."

The guys stayed quiet, watching me as I pushed more energy at it.

"It's like, it needs me to do something, but I'm not sure what." Lavender moats danced along the blade and sank into the crack in the hilt. "The blade obviously has, or had, some sort of magic, or it wouldn't have been able to block that spell."

I fiddled some more, moving the magic around, playing with *something* in the blade.

"Yeah, I don't think I can fix it." I shrugged and pushed one last time with my magic.

Yelping, I tossed the knife away from us as magic flared. Ed threw himself across my lap, pinning me to Allan, who was also trying to protect me. Doc had jumped in front of us and held his hands up, the air shimmering with a shield, one of the handful of spells he knew how to cast with borrowed magical energy. In this case, my magic.

Doc swore.

I tried to free myself from the tangle of werewolves and peek around Doc, but Ed was still convinced we were under attack.

"Ed, Allan, let her up. I think it's safe."

Doc dropped the shield, and I finally managed to crawl free of the wolves. I came over next to Doc and couldn't resist putting my arm around his bare waist, but the body on the floor had most of my attention.

"What the hell?"

None of us spoke after that, studying the person that had materialized out of the knife, however that was possible.

The body was definitely male, had olive toned skin and shoulder length dark hair. I couldn't see much more than that, though his features didn't seem to be Caucasian. He wore some kind of long, divided, brocade coat thing lined in fur. His boots were leather and of a style I didn't even recognize. If it wasn't for the large bloodstain on the back above his kidney, the jacket would have been really nice. The stain looked fresh.

"Is he still alive?" I managed to say around the shock.

That got the guys moving. Doc knelt next to him. "Barely. Sofia, come here, see if you can help me heal him."

"Me?"

"I know the basics. I just usually don't have enough magic stored up to do more than take care of a stubbed toe."

"You sure you're not a mage?"

"Just been around a while," Doc muttered, clearly distracted as he rolled our guest onto his side.

I sank down next to him and offered him my wrist. Doc glanced at me and smiled. "Let's see if I can guide your magic first."

"Okay."

"Just put your hands on him and call on your magic and see if you can follow what I'm doing."

"Sure." I hoped I wouldn't cause whoever this was to die, because I had no idea what I was doing.

I put my hands on the stranger's arm and called on my magic. I poured it into the guy. Lavender sparked across him, and blue sparkles rose to join them. I nearly lost my concentration in surprise.

"He's a mage," Allan exclaimed.

"Looks like it," Doc replied tightly. He put his hands on top of mine, and I let him direct my magic. We sank deeper into the unconscious man's body. The wound pricked at me, as if leaching energy from anything that touched it. Not only had he been stabbed, but he'd been poisoned, too. Doc showed me how to use my magic to repair the wound, and then he withdrew from the connection.

"He's going to need more than that to recover," Doc said. "That poison is nasty, whatever it was."

"Are you going to save him?" Allan sank down next to us.

Doc sighed and pulled one of the beaded bracelets off of his arm. He wore identical wide bracelets on each wrist. They stored a little magical energy, giving him an extra edge against mages in combat. Not that the half-vampire normally needed much help unless he was also defending others. They had been his mother's, a Navajo vampire hunter at the turn of the last century.

"Suppose we should try."

Doc's energy changed as he let his vampire half take over, and he bit down on his wrist. Vampire blood had a lot of nifty qualities, one of them being that it could help heal the poor sod on our floor. It wasn't well known, and vampires preferred it that way. They were one of the more powerful supernatural beings, and one of the more reclusive.

Blood welled on Doc's wrist, and Ed rolled the guy over and tilted his head back.

Though the wound was slowly healing, the guy's life force faded as the poison worked.

The moment Doc's blood hit the guy's system, a jolt ran through my entire body, transmitted from the injured guy. He sucked in a breath, shuddering as Doc's blood helped me combat the poison, though he remained unconscious.

For a few moments, I wasn't sure it was going to be enough, that we were too late. I poured more magic into him, determined to save him, though I had no idea who he even was. My hold on my magic weakened. It was only in the last couple of weeks that I'd even tried to do anything on purpose other than fix my hair, and I still really didn't know what I was doing.

I lost my grasp on the lavender motes of magic and collapsed across the newcomer, trembling with exertion.

Doc pulled me into his arms, and I shivered. "Were we too late?"

"No, I don't think so," Doc replied. "Ed, Allan, see if you can get him into my room."

Doc helped me to my feet and brushed a strand of my short hair out of my face. It stuck to my face, and my shirt clung to my body. Everything was soaked, as if I'd run a marathon in the Nebraska summer. Exhaustion tugged at me.

Protesting when Doc swept me off my feet earned me a kiss on the forehead.

"You're beat, let me carry you. We'll get our guest cleaned up, and you can rest."

I rested against Doc's shoulder and enjoyed being held in his strong arms. "So, does this happen often? Strange men appearing in your living room?"

Doc laughed. "No. Unless I'm forgetting something, this is certainly a first for me."

"How, exactly, was he in the knife?"

"Hopefully, we'll be able to ask that question soon." Doc put me down on his king-sized bed. When you shared with two werewolves and now me, you needed more space than a queen allowed. He kissed my forehead and went over to the other side where Ed and Allan stared at the stranger.

"Let's see if we can get his shirt off and check his wound. We can see if Sofia got it closed up and check to see if it looks infected," Doc ordered.

Between the three of them, they had the stranger's shirt off in short order.

"That looks like it hurt." Allan winced, pointing to the guy's chest. A diagonal scar ran from his collarbone to the opposite hipbone.

"Sword," Doc commented before gently rolling the guy over onto his stomach and looking at his back.

We all flinched.

The knife wound was closed, but whoever had stabbed him hadn't done it cleanly, and while the scar wasn't too bad, the person had done more than just slide the knife in, they had twisted it.

"Wonder what he did to deserve that," Ed puzzled.

"Pissed someone off," Allan replied.

Doc put his hand over the wound. "It's not hot, so we probably got all of the infection, and his heart is beating normally now, so he'll probably recover."

"He looks Asian," Ed suggested when they rolled him back over onto his back and covered him with a blanket.

"Not quite," Allan replied.

"Yeah…" Ed trailed off. "Strange."

"Well, whoever he is," I said. "I hope he's friendly." He didn't look much older than the rest of us, though I knew that could be deceiving.

The guys looked at me, then back at the guy on the other side of the bed. Their expressions darkening from curiosity to suspicion.

"Let's hope," Allan agreed.

∞ ∞ ∞

I drifted in and out of consciousness, recovering from the magical exertion, while Ed, Allan, and Doc rotated keeping watch on us.

Warm hands caressed my cheek, and I opened my eyes. Ed pressed his lips to mine gently before whispering, "Allan and I are going to go run. If he's not awake by the time we get back, join us in my room?" His eyes shone with hope.

"I will."

Ed's sky-blue eyes lit up with joy, and I couldn't help but smile.

He kissed me again before leaving the room.

Thirsty, and wanting a shower after being drenched in sweat earlier, I got up.

Doc glanced up from the tablet he was staring at, the light from the screen illuminating his face in the otherwise dimly lit room.

"Whatcha doing?" I came over. He put the tablet down in his lap and put his arm around me until I was leaning against him and the chair he sat in.

"Grading papers from one of my upper level classes."

"You know, you have yet to give us anything other than reading assignments."

Doc cleared his throat, looking uncomfortable. "This may be the year my freshman history class gets A's for showing up."

"Oh?"

"Yeah. I find myself not wanting to grade a certain student's assignments."

"Oh." I blushed. "Sorry."

"It is far more my fault than yours, Sofia. I'll have to give a final, just don't fail that, and it should be fine."

I laughed. "Sure, Mr. Cassidy."

He groaned. "Gods, please don't call me that."

"Ha." I planted a kiss on his cheek and headed for the bathroom.

The hot shower drained away some of the stress and tension from my shoulders along with washing away the sweat from earlier. I didn't linger, not really wanting to leave Doc alone with the stranger for too long. Not that he couldn't take care of himself, but it still worried me. As soon as I turned the shower off, I heard voices, so I hurried through drying off, threw on a pair of Doc's flannel pants and one of Ed's shirts, though they were all a little too big, and stepped out into the bedroom.

The newcomer was sitting up in the bed, back pressed against the headboard, looking terrified.

Doc hadn't moved from his chair, but he had put the tablet down, and I knew from experience he could cross the room before any of us could blink.

The new guy turned to look at me, but Doc kept his attention directed toward the potential threat.

"Hi." I tried to sound welcoming.

He tilted his head, as if trying to figure out what I said.

Finally, he replied. It sounded like a greeting, but I didn't know the language. I looked at Doc. "Do you understand him?"

"No. Sounds Russian, though."

I pointed to myself. "Sofia."

That he understood. He said something, then my name, following with pointing at himself. "Nikolai Orlov."

"Nikolai. This is Doc." I pointed.

"Doc." Nikolai nodded his head. He relaxed a little, but his shoulders were still tense and his eyes darted around the room. He said something else that, to me, had the cadence of where am I.

"There doesn't happen to be any magic that will help you understand us, is there?" I really didn't know the full extent and limitations of magical power. I only knew the stories people told. Growing up in a non-magical family, even though I possessed the ability, had a lot of disadvantages. Including being completely untrained.

Nikolai stared at me, and I got the idea he was trying to decide if he was safe or not. As long as he was friendly, he was safe, but he had no way to know that. Though hopefully waking up healthy and not restrained was a clue. Though, by the way he eyed Doc, he knew the other man was dangerous.

I held my hands up and let lavender sparkles dance across my palms.

Nikolai's eyes went wide, his gaze darting between me and Doc. If anything, he pressed himself further into the headboard.

Pulling my magic back into myself, I dropped my hands and tried to look non-threatening.

"It's okay. We're friends."

He studied both of us for a few more minutes while I tried not to move. I was guessing he was a trained mage, but either he had an idea that Doc could get to him before he could cast a spell, or he was still exhausted from whatever had happened to him, because he didn't look like he was about to try and do any magic.

Finally, he held out his hand to me, though he kept his fearful gaze locked on Doc.

I glanced at the vampire as well. Doc frowned and fluidly rose from the chair. He usually managed to keep his movements more on the human side, though he moved with a fighter's grace all the time. Right now, he wasn't trying to blend in.

Nikolai paled and babbled something that definitely sounded like a version of vampire.

Doc put his hands on my shoulders, claiming me. Nikolai nodded somewhat frantically before holding his hand out to me again.

"I don't think he's going to hurt me," I said.

"I'm not getting that impression, either," Doc replied. He kissed my cheek and then stepped back.

Heart beating a little faster, I closed the distance between myself and Nikolai. I put my hand into his. Though his fingers were long and elegant, his palms had rough callouses, and his gentle grip did nothing to disguise the strength in his hands.

He climbed out of the bed, letting the blanket the guys had covered him with fall away, and stood in front of me. His pants looked to be of some sort of fine linen, and they hugged his hips. Nikolai's muscles were a little more defined than Doc, but not nearly as muscular as the wolves. I met his dark brown eyes and noticed a shine of the same rich blue as his magic.

Nikolai glanced at Doc, clenched his jaw as if frustrated, and said something that sounded like he was trying to reassure both of us. Then he cupped my cheeks with his hands and blue motes of magic filled the air around us.

My magic responded on its own, or Nikolai was doing something to call it up as well, until we stood in a small light show of our own making.

"Sofia?" Doc murmured softly.

"It's okay," I answered.

The magic tingled through us, pulling at me. I let it tug me along, pull me into Nikolai's gaze, until he blinked and let go of my face.

I took a step back and raised my eyebrows as I looked around. We stood in an ornate room I had never seen before. The floor looked to be white marble. The pillars, probably also marble. Gold gilt covered the walls, and lamps in sconces lit the space. For all of the ornateness of the building, there weren't any pictures on the walls, and that surprised me.

"Where are we?"

"I have that very same question."

I jumped, not expecting to understand Nikolai.

"Your vampire, he will not attack me for this?"

I brought my attention fully back to Nikolai. He was fully dressed in the same clothing we had found him in. "How did you know?"

"He is not the first vampire I have met, and I could taste blood in my mouth when I woke. I assume the two of you healed me?" He winced, probably with the memory of being stabbed in the back.

"Yes, we did. And no, as long as he doesn't think you're hurting me, he won't."

He sighed in relief. "They can be very territorial. And to answer your question, we are still standing in that very strange room I woke in, but I've brought our consciousnesses to a place where we can converse. It is a thing mages do. You are not familiar?"

I shook my head. I didn't want to admit I knew next to nothing about magic, but I was probably going to have to tell him.

"I would echo your question. Where have I woken?"

"Colorado."

He frowned. "I'm not familiar with this place."

"It's in America."

Nikolai still obviously had no idea what I was talking about.

"Um, where are you from?"

"Most recently, Moscow. I'm the high mage of Prince Ivan Vasilyevich. Well, he is the regent for Vasily, but he will soon be fully in charge."

I stared at him.

"You know these names?" He sounded hopeful.

"Well, I mean, I know Moscow."

"Perhaps I should ask what year it is," he inquired hesitantly.

I told him.

He paled.

"Nikolai?"

"Tell me, does Russia still stand?"

I raised my eyebrows, but I nodded.

"And the Mongols?"

"There is a Mongolia, but if you're talking like, Genghis Khan type Mongols, not really." I knew very little about that region, but Nikolai's shoulders eased, and he took a breath.

"So, what time are you from then?"

"Fourteen fifty-five."

"Oh."

"It appears I was trapped for a very long time." He sighed. "Damn Roza, anyway."

"What happened?"

"I believe I will be answering this question many times in the near future. Perhaps it would save a bit of time if I answered you and, did you say his name was Doc? At the same time."

"Yeah. Well, it's Roy Cassidy, but Doc's his nickname."

"Curious. Well, I do not believe I can bring you here every time I need to have a conversation with someone so that you can translate for me, as much as I am enjoying having you in my space." He winked at me. "Would you be willing to give me your language. I will trade, of course."

"Give it to you?"

"I can take the knowledge of your language and transfer it to myself. It is common knowledge in my day, but perhaps it has been lost to time? It's not a perfect solution, still takes time to fully adapt to the new language."

I shrugged. "I still retain my knowledge, right?"

"Of course. And I will trade you. I know several languages. What would you find most useful? I speak Russian of course. The Mongolian tongue. Many regional dialects that will probably be less useful to you. I do not know enough Chinese for it to be a fair trade. Perhaps Russian?"

"I, uh, sure. Though I'm willing to bet the language has shifted quite a bit since you learned it."

"Perhaps, but you will always be able to understand me."

That idea pleased him, so I shrugged. "Sure, why not."

He tilted his head as if trying to understand my phrasing. "Thank you. I'll bring us back so you can explain to your friend. I don't want him to worry."

"Sure."

He stepped back over to me and cupped my chin and drew me back into his gaze. After a moment, I could tell we had shifted back. I felt heavier, though I hadn't noticed the lightness before.

"Sofia?" Doc did sound worried, so it was probably just as well Nikolai had returned us to a normal state of consciousness.

"It's okay. So, uh, Nikolai is from Russia. Like, fourteen fifty's Russia."

Doc swore.

"Yeah, that's kind of what he said when I told him what year it was. He's going to, uh, trade me languages so we can talk."

"Convenient," Doc replied.

"Well, I'm glad we won't have to teach him English the hard way."

Nikolai watched our exchange, eyes wide with worry.

"He definitely knows you're a vampire, though."

"I could tell," Doc said tightly.

Nikolai still cradled my face in his hands, and his hands tensed at Doc's tone.

I put my hand on Nikolai's muscular forearm and squeezed, trying to reassure him.

I wasn't sure it worked, but he tore his attention away from Doc and met my gaze.

He asked something that was probably the equivalent of 'ready.'

I nodded.

Our magic spiraled around us again, tingling through us. My eyes widened when Nikolai leaned down and pressed his lips to mine.

Chapter 4

Sofia

I wasn't sure how long we stood there, the magic connecting us as whatever spell Nikolai had cast worked, but when the magic finally released us, my legs trembled and my limbs dragged at me. Nikolai stepped back and dropped his hands, though he grinned and winked at me.

I smiled, though he hadn't really kissed me so much as pressed his lips to mine, as if transferring the languages through the contact. Maybe that's what he had done.

"It takes a little while for the language to fully integrate," Nikolai explained in Russian. "You should be able to understand me right away, but speaking properly will take a little practice."

I nodded, grinning. It wasn't that the words translated to English in my head, so much as I automatically just understood them like I did English. "Neat!" It came out in Russian, and I clapped my hands over my mouth.

He laughed. "Your accent is atrocious."

"Because yours is going to be any better?" I grumbled that in English.

"Perhaps," he answered slowly.

Oh, I was so wrong. Russian colored the way he spoke the word, and it pleased me to no end.

Nikolai arched an eyebrow. I just shrugged, trying not to grin.

A low growl interrupted us. We both turned sharply.

"Ed," Doc warned quietly.

The werewolf subsided, but both blond werewolves glared at Nikolai.

"You have werewolves, too?" He said that slowly in English, as if testing the words as he spoke them.

While I enjoyed Doc's heavier western drawl, and Ed and Allan's light one, I could listen to Nikolai speak all day and I'd never get tired of it. Of course, I never got tired of listening to Doc, either. If I could find a way to do it without it being totally weird, I'd have to see if I could get him to keep the accent even if he learned to speak without it.

Clearly, I would have to work on mine, however.

"Uh, yeah, we're one big happy pack," I replied.

"Don't look terribly happy." To his credit, he didn't step behind me, but he probably wanted to.

"Well, you know, possessive."

He nodded.

"So, Ed," I pointed at the lighter colored werewolf, "Allan." I pointed at the slightly darker blond wolf. "And you've met Doc. Everyone, this is Nikolai."

"Hello," Nikolai ventured hesitantly.

Ed growled again, turned, and stalked out of the room. Allan huffed and followed his brother.

"Would you like something to eat?" Doc glanced at both of us.

"Please."

I nodded.

"Is there a shirt I can borrow until I repair mine?" Nikolai touched his back where the knife wound had been, fingers tracing the scar.

Doc, not looking completely happy, though less upset than the werewolves, dug in his dresser and tossed one of his T-shirts to the mage.

"My thanks."

"Sure. Sofia, would you mind making something? I would subject Nikolai to my cooking, but he did just recover from being poisoned. I'd hate to poison him again." Doc half smiled at his joke.

"Okay."

After studying the shirt for a moment, Nikolai pulled it on, and I couldn't help but notice the way his muscles bunched and rippled as he put the shirt on. It was one of the many plain T-shirts Doc owned. This one was blue. They were similar enough in size that Doc's clothing would probably fit Nikolai, though we might need to take him shopping.

I paused on my way out the door. Nikolai literally had the clothing on his back and that was it. Well, and his magic. He didn't even have knowledge of the world today. He had probably already figured that out, but it couldn't be a good feeling.

"Do you not have servants?" Nikolai followed closely behind me, glancing over his shoulder. Doc stalked after us.

I didn't know if the guys were picking up some vibe I was missing or if they were simply acting protective, but I didn't sense any ill intent from our guest.

"Servants? Um, no?"

He sighed, though I got the impression it was from his lack of knowledge, not our lack of servants. I could have been wrong, though.

Nikolai stayed silent, but I could see him looking around curiously. I wondered how the guys' cabin compared to what he was used to. Clearly, it wasn't the palace or castle or whatever he had lived in back in his own time, but it was a nice cabin. Most of the lights were off, though the lamp by the couch and loveseat was on. Doc didn't seem to need light at all to see easily, and Allan and Ed didn't need much more. They had probably left the light on more for me than anything.

Nikolai studied the lamp but then the window caught his eye. Though it was dark outside, he walked over to it. He touched the glass, pressing his fingers against it, before looking out. The living room overlooked the valley, and the lights from the small town and the college glittered in the distance.

I flipped the light on in the kitchen. I could navigate the cabin in near darkness, but I needed light to cook.

Nikolai came in and studied the light fixture before frowning, his gaze sweeping over the appliances. His shoulders sagged.

"Grab a seat."

He did, studying the table. The werewolves padded into the kitchen. Ed laid down near the refrigerator. Allan laid down near

Nikolai. Doc leaned against the far wall, arms crossed, studying Nikolai.

"What do you like to eat?" I had no idea what to make for a Russian from the fourteen-hundreds.

"I shall have to be adventurous, I suppose."

I glanced at Doc. He shrugged.

Ed got up and stuck his head in the fridge. He touched a package of hamburger with his nose before glancing up at me.

I rubbed his ears, and he dropped his jaw in a wolfy grin.

"Hamburgers it is."

"Do you think you're up to telling us what happened to you?" Doc's voice carried its normal friendly cadence.

"Yes."

I got a glass of water for Nikolai and handed it to him.

He glanced at me, hesitated as if trying to figure something out, before he nodded. "Thank you."

"You're welcome."

"I am…" He paused before shaking his head. "I was high mage for Prince Ivan Vasilyevich. Quite a nice post, but not without dangers. We are—were fighting off Mongols and were often out in field, but earned place at court finally, as the fighting began to settle down."

"Is that how you got the scar across your chest?" I squished the ground meat into individual patties and threw them on the griddle. It would have been better to use the grill, but I didn't want to miss the story.

"Yes, unlucky blow. Fortunately, Peter was there to save me."

He didn't elaborate, and I saved that question for another time.

"With many mages dying in combat, I needed to train others and had several students. One in particular, Roza, showed quite a lot of promise."

I wasn't sure if Nikolai was lost in his memories while he spoke, or if he was ignoring the werewolves. Both of them perked up when he mentioned students.

Doc glanced at me. I shrugged.

"Turns out, along with quite a lot of promise, she had quite a lot of ambition. Ivan was a friend of mine and it was highly unlikely he would replace me. I was popular with many of the nobles, despite my mixed heritage. Father was a Tatar invader. Mother a Russian noble. She killed him escaping from his camp and made it back to Moscow. It is rather fortunate I turned up with magical abilities, or my life may have been quite different and likely much shorter.

"Roza somehow devised a nasty trap, stabbed me in back, and well, now am here." He took a drink of the water.

Doc pushed off the wall and went into the living room, returning a moment later with the broken knife. He put it on the table.

Nikolai shuddered. "How did you come to be in possession of that?"

"I stole it from some mages," I explained. "They kidnapped me, and I used it to escape."

Nikolai smiled.

Knowing he would ask, I continued as I flipped the burgers. "I actually used it to block a spell, which is how it got so damaged. I've had it for about a week, and I was poking at it with magic and I think I unlocked it."

"Thank you both for saving me. I appreciate it. Though, I don't know what to do with myself now." He stared at the table again.

I made a burger for him, since I doubted he would have much experience with them, then I made one for myself and brought them both over to the table.

"You guys hungry?" I looked at the wolves.

They traded a look before giving me the wolf equivalent of 'no duh.'

Laughing, I put a couple of burgers on plates for them. "Floor? Table?"

"They can eat on the floor. The chairs aren't really big enough for wolves," Doc said as he went over to the refrigerator and pulled out a protein drink.

I put the plates down, petting both of the wolves, before sitting at the table. Doc joined us. Nikolai watched me while I picked up my burger and took a bite. He did the same, eyes raising.

We ate in silence. Though it was quite late, we were all hungry, and the food disappeared quickly.

"Nikolai, you can stay with us for now," Doc offered after we had finished. "It would be terribly unfair to turn you lose on the world as it is right now." He smiled.

"My thanks. I will try not to be too much of a burden."

"You can repay us by teaching Sofia magic."

Nikolai looked at me and frowned, a faint hint of panic crossing his face before he shook his head. "I can't," he replied.

"Why?" Doc's voice had taken on a hint of danger, though at the moment, Nikolai looked more afraid of me than the vampire.

"Surely she's already trained. She's an adult."

"It's a long story we'll tell you later, but she's not."

"I see. I suppose." He looked confused again but finally shrugged. "I do not train people who are already in relationships. Is unnecessarily complicated. Nearly got me killed. Twice. I was not even trying to interfere in their relationship." He sipped his water.

The wolves both growled.

"Guys, we'll talk about it later. The poor guy has had his entire world turned upside down, and I'm sure we're all tired. Let's get some rest," Doc said.

"Doc, do you maybe want to show Nikolai how to use the shower and everything? Spare toothbrush, things like that?"

Doc's eyes widened, and I wasn't sure he had considered the implications of Nikolai's predicament until just then. The Russian mage was handling himself well, but there was almost nothing familiar for him in the modern world.

"Yes. Ed, Allan, which one of you wants to give up your room?" Doc stood.

The two wolves looked at each other before Allan huffed and nodded.

"Nikolai, wait here a moment, and I'll get some clothes for you," Doc ordered as he left the kitchen.

The mage nodded, pressing his hands together on the table and staring at them.

I couldn't even imagine how he felt. I put my hand on his shoulder and squeezed. He shot me a grateful look.

Doc returned quickly, a pile of clothes in his arms. Nikolai followed Doc out of the room.

I sighed, exhausted. "Come on, guys. Let's go to bed."

The wolves padded along behind me, and I climbed into bed. Ed lay with his head on my chest, and Allan trapped my legs. They left one side open for Doc, but it was almost an hour before he joined us. He curled up around me, his face buried in my hair. The wolves were solidly asleep, but I woke up.

"He going to be okay?"

"Probably. He doesn't seem like the type to give up." Doc kissed my neck.

"Starting shit?" I grinned.

"I'm exhausted. You're exhausted. I just wanted to kiss you, and you're trapped under a couple hundred pounds of werewolf." I could hear the smile in his voice.

"Damn."

He laughed.

"But you're right. I'm beat."

Doc slid his hand under Ed and hugged me against him. "Good night, Sofia."

"Night."

∞ ∞ ∞

As usual, the wolves were up before me the next day and Doc had stayed curled around me, holding me until I woke. The smells of breakfast were probably what had pulled me out of one of the deepest sleeps I'd managed since I'd found out why the magic mafia—my term for the local group of black market mages—was after me.

"Morning," Doc mumbled into my hair.

"Were you waiting for me to wake up?"

"Maybe," he drawled.

"You don't have to, you know." I felt bad keeping him.

"I like waking up with you in my arms, and I didn't want you to wake up alone." He nuzzled my neck.

"I like it, too," I replied a little breathily, heart fluttering in my chest.

"Good." He trailed kisses along my jaw.

I rolled over to face him, tangling my legs in his and burying my hand in his hair, pulling him in for a kiss.

We enjoyed each other for a moment, but it didn't take long before we broke apart. My stomach was growling despite the late dinner, and we both wanted to make sure Ed and Allan hadn't traumatized Nikolai too much.

After a quick trip to the bathroom, I joined everyone in the kitchen. Nikolai was sitting stiffly in a chair against the back wall, watching. He looked uncomfortable wearing Doc's jeans and T-shirt, but they fit well enough. Maybe a little tight across the shoulders. Doc stared at a tea kettle, boiling water for tea. I was glad he was a tea drinker. I hadn't been able to touch a latte since Alex had spelled me with one when they had kidnapped me.

Doc glanced at me, lifting an eyebrow. I nodded.

Allan and Ed were busy making a mountain of food. I really did wonder how Doc managed to afford to feed them sometimes, but then he didn't eat much himself, so maybe it balanced out.

Ed saw me, and his eyes sparkled. He came over, grabbed my hand, and tugged me to my normal chair before planting a kiss on my cheek.

I happened to glance at Nikolai. His eyebrows were raised and his eyes bounced from us to Doc.

Right, so we were going to have to have that conversation sometime soon. Oh well.

Allan dropped a Sofia sized helping of pancakes, bacon, and eggs in front of me. Ed brought me juice, and Doc put a mug of black tea with a little sugar in front of me. They always took care of me, but this was a little over the top. Either they were as glad my parents were gone as I was, or they were feeling extra possessive.

Except then, Ed went and did something really weird. He invited Nikolai over to sit next to me. I really didn't think he was trying to hook me up with the Russian mage, even though the behavior was similar to when he was trying to hook me up with

Doc. I traded a confused look with Allan, who shrugged. Finally, I just decided I might not actually ever understand Ed and just went with it. It was his spot he had given up. Doc sat next to me, a slight frown on his face, and Allan sat on the other side of Doc like normal.

Nikolai didn't say much, just watched what we did with our food before also eating. Doc had also given him a mug of tea, and Nikolai sipped it thoughtfully.

"So, what are we doing today?" I leaned back once I had finished as much food as I could eat. The original plan had been to head to the lake, but I guessed that had changed.

"You, Nikolai, and I are going to head to town and get him some clothing and boots. Believe it or not, it will snow in a couple of weeks," Doc answered. "Ed and Allan are going to stay here and burn energy."

I raised my eyebrows. "No way."

"Always snows before Halloween, and it's almost October."

The weather had cooled significantly since I had arrived only a few weeks ago. The air had a bite to it that it hadn't had when we first arrived, and I was finally starting to remember to dress in layers.

"And then we're going to stop by the college and see if we can get Nikolai permission to audit classes for the rest of the semester. Maybe call him an exchange student or something. He needs to start getting used to the world as it is now, and that will be a decent place to start. I need to get him an ID, too. I know someone who can help. We will get that sorted this week."

"College?" Nikolai ventured dubiously.

Doc nodded. "Also, Nikolai, you need to understand, you cannot under any circumstances tell anyone you're a mage, or mention that any of us aren't human."

"I cannot?" He frowned. "Why?"

"You have a lot of history to catch up on, but the short version is that shortly after you vanished into your magical prison, the Renaissance happened. The church turned humanity against the supernatural world, and those who didn't go into hiding were killed. It's only been recently that any supernatural beings have reemerged, and it's still not safe."

"Oh." He stared at his hands for a moment. "I will, of course, not say anything."

"There's a lot more you need to know, but for now, just pretend you're a friend of mine from Russia. Maybe instead of a student, I'll say your visiting and wish to observe American classes. Then you can shadow all of us."

"I will attempt to be unobtrusive," he offered tightly.

Nikolai was clearly unhappy, but I could think of a lot of reasons why that might be, so I didn't question him.

Chapter 5

Sofia

"How do you do it?" Nikolai asked when we stepped outside.

"Do what?" Doc glanced at the Russian mage.

"Go out in the sunlight."

"Oh. I'm only half-vampire." Doc opened his door and climbed in the cab.

Nikolai stared, his gaze darting between Doc and the pickup. "What…I don't even know what to ask right now." He sighed and rubbed his forehead

"It's called a truck," I explained. "Here, you can sit up front so you can see better."

Nikolai jumped when Doc turned the diesel on, glared at the vampire, then followed me to the passenger side door which I opened for him.

He awkwardly climbed in. Not admiring Nikolai's very fine ass while he got in was impossible with the way the borrowed jeans fit him, and I just hoped no one noticed my attention.

I hopped up on the running board and grabbed his seatbelt. "Need to strap in. I'll show you this time."

I leaned across the mage and slid the buckle into the slot. "You release it by pushing this button here."

He looked down and touched the button. "Thank you."

"Sure." I hopped off the running board and shut his door for him and then climbed in the back.

Nikolai looked like he was trying to stare at everything as Doc drove down the narrow dirt driveway.

My phone chimed, and I pulled it out.

Victoria: Girl! How's it going with all those hot guys?

I couldn't help myself. I giggled as I replied.

Sofia: Picked up another hot guy.

Victoria: What!

Sofia: LOL. Long story short…actually, I don't think I can explain over text. I'll tell you tonight. Not dating him or anything.

Victoria: You'd better.

Sofia: We're actually headed to town if you want to join us.

Victoria: Naw, catch you tonight. Working on a paper.

Sofia: Later.

Victoria responded with a thumbs up icon.

Nikolai had twisted around and was watching me, but he didn't ask what I was doing. He had so much to learn about.

"Hey, Nikolai, can you do the language transfer thingy with other knowledge?"

"Thingy?" He drew the word out as if trying to figure out what it meant. After a moment, I thought he gave up. "Yes."

"Do you want to, you know, just grab a bunch of my memories and see if that helps you get up to speed with the world as it currently is?"

"Ah. I believe I will be able to manage on my own."

"Okay, cool." I wasn't as convinced as he sounded, but he could always ask me later if he changed his mind.

"I'll teach him to use the internet," Doc said.

Nikolai was again glued to the window as we pulled into town. Doc drove through the downtown touristy area and headed toward the outlet shops. Before long, he parked, and Doc and I got out. Nikolai managed his seatbelt, but he couldn't figure out the door. I tried not to laugh, it really wasn't funny, and opened the door for him. "Here's the latch for next time." I demonstrated, and Nikolai nodded stiffly.

Fortunately, the store wasn't very busy. It was very interesting to watch Nikolai's reactions to everything. He had literally never seen or even imagined most everything he was experiencing. He walked nearly on top of me, tense, but not saying anything.

Finally, after a quick glance at Doc, I took Nikolai's hand, uncurled his fingers, and slid my hand into his. Doc nodded his approval and went back to throwing things our Russian friend might need into a cart he pushed.

"I'm glad you're basically my size," Doc mused. "We don't have to try anything on."

As we worked our way through the store, Nikolai relaxed a little, though only so that he wasn't crushing my hand in his grip. He certainly wasn't comfortable.

I eyed a lavender flannel shirt that matched my magic. Doc noticed and grinned at me, tossing it in the cart with everything else.

It took a little time to work our way through the various outlets, but by the time Doc was done, Nikolai had clothes for the season, a couple of different jackets, a pair of hiking boots and a pair of winter snow boots, gloves, and a hat.

"Hungry?" Doc asked after putting the bags in the truck.

I hadn't been until he mentioned it, but then I was ravenous. "Yeah."

Nikolai didn't answer, but he had to be hungry.

"What do you want, Sofia?"

"Um," I glanced at Nikolai. He looked stressed. "Let's just grab fast food, hit the college, and get back."

Doc followed my glance to Nikolai and nodded. "Drive through it is."

Nikolai clutched my hand so hard, I thought my fingers might be turning blue.

"You have another boyfriend?"

I yelped at a very familiar and unwelcome voice and spun around. Doc was already in front of me, and I stepped in front of Nikolai, though he was probably more than capable of defending all of us. Alex stood a few feet away from us, arms crossed, glaring at me.

We had the truck at our backs, but I hoped Alex wasn't going to start something. I couldn't help the tremors of fear as my heart started racing. Seeing Alex reminded me too much of being kidnapped. Nikolai put his hands on my shoulders as I pressed him into Doc's truck with my back.

"No, why?" I managed to stammer.

"You were holding his hand."

"Some cultures hold hands with friends, Alex," I growled. "Nik is an old friend." Pitching my voice low and switching to Russian, I whispered, "Don't talk if you can avoid it." Doc still blocked most of Alex's view of me, so he probably didn't notice.

Nikolai squeezed my shoulders in agreement.

"You're looking pretty good for someone who got stabbed a week ago." I managed to get my voice back under control, and it came out sounding strong and pissed. I certainly was pissed.

"Fortunately, I wasn't alone." He glanced around. "You look good for someone who's sleeping with a vampire. Not anemic?"

Doc growled.

"Can I roast him," Nikolai whispered in Russian.

"I wish."

Alex, his warning delivered, smiled and left. The reminder that he, and the others, knew our secrets, sent chills down my spine and made my heart race in fear.

Nikolai held me against him while we watched Alex get into his red Mustang and drive off.

Doc finally took a breath and turned toward us. He didn't even seem upset that Nikolai was holding me while I shook.

"Fuck," I growled after a minute.

"Why did we not attack him, if he is so dangerous?"

"Unfortunately, in these days, if we got caught, it could really land us in trouble. Like, jail or dead." I hugged myself.

Doc nodded. "We need to solve this particular problem before it blows up for all of us. Unfortunately, I don't know how." He clenched his fists and glared in the direction Alex had driven.

"Yeah, well, not going to happen on an empty stomach. Let's go."

Doc opened the door for Nikolai, and the mage climbed in a bit more gracefully this time.

I got in the back, and Doc got in the driver's seat.

Nikolai turned to look at me once the diesel was running. "Who was that?"

I sighed. "Someone I'm really glad I didn't end up dating."

The mage laughed. "Yes, he seems disagreeable."

"Very."

Doc and I filled Nikolai in on that part of the story while we got food and parked in a valley overlook to eat.

∞ ∞ ∞

Doc left us alone in the truck while he ran inside the admin building. It was Sunday afternoon, but he thought he could at least get a guest pass for Nikolai for the next couple of days.

"There is something I cannot figure out," Nikolai said, switching to Russian. The language caressed my ears.

"Only one thing?" I answered slowly, testing the words, enjoying my ability to speak the new language.

"Ah. Yes, many things. But one question for now, I suppose. You and Doc are married, yes?"

The question took me by surprise, leaving me speechless for a moment. "Well, we're together, anyway." Marriage hadn't even crossed my mind yet. How on earth would we handle something like that? If we even decided to go there. That was a conversation we needed to have sometime in the future.

"Ed and Allan? They…" He trailed off as if unsure how to continue. He waved his hand around for a minute before sighing.

"I'm with all of them."

"Married to all of them?"

I thought about letting him flounder for a while, but his life was hard enough right now. Those questions were a little personal, though I supposed he was living with us, so he needed to know our dynamic. "No, just together. Like I said, one happy wolf pack."

"Ah. Werewolves and their packs. I see. Though I am surprised Doc went along with it. The supernatural community does treat such things a bit different than regular humans. I suppose that hasn't changed much."

"He's been part of their pack longer than they have known me."

Nikolai nodded. "I see. You truly are untrained?"

"My birth parents died about the time I was born. Somehow, I was adopted into a non-magical family. Apparently, my parents actually tried to find someone to teach me, but couldn't."

Nikolai nodded. "Mages can be particular about who they train, when they have the luxury."

"And you won't teach me?" I didn't want to push, but I needed to know his reasons.

"Sofia, to teach you properly, I will have to spend a great deal of time with you. Our magic resonates. It will draw us together. Even if we decided we hate each other, if we continue to work magic together, it will bring us closer. I can teach you basics without risking that, but not more. I do not wish to incur the wrath of your pack. Nor would I wish to cause any difficulties. The time we will have to spend together for you to learn the basics will probably push their limits as it is." He looked sad. "Also, I'm not so certain I'm ready for another student. The last one nearly killed me."

"What if our magic didn't resonate?"

"Finding someone who resonates with you happens now and again. It's not terribly rare, but it's also not so common that it is to be taken lightly. If it did not, I would be able to teach you the basics and maybe a touch more, but that would be it. Families typically have resonance, which is why you are usually trained by family. When mages search for their own mate, they typically look for someone who has resonance with them. Resonance means that we cast magic in similar ways. If we did not resonate with each other, sharing languages would have been more difficult, not impossible, but not as easy, and I would have waited until I had recovered more to attempt it." He shrugged.

"Not everyone casts magic the same?"

"Yes and no. Magic is basically the same for all mages. However, the small details of how a mage shapes spells varies. It may have something to do with bloodlines. I don't truly know."

"Okay. Well, will you teach me some of the basics at least?"

"Though I'd rather refuse, I do not believe I can. You are all doing quite a bit for me. I will try."

Notes of fear entered his voice again, but before we could talk anymore, Doc returned.

"Guest pass acquired. You can shadow one of us for the week, and I'll work on seeing what we can do about the rest of the semester." Doc started the diesel, and we headed back to the cabin.

It might have made sense for me to stay on campus, since it was late in the day and they would have to bring me back down in a few hours anyway, but I wasn't ready to go back to the dorm and Doc didn't suggest it.

The trip back to the cabin was quiet. Doc was lost in thought, and Nikolai was probably overwhelmed. I didn't have anything left to say.

Ed and Allan came out of the woods to meet us when we arrived. Ed practically pulled me out of the truck, a big grin on his handsome face. He swung me around before setting me on the ground and putting his arm around my waist.

Allan helped Doc grab the bags, and Nikolai, still looking a little lost, followed after them.

Once inside, I collapsed onto the couch.

Ed sat next to me, and I pulled my feet up and set my head in his lap. He ran his fingers through my hair.

"How'd the day go?"

"We ran into Alex. It was okay until then."

Ed growled.

"Pretty much. He happened to remind us that he knows our secrets. We know his, so it might be an empty threat, but it's hard to tell."

"Asshole."

"Yeah."

Ed continued to play with my hair, soothing me.

Allan came back and gently lifted my legs, sliding under them so my calves were lying across his lap. "Doc and Nikolai told me what happened with Alex," he grumbled. His soothing touches joined Ed's.

I sighed.

"It'll be okay, Sofia. We'll figure something out," Allan tried to reassure me.

They had lulled me to a half drowsy state by the time Doc and Nikolai joined us. They sat on the loveseat. Doc was showing Nikolai how to use a tablet and explaining the internet.

"I have so much to catch up on." Nikolai sounded a bit overwhelmed.

"You can stay with us as long as you need to," Doc offered again. "Of course, you may be better off somewhere else. I suspect things with the Andersons are going to get worse before we figure out how to resolve the issue."

Nikolai waved his hand dismissively while he stared at the tablet. "I am battle mage. Yes? I may as well fight. Besides, Alex is a…" He hesitated, muttered something in Russian that must have been slang because while I understood the word, I didn't know what he meant. "I will learn the modern equivalent. He is not as powerful as he believes he is." Nikolai looked up, eyes scanning all of us. "I suspect much was lost in the Renaissance. I am…" He hesitated again. "I used to use magic constantly. It makes a large difference." He focused on me, seeming to ponder before shrugging. "It is problem that you cannot. It will keep you from reaching your full potential."

I didn't reply, certain he was right. Though really, my short-term goal was simply not to get turned into a host for a greater demon.

Chapter 6

Sofia

"So, spill," Victoria ordered when I returned to my dorm room that evening. She had already changed into pajamas. She had a towel wrapped around her head, covering her fro, and a light-colored face mask contrasted with her dark skin.

"You gotta try this." She tossed a bottle at me.

I studied the ingredients. Lavender featured prominently.

"It's supposed to help reduce anxiety." She beamed at me.

"Do you have anxiety?"

"No, but I figured you might have a little extra stress in your life right now, so I got it for us to try."

"Aww, thanks." I returned her grin. "I showered at the cabin."

Her grin widened.

"So, I can try it after I change," I continued, trying to ignore her expression or the blush that spread across my face.

"Great. Who's the new guy?"

I laughed, dropped my bag onto my bed, and pulled my sleeping clothes out of the dresser. Our room had a divider down the middle where the two desks were, and the closets sat back to back. The beds were on the outside walls, and we each had a window. We had a corner room, so I had an extra window since I was on the outside wall. Our room was protected by wards that Doc, using borrowed magic, had placed for us, and it was reasonably secure, so I felt comfortable talking.

Victoria sat in my office chair and turned her back to give me a bit of privacy while I changed.

"So, do you remember that knife I, uh, stole from the Andersons?"

"Yeah."

"I was poking at the knife with my magic and somehow triggered a release or a key or something, and suddenly we had a nearly dead Russian mage on our floor."

Victoria cursed. "And he was trapped in the knife? How?"

"Turns out back in like, fourteen fifty-five or something, one of Nikolai's students—he's the new guy—decided she wanted his position. So, she made a magical trap with the knife as a trigger. Then she stabbed Nikolai in the back. Literally. She also poisoned him, just in case the rest wasn't good enough. Fortunately, the magic put him in some sort of stasis."

"You're shitting me." She stared, incredulous.

"No, I'm totally not. Doc helped guide my magic, and I managed to heal him." Victoria didn't know that Doc was a half-vampire, and it was safer if she didn't find out. Not that we didn't trust her, but some secrets were pretty important to guard. Vampires in general were one of the most dangerous of the supernatural community. They tended to avoid humans except for food and dealt with discovery with lethal finality. Doc had started life as a vampire hunter with his father, and likely wouldn't be popular with a full vampire regardless, but the fewer people who knew, the better. It was bad enough that the Andersons knew.

Somehow, Doc had come to an agreement several years ago that the Andersons, who ran the local branch of the magical black market, would leave him, Ed, and Allan alone. Until I came along and disrupted all of that, the truce had held. He hadn't told me what he'd done to get them to agree, but I knew the older Andersons were afraid of him. Alex didn't seem to share that fear. Unfortunately.

"Anyway, he's grateful we saved him. Seems pretty nice. And has a lot of catching up to do. We took him shopping today. He handled it well, but it was pretty stressful for him."

"That's insane."

"Yeah." I flopped down on my bed and opened the face mask bottle. "Oh, this smells good."

"Try it."

I did, and soon we were both laying on my bed, enjoying the lavender aroma.

"Okay, so I have to ask. Is he hot?"

"Nikolai?"

"He's the only new he, right? We already know the other three are hot." Victoria giggled.

"You are terrible."

"Well?"

"Yeah, he's pretty hot. Shoulder length dark brown hair. Dark brown eyes. A bit more muscular than Doc, but leaner than Ed and Allan. His hands are interesting. They're long and slender but also calloused. He told us he fought in a lot of wars, so I imagine they're like sword callouses or something."

Victoria turned her head and looked at me. "Girl…"

"What?"

"That's a level of detail I was not expecting."

"Um, well, you asked. I was holding his hand for a large bit of today. He was pretty nervous."

Victoria laughed.

"Anyway, he's half Russian, half Tatar."

"Interesting. Think the guys will adopt him into the pack or just keep him around long enough that he can function on his own?"

"It's going to take a while to get him on his feet. If he doesn't want to stay with us, we may have to find someone else to help."

"Well, I'm looking forward to meeting him. Wait, if he's from fourteen fifty-five Russia, how are you talking to him?"

"Oh, good question." I laughed. "He traded me languages. Apparently, there's a spell where you can do that. I speak his version of Russian now. Badly. Apparently, fully being able to speak the language takes a while."

"No way." She propped herself up on her elbow and stared at me.

"I'm not lying to you," I said in Russian.

"That's so cool." She flopped back down on the bed and stared at the ceiling. "Is he going to teach you magic?"

"Some. We'll see how it goes."

"What's he going to do while everyone is in classes?"

"Doc got him a guest pass, so he'll shadow us this week. We're still trying to figure all that out. I mean, he may just want to hide in the cabin for a while after he spends a week following us around school. I think Doc showed him the internet."

"He's doomed now." Victoria laughed.

I echoed her laugh, though I was very curious to see what Nikolai thought of the modern world once he got somewhat of a handle on the past several centuries. Poor guy.

Chapter 7

Sofia

The next morning Victoria and I stumbled through our morning routine and then headed to the dining hall together. The cool morning air caught my breath and carried it away.

"Won't be long before it snows," Victoria informed me, grinning.

"You're crazy."

"If you don't like snow, you came to the wrong college."

I sighed. "Very true. I think it's more that you all talk about it as if it's a national holiday or something."

"Around here, Sofia, it is. This town survives on ski season. Well, and beef and the college, but ski season is what really brings in the tourists and the money."

The warm air of the dining hall was a bit stifling after the cool crispness of outside. My stomach grumbled, and I hurried to the buffet, Victoria right behind me.

Briefly, I considered trying some coffee, but the thought still turned my stomach, so I got hot water and a tea bag instead.

"It's not going to bite you," Victoria said.

"What?"

"The coffee maker. You're looking at it like you can't decide if you want to blast it out of existence or make sweet love to it." She giggled.

I groaned, trying not to think about the images my brain came up with. "It's too early for that."

"Too early for what?" A familiar Russian accent caressed my ears and caused a few butterflies unrelated to the coffee maker in my stomach.

I turned, eyes wide. Ed and Nikolai had come up behind us. Ed had a tray full of food. Nikolai looked curious, but Ed was looking at the coffee pot as if trying to figure out what it had done to deserve Victoria's comment.

"Nothing. Good morning, Ed, Nikolai. Let's grab a table."

Victoria studied the Russian mage, eyes sparkling with amusement.

We found an empty round table. Victoria sat on one side of me, Ed on the other, and Nikolai across from me. Much of his attention was focused on me, but he looked around quite a bit as well, though he wasn't as wide-eyed as he had been yesterday.

Ed leaned against me for a minute, and I returned the gesture, tilting my head for a quick kiss from my handsome wolf.

Victoria nudged me and nodded toward Nikolai. Oh right, introductions.

"Nikolai, this is my good friend and roommate, Victoria. Victoria, this is Nikolai."

He brought his attention back to the table and focused on Victoria. I saw her eyebrows raise, and I thought she might have blushed a little. It was hard to tell with her darker complexion.

"It is nice to meet you." He smiled warmly at her.

I thought I heard Ed sigh a little and glanced at him, but by the time I looked, he was focused on his food.

I tilted my leg so I could touch his knee with mine. He returned the pressure but kept eating. I understood. Werewolf metabolism. Food was one of the more important things in his life.

"It's nice to meet you, too. I look forward to chatting when we're not around so many other people." Victoria smiled back.

Nikolai glanced at me and tilted and eyebrow. I was pretty sure he was curious to know how much she knew, so I nodded slightly.

He switched to Russian. "It is safe to talk around her?"

"Mostly," I replied in the same language.

"That is so cool," Victoria exclaimed, cradling her coffee.

I leaned away. It wasn't a latte, but even the smell of coffee was turning my stomach. It was possible it was time to break the caffeine habit.

Nikolai noticed, but I shook my head when he gave me another questioning look.

"So, why live here, not at the cabin?" Nikolai studied me while I sipped my tea.

"Um, well, it's kind of complicated, but long answer short, my parents probably wouldn't be comfortable with that, I haven't known Ed, Allan, or Doc long enough to invade their space that completely, and it's easier to get to morning classes when I'm down here."

"I see." His tone conveyed confusion though, and I guessed he didn't really understand.

I picked at my food, knowing I would be hungry later, and was staring remorsefully at my plate when Victoria gasped.

We all looked in the direction she was.

"I wonder what he's doing here," I exclaimed, surprised to see a familiar looking Viking with husky blue eyes wandering toward us with a tray of food and an angry scowl on his face.

Ed watched him warily, but didn't seem as concerned as I thought he should have been at seeing the Andersons' pet demon walking toward us.

Ash clearly wasn't happy about being here. He hooked the chair with his foot and pulled it out, before nearly dropping his tray on the table and sitting next to Nikolai.

Victoria was shooting wide-eyed glances between us, so I put my hand on her arm and squeezed reassuringly before nodding toward Nikolai. If nothing else, I was certain he could protect us.

The Russian had noticed our reactions and studied Ash closely, his hands on the table, and I got the impression he was ready to defend us if necessary. We had mentioned Ash to him the previous day.

Ed went back to eating, though he had his attention on the demon.

"Hi, Ash." I could at least try to be polite. He wasn't exactly an enemy, according to Doc. A smile tugged at my lips when I pictured the grumpy demon kissing Doc. I wasn't sure how I felt about it, but I certainly wasn't going to argue with someone who could probably incinerate me. At least not while he was under someone else's control.

He grunted irritably.

"You're back in classes?" We needed some information from him.

"I have been instructed," he growled out, "to find out more about this new friend of yours." He turned his glare on Nikolai. "The school was informed I was sick. My absence was excused. It's all very tidy." He shoved some eggs in his mouth and chewed angrily.

"No more hunting us down?" I wondered if they had changed his orders.

"Not right now." His voice lightened a bit.

"Is he not the enemy?" Nikolai asked me in Russian.

Ash looked like he was in pain for a minute before he grunted again. "I was not instructed to hide from you my knowledge of many languages."

Nikolai raised his eyebrows and smiled. "You know," he continued in Russian. "I think we might get along just fine."

The demon's glare faded slightly, and he sighed, but didn't reply.

Victoria stared at me.

"It's…" I hesitated. "A long story. You know most of it. Ash isn't the enemy."

"You cannot trust me," he grumbled, staring at the table.

"No. Of course not," I answered softly.

My roommate shook her head and went back to her coffee.

I tried to focus on the bergamot aroma of my tea and ignore the rich coffee scent that made me want to hurl.

∞ ∞ ∞

"Ed acted anxious to get rid of me," Nikolai stated once we were headed for Doc's history class. Ed had left the Russian with me and went off to his own class. Victoria headed toward hers, and Ash trailed along behind us, scowling.

I wasn't terribly comfortable talking about anything with Ash around, so I shrugged. "Maybe he just wanted you with me."

"Why?"

"Protection?" I whispered as quietly as I could and hoped the demon couldn't hear me.

"Perhaps."

A thought occurred to me. If Ash was back in classes, what about Alex?

"Hey, Ash?" I spoke a little louder, but he didn't reply. Maybe he hadn't heard?

"Ash?" I turned to face him.

He glared at me but took a few steps closer.

"Is Alex back at school, too?"

His expression turned murderous, and I forced down the urge to hide behind Nikolai while we walked.

"Yes."

"Great," I grumbled sarcastically.

The demon nodded. He moved next to me, and Nikolai dropped behind as we went inside the history building and climbed the stairs to the classroom.

Ever since I had drunk a fair bit of Doc's blood laced with Ash's demon magic, the altitude didn't bother me at all. When I had first arrived from Nebraska, a set of stairs had winded me, but now I could probably run up them with no issue. Hopefully, that was the only side effect I would experience. So far, it was the only thing I had noticed. I think it had more to do with the healing aspects of vampire blood than anything else, but I wasn't sure.

Nikolai was breathing a little heavily when we reached the top, and I hoped the guys had thought to warn him about the altitude.

We walked in, and Doc just about dropped the notebook he was holding, his eyes widening with alarm at the sight of Ash. The handful of other students already in the room turned to look at us, but other than Nikolai's presence, they couldn't tell there was anything unusual with Ash's return. The class size wasn't large, so they would have noticed Ash missing from class.

I shook my head, and Doc cleared his throat. "Welcome back to class, Ash. I trust you're feeling better?"

I happened to glance at Ash when Doc addressed him, and the unmasked desire on his face surprised me.

"Yes," was all the demon said.

I looked back at Doc to find a distressed look on his face, like he might be trying really hard not to blush.

"You know, Ash," I said in Russian as I sat down. "You might not want to look at the teacher like you want to eat him."

Ash dropped his gaze to the desk, and Doc took a deep breath, looking relieved.

"You're one to talk," Ash replied in the same language.

It was my turn to blush. Nikolai laughed.

"If the foreign language department is ready, we'll start class," Doc chided, eyes shining with mischief.

"Carry on then," Nikolai replied imperiously in English.

Doc rolled his eyes, but he also laughed. "By the way, class, we have a visitor from Russia with us today. He's a colleague. He'll be shadowing a handful of students for the week, so make him feel welcome."

Nikolai wasn't completely comfortable with the attention, but he nodded politely while the students greeted him.

Class itself was uneventful, but when Doc dismissed us, several of the students came over to talk to Nikolai.

Ash grumbled and left before I could say anything to him, but he was in a couple of my other classes, so I would see him later even if he wasn't actively following us. Of course, I would see Alex later. The thought made me shiver.

Nikolai noticed and put a hand on my shoulder. "All right?"

I nodded.

"What's Russia like?" One of the students surrounding us asked.

"What do I say?" he asked in Russian, sounding desperate.

"Be vague," I replied in the same.

"Cold," he finally replied. "Always cold. Snow everywhere. Buried in it." He grinned, and the student laughed.

He managed to answer a few other questions before Doc chased everyone off.

"Are you two doing okay?"

"Yeah," I replied. "Well, I am anyway."

"Surviving," Nikolai answered.

"You can come with me, if you want, or stay with Sofia. It's up to you."

Nikolai considered both of us before he answered slowly. "She mentioned it might be useful to have me around as protection."

Doc nodded.

"Then, if no objection, I will stay with Sofia."

Doc tightened his lips for a moment before nodding. "If I don't see you before, I'll catch up to you this evening. Try to keep the Russian to a minimum. I'm pretty sure they don't speak your dialect anymore, but there are a few Russian speakers on campus."

"Sofia was merely warning Ash that he looked like he wanted to eat you and that might be considered inappropriate."

Doc's face turned all sorts of red, visible even through his darker skin tone.

Nikolai chuckled.

"Yeah, well, uh, thanks," Doc stammered.

"You do seem to have caught the demon's attention."

Doc shrugged uncomfortably. "Apparently."

"This is a good thing," Nikolai said. "Means he is less inclined to kill us all once we free him."

Doc raised his eyebrows.

"You mentioned that was part of plan."

"Yes, if we can figure out how."

"I will put some thought toward it," Nikolai stated.

The two men shared a glance I couldn't interpret.

"Guys, I need to get to my next class."

"Quite right. Lead on."

We said quick goodbyes and then left the classroom.

Allan caught up to us once we were outside.

"Sofia!"

"Hey!" I hugged him and gave him a quick kiss.

"Hi, Nikolai."

"Allan," the Russian replied.

"How are you two holding up?" Allan glanced at Nikolai.

I took his hand, and we walked together, arms touching.

"We're fine," I answered.

Allan clenched my hand and growled softly. I saw where his attention was and sighed.

"Less fine," I amended.

Alex sauntered toward us. He didn't say anything, just met my eyes deliberately, the sneer on his face a sharp contrast to his short blond curls and sapphire blue eyes. He walked past, as if he didn't have a care in the world, though he did eye Nikolai.

"Quite certain I cannot blast him?" Nikolai whispered once Alex was out of earshot.

"I wish," Allan answered for both of us.

He chuckled, and Allan squeezed my hand.

At least I wasn't facing him alone.

Chapter 8

Sofia

I did end up having to hand Nikolai off to Doc later in the day so he could go meet with some of the administrators. Doc was going to see what options they might have for letting him continue to shadow us for the rest of the semester. It would be a good way to get him used to everything. After that, we would have to see what happened.

Victoria and I were in our dorm room working on homework when my phone chimed that it had a text.

Doc: Nik wants to check the wards on your dorm. Where are you?

Sofia: Conveniently, my dorm.

Doc: We'll be there in a minute.

Sofia: Ok.

"Victoria, Nikolai and Doc are going to sneak up here and check the wards."

"Good."

A few minutes later, I heard a soft knock on the door and got up and opened it.

Nikolai looked annoyed, and Doc had a carefully neutral expression on his face. Uh oh.

Nikolai studied the room for a minute before shaking his head. "You did well enough, but only warding her room makes it fairly obvious where she is."

"I did the best I could," Doc muttered through gritted teeth.

"Yes, yes, of course you did." Nikolai waved his hand dismissively. "Wards are fine. Simply not enough of them. I'll return."

I stopped him with a hand on his arm. "Where are you going?"

"Yes, I must ward entire building. I will be discreet." Nikolai held his hand over his head for a moment, then I saw a faint hint of blue sparkles before he vanished.

"Whoa," Victoria exclaimed, eyes wide.

"Invisibility spell," Nikolai said from the doorway.

Doc stared at the space the mage had occupied before growling.

"He's going get stuck in the elevator or something," Doc muttered, and followed him out into the hallway.

Victoria laughed.

"It's funny, but at the same time, I really do feel sorry for Nikolai. There's a lot to catch up on."

"Yeah, no kidding. I can't even imagine."

Doc came back after a minute. "He took the stairs."

"You okay?" I went over and wrapped my arms around him.

Doc hugged me back, but not with his usual enthusiasm.

"Yes. He's just…" Doc shook his head. "You do realize he's actually the next thing to royalty?"

"I guess I hadn't made that connection."

"He seems to be trying to rein it in, but he's used to having servants, and it's pretty obvious." He slipped into a fair imitation of Nikolai's accent. "You did fine, Doc, this is wonderful," Doc snapped.

I raised my eyebrows and shared an amused look with Victoria while Doc went off on a fairly detailed rant about Nikolai, all in a Russian accent. I tried really hard to be sympathetic, but Doc's drawl mixed with the Russian in an extremely pleasing way, and it was kind of turning me on. Unfortunately, I knew at some point he was going to notice my arousal, and that just made the flutter in my stomach harder for me to ignore.

He finally stopped and glanced at me, eyebrow raised.

I blushed and shrugged, putting my hands up in a helpless gesture.

"Ugh." Doc rolled his eyes and flopped onto my bed dramatically.

Victoria laughed. "Are you going to be all right?"

"Yes. It will be just fine. He really is trying. He's quite grateful we saved him, if nothing else."

"I thought Sofia saved him?" Victoria said.

Doc opened his mouth to reply, snapped it shut, sighed, and nodded. "Yeah, that's what I meant."

"Sorry," Victoria backed off, realizing she had touched on something we didn't want to talk about.

"And of course, now Ash is back in class." Doc changed the subject. "The Andersons are getting restless, and who knows what they're going to do next."

"I'm curious about Ash. You know he's working for the Andersons, but you all actually seem okay with him. That's…a little strange," Victoria questioned.

"He likes Doc." I shrugged. "And he hates the Andersons. He's not working for them willingly. Seems like he's trying to help us."

"Why does he like Doc? That also seems kind of weird."

"I—" Doc snapped his mouth shut again. "I was nice to him when I could have killed him. Guess it made an impression." Doc cleared his throat and glanced away for a moment.

I laughed, I couldn't help it. 'Nice' was a bit of an understatement.

Victoria tilted her head at me, but I shook mine. It was too complicated to explain without telling her things it was safer for her not to know.

"I'll try not to ask awkward questions, but it's hard to know what I can and can't ask," she said.

"It's fine, Victoria. We're all grateful for your friendship and understanding," Doc answered.

"Aww!" she gushed.

A soft knock on the door interrupted us, and Victoria went and answered, letting Nikolai in.

"Thank you," he nodded to her before coming in and taking my office chair. The rollers didn't seem to faze him, so he must have encountered a rolling chair already.

He was taking most things in stride today.

"You warded the entire dorm?" Victoria sat down on the bed by Doc's feet.

"Yes. It should be quite safe from magical attacks."

"Thanks, Nikolai."

He smiled at her praise. "You are most welcome."

"Do you want to join us for dinner, Victoria?" I adjusted my position against the wall.

"Where are you going?"

"Nikolai has never experienced the joys of pizza." I smirked.

Victoria smiled back. "I'm in. Maybe you'll let me out of our normal Friday dinner then? I need to head home for the weekend."

"Sure, no problem. I'm quite certain the guys won't mind me showing up a little early this weekend."

"Not in the least," Doc drawled. He took my hint though and sat up on the bed.

I grabbed my backpack purse and a jacket. Victoria grabbed her bag and coat, and gestured for the guys to precede us out the door.

Nikolai and Doc snuck out ahead of us, and we waited about thirty seconds before following.

"Well, he's cute." Victoria nudged me as we walked down the staircase.

"Yeah, he is," I agreed, but I wasn't focused on the conversation.

She nudged me. "Are you okay?"

"I think so. There's just so much going on right now that I never expected. Don't know why it's hitting me now, but it is."

"Maybe it's because your guys suddenly aren't all getting along."

"Ed, Doc, and Allan are getting along fine," I protested.

"Right, but now you have Nikolai."

I raised my eyebrows and gave her a confused look.

"You may not have noticed, Sofia, but he looks at you just like the guys do. And you're giving him puppy dog eyes."

"I am not."

She snickered. "Are too."

"And we literally just met."

"You just met the others, and you fell pretty hard."

I sighed.

"And I wouldn't have pushed you to date them all if I didn't think you liked them," Victoria added. "And you like Nikolai, too."

I sighed again. He wasn't part of the pack, and he'd already told me he didn't want to cause problems for us. I didn't want to cause problems for us, either. Our relationship was so new, any misunderstandings might be hard to deal with.

She gave me a quick hug before we went outside to meet up with the rest of the guys.

Chapter 9

Doc

You've already lost her, Roy.

The words echoed in his head as he drove Nikolai, Ed, and Allan back to the cabin after dinner with Sofia and Victoria. Sam, the mage who ran a curio shop in the main strip of the tourist part of town, had stopped by the pizza place and come by their table. She had known Doc, Ed, and Allan for several years, though, to his knowledge, she hadn't guessed he was essentially a vampire. Being able to go out in sunlight unlike a full vampire and likely being the only half-vampire in existence, at least in the States, made it pretty hard to figure out what he was. Of course, Nikolai had known, but Nikolai claimed to have known several vampires, so maybe it was more obvious when you knew what to look for.

Sam had pulled him away from the table and outside after a quick round of introductions.

"Where did you find a mage?"

Doc shrugged. "Kind of dropped into our lap."

"You know you'll lose her to him, right?"

"What?"

She smiled grimly. "Everything you just gave up for that girl will be for nothing. He's suited to her. Their magic will draw them together as he teaches her."

Doc's heart stuttered, and he clenched his fists, struggling to hide his reaction to her words, but also unable to take a breath.

"Which one of you is dating her, anyway? I thought it was you, but the way Ed and Allan look at her made me wonder."

"Uh." Doc ran his hand through his hair, which he was currently wearing down because Sofia liked it that way.

"Wait, no. I don't want to know." Sam shook her head wryly.

"None of us want to see her hurt, Sam," Doc said, voice low. "If losing her to Nikolai will keep her safe, then we'll just have to deal with it."

"You know the Andersons won't leave you and the boys alone after this. Even if Sofia is gone. Right? That truce you fought so hard for is gone, and the reason for it will be, too." Sam crossed her arms and gave him a look that almost seemed smug.

"Why do you even care so much?" Doc glared back, voice rising slightly.

She took a step back, fear flashing across her eyes.

Doc took a deep breath and tried to tone his emotions down a little.

"I just don't want to see any of you get hurt. Look, I didn't think any of you would know. She may not even know. I'm quite certain Nikolai does."

He shrugged, shifting his feet, and staring at the ground. "It'll be what it will be."

"Their auras have already mingled. You've already lost her, Roy. She just doesn't know it yet."

"Doc?"

He snapped his attention back to the present, braked hard to make the turn off, and focused on the small dirt road to his cabin. He wasn't sure who had spoken to him, but it didn't seem to matter. Did anything matter? He didn't want to lose Sofia. Was it already too late, as Sam had claimed?

They reached the cabin, and he shut off the truck. Everyone climbed out into the dark evening.

His eyes adjusted almost immediately, and he did a quick scan of the area, looking to see if he sensed anything disturbed in the area.

Ed and Allan did the same but didn't appear worried as they headed to the house. They kicked off their shoes, and both sprawled on the couch.

"What's up?" Ed asked when Doc sank down onto the loveseat.

Nikolai sat in the armchair near the window.

"What do you mean?" Doc leaned back and stared at the ceiling, stretching his legs out in front of him.

"Whatever Sam said bothered you. You've barely said a word all night," Ed answered.

Instead of answering Ed, he turned his attention to Nikolai. "Why won't you train Sofia?"

Nikolai answered after considering Doc for a moment. "I already told you, I do not train people already in a relationship. It goes badly. I will teach her a few basic things."

"What about it goes badly?"

"Typically, the other half of the relationship grows jealous of the time the student spends with the teacher."

"That's it?"

"No. I have already spoken with Sofia. She understands."

"But you don't want to tell us?" Doc crossed his arms.

"It is not particularly pertinent." Nikolai shrugged. "It doesn't work well, and I am not going to do it."

"What if it's the only way to keep her safe?"

Nikolai sighed, looking resigned. "The difficulty is this, if you must know. Our magic has resonance. I can teach her beyond basics, but it will draw us together, even if we don't want it. I do not want to cause problems with all of you." He clenched his jaw and frowned.

"Surely you can keep your hands to yourself," Ed grumbled.

"Yes, of course I can." Nikolai shook his head. "It is difficult to explain unless you've experienced it."

Doc thought he knew what Nikolai was talking about. When he had helped Sofia first access her magic more deliberately, her magic had washed through him. They'd had no reason not to act on their impulses, and he hadn't thought anything of it. If that was what Nikolai was talking about, he understood why the mage didn't want to get involved, but according to Sam, it was too late.

He brought his attention back to the conversation when he heard one of werewolves growl at Nikolai.

The mage held his hands up. "No, I would not deliberately steal her from you. I do not wish to. It is simply the way magic works."

Ed glared. Allan glanced at Doc, as if looking for help.

"I will demonstrate, if that's what it will take to convince you." Nikolai shifted his attention from the angry werewolf to Doc. He stood up. "Come here."

Mildly annoyed at being ordered around, but not having the energy to argue about it, Doc got up and went over to the mage.

"Thank you. Now, call on magic you carry in reservoir."

Doc hesitated.

"I will replenish it for you, if necessary."

Doc took a deep breath and hoped he wasn't going to regret being the demonstration. Touching Sofia's magic stored in his mother's bracelets, he called it into himself.

"So, see, Doc is using Sofia's magic. The only thing I will do is push my magic into him, as if teaching him new spell."

Before he could even remotely prepare himself, Nikolai pushed a tendril of his rich blue magic into him.

He gasped, Nikolai's magic rushing through him like electricity. Hunger warred with desire as his body instantly aroused. He couldn't even think for a minute, and he nearly went for Nikolai's neck as he practically lost control of himself.

"How do you even get anything done if it's like this?" He trembled with the effort of keeping his hands off Nikolai. It didn't help that the mage's heart was racing, and he didn't seem to be able to move his eyes away from Doc, either.

"This is why family usually teaches each other. It is different with family." The mage's voice was strained. "It is not this bad after the first few times, though it does not get appreciably easier without lots of practice." He bit his lip. "Maybe I should have tried more explanation before resorting to demonstration."

Doc's teeth ached, the need for blood raging through him. It hadn't affected him this strongly in years. He growled softly.

"Go ahead." Nikolai tilted his head, further exposing his throat.

He wanted to resist, almost managed to, until Nikolai stepped forward and put his hand on Doc's chest. The physical contact snapped the last amount of self-control he had left.

Nikolai groaned as he sank his fangs into the mage's neck. He wasn't gentle and was certainly going to leave more of a mark than normal. Nikolai pressed into him, hands clutching at his back.

He managed to stop before he risked actually hurting the other man, leaning back, trembling with his reaction. He still wasn't satisfied, but the blood had taken the edge off of his arousal, though he still couldn't get his fangs to retract, and he might need to talk Allan or Ed into giving him a bit more later. Probably Allan.

Nikolai's dark eyes nearly glowed with the blue of his magic when he met Doc's eyes, though they were slightly unfocused. A smile curled his lips. "My self-control is not so good as yours," he warned before he pulled Doc to him and pressed his lips to the vampire's, clearly not minding the blood.

That did the last of his restraint in. The magic coursing through both of them demanded some sort of release, and he was helpless to deny it. Not breaking off the kiss, he shoved Nikolai back until he was up against the wall, opening his mouth when the mage pressed against his lips with his tongue. Groaning, he lost himself in Nikolai's embrace.

Chapter 10

Allan

Allan watched his friend make out with the mage and couldn't decide if he was turned on or jealous. Maybe a bit of both. He ground his teeth, wondering if he should intervene. If Sofia had been there, it would have been perfect. She could have said if she minded or not, and then he wouldn't feel conflicted. Though he hadn't been thinking of Nikolai in those terms until he'd provoked Doc.

"I don't know if we should just leave them to it, or throw a bucket of cold water on them," Ed joked, though Allan heard the underlying tension and confusion he felt echoed in Ed's voice.

Allan wrenched his gaze away from Nikolai and Doc and turned his attention to his brother. "To be honest, I think Sofia's self-control is better than Doc's, but his is pretty good, and if he can't keep his hands off of Nikolai, then we can't expect her to, either."

Ed sighed, his eyes reminding Allan of a sad puppy. "We're going to lose her, aren't we?"

Allan returned his attention to Doc. Nikolai was currently digging his hands into the vampire's very fine ass.

Nikolai finally leaned back, gasping for breath. "Roy," he groaned.

Doc ignored the mage, or didn't hear him. He had his face buried in Nikolai's neck, and the expression on the mage's face showed he certainly didn't mind, though he was trying to get Doc's attention.

"Roy!"

The vampire growled but managed to get a hold of himself. His breath came in heavy pants. He stepped back, putting one hand on the wall and leaning on it.

Nikolai sagged back, letting the wall support him. Allan didn't think the mage would be upright otherwise. His eyes were glassy, and bites bruised both sides of his neck.

Allan winced. That wasn't going to feel good later.

"Sorry," Doc apologized after a minute.

"I knew what I was doing," Nikolai breathed. "I should be the one apologizing."

They both had blood smeared around their lips.

Doc nodded, put his hand on Nikolai's shoulder, and squeezed gently before turning away. "Excuse me." He nearly fled to his bedroom.

Nikolai closed his eyes and sank to the floor, back sliding along the wall.

"Are you okay?" Allan felt he had to ask, though the mage had admitted he knew what he was getting into.

"I'm quite fine. Just lightheaded." Nikolai touched his throat. "Do you think he's angry with me?" He managed to sound worried, despite his endorphin induced haze.

"No, probably not," Allan answered. "He's probably just confused." Allan knew he was.

"Good."

"How much blood did you lose?" Ed asked.

Nikolai waved his hand. "I know a spell to fix that. I spent many military campaigns with a couple of vampires. It's not so easy to keep them fed unless we're in battle. Not many people are as open minded about being food as we are."

Allan shivered at the implications.

"How do vampires on military campaigns manage sunlight? Seems dangerous," Ed asked.

"I have a spell for that, too," the mage replied. "Would one of you help me to the bathroom? I should probably wash the blood off and heal myself."

"He tore you up pretty badly." Ed sounded surprised. He stood and went over to the mage.

"Yes. I assume he is not usually so rough."

"No, he's not," Allan answered.

Nikolai actually smiled while Ed helped him up.

They left Allan alone in the living room, and he stared at his hands, not sure what to do with himself now. Finally, he decided to go check on Doc.

His pack brother was leaning against the wall, staring out the window into the black night. The lights weren't on, but none of them needed light to see well.

"Are you okay?" Allan came up next to Doc, standing so that he almost touched Doc, but not quite.

Doc had wiped the blood from his chin, but he hadn't made it so far as the bathroom to clean up. He still had some smeared on his cheeks, and Allan could smell Nikolai's blood on the vampire's breath.

"Yes. Is Nikolai okay? I got a little carried away."

Allan did his best to imitate the Russian's accent. "I have a spell for that."

Doc laughed weakly. "Of course there is."

They stood there for a few minutes in silence before Doc broke it. "I'm sorry, Allan."

"For what?"

"I don't know. I just feel like I should apologize to you. I know you like guys, and you let me take your blood pretty frequently, and, well, you never get anything from me in return."

Allan shrugged, the motion brushing his arm against Doc's. "I have a hand. Two in fact."

Doc's eyebrows rose, and he glanced at Allan.

He blushed. "I, uh, broke my arm once when I was still human. My dominant arm. So…I had motivation to train my other hand."

Doc chuckled. "Still, I'm not sure that's really fair. I know Ed would prefer I kept my hands to myself, but you should tell me what you want."

"Really?"

"I mean, we might want to run it by Sofia." He shrugged. "But I honestly don't think she's going to mind."

"What about you?"

"What do you mean?"

"I never really got the impression you were into guys."

"Allan, until just recently, there was a significant lack of any romantic interests in my life. I'd never really thought about it. While I'm pretty sure I prefer women, I'm apparently not having any issues kissing guys, either."

"Yeah, you seem to be surrounded by interested parties these days."

Doc shook his head ruefully.

"Let's figure out what to do about Sofia before we worry too much about you and me, okay?"

"Sounds good."

Doc put his arm around him and pulled him into a side-hug.

"What are we going to do about Sofia?" Allan leaned against his pack brother. "She needs to be trained, but we'll lose her."

"Sam says we've already lost her. She just hasn't realized it yet."

"That's why you were so upset earlier?"

Doc nodded. "Think Nikolai will share her?"

"I don't know. He seemed adamant he wouldn't train her." Allan replied.

"I'm actually wondering if he didn't think we would be willing to share her with him."

"Are we?" Allan wasn't sure he was comfortable with the idea, but then, he had just watched Nikolai make out with his best friend and it had only bothered him a little, but would it be different if it was Sofia?

"We'll need to talk to Ed, but if it means we can protect her and keep her, it might be the best option."

Allan nodded. "We'll have to talk about it." He smiled slyly. "So, who's a better kisser, Ash or Nikolai?"

Doc sputtered.

"No really, I kind of want to know," Allan surprised himself by saying.

"Uh, probably Nikolai."

Allan laughed. "You both looked like you were enjoying yourselves."

Doc shivered and folded his arms across his chest. "Yeah."

"If you're worried about Sofia, I don't think she'll be mad."

"No, she'll probably understand."

"Nikolai was worried you're mad at him," Allan added.

"Not mad."

"Good. Why don't you go take a shower and change? You can't avoid everyone forever, anyway."

"I just needed a minute alone to calm down."

"Good, well, I think Ed and I are going to go run. If we don't see you before we leave, we'll see you when we get back."

Doc surprised Allan by pulling him into another hug. This one was a proper hug, and he squeezed tightly.

"Whatever did I do to deserve the two of you in my life?"

"Pissed someone off, I'd imagine," Allan replied with an amused smile.

Doc looked at him. "You know that's not what I meant."

"I do. We're grateful for you, too. We're pack."

Doc nodded. "Go run. I'll see you tonight. Be careful."

He tightened his grip for a moment before releasing Doc and leaving the room.

Ed had already changed and was waiting for him by the door. He went into the smaller bedroom he currently shared with Ed and shifted into wolf form. The forest called to him, and he intended to answer.

Chapter 11

Doc

Nikolai sat in the armchair, staring at the tablet they had given him. He looked up when Doc scuffed his foot so he wouldn't startle the mage as he returned to the living room.

He was surprised when the mage blushed, but Nikolai didn't say anything when he stretched out on the couch. Doc wasn't even sure how to define his feelings at the moment, but the mage still pulled on him in a way that was more than the delicious taste of his blood.

"I'm sorry," the mage finally admitted, touching his neck. "I pushed you harder than maybe I should have."

"I'm not mad, though I was pretty rough with you." He didn't quite apologize for it. The mage's neck was bruised, but it didn't look as bad as Doc had feared it might.

"I will heal quickly." He shrugged. "So, now you see why I should not teach Sofia. I would never do anything she didn't want, of course." Nikolai hunched his shoulders. It was obvious what he meant.

"We will have to talk about it more," Doc replied. "There are a lot of things we need to consider, but the most important thing is her safety." He hesitated. "We share her with each other. Maybe we need to expand our pack a little more."

Nikolai's eyebrows rose in surprise. "I had not considered that possibility."

"We would have to talk to Ed and Allan." Doc said. "Then Sofia, if we're all in agreement."

"I will think on it."

He nodded. "Of course." Doc's cheeks flushed as he pushed further. "And you'll have to ask Sofia if she's willing to share me."

Nikolai's jaw dropped for a moment, but he knew he hadn't misjudged the other man, especially when he smiled. "I may have to do that."

They fell into a relatively easy silence after that. Nikolai surfed the internet, and Doc finally pulled out his school tablet and tried to focus on grading papers. He had actually drifted off to sleep when the front door banged open. He was on his feet before he was fully awake.

Allan barked urgently, a sound he had never heard either of the werewolves make. The darker blond wolf collapsed to the ground and shifted back to human form.

Doc had seen them shift many times, but the process always fascinated him. It looked painful, but neither of them had complained as bones reformed, fur receded, and muscles pulled their shape back to a human one. It was different when he did it while borrowing their powers, so he didn't know how it felt for the wolves.

He looked around for Ed but didn't see the other wolf. Something must have happened. Especially if Allan was forcing himself to shift back to human form. It was easier if they just let it happen naturally while they slept.

Once he was done, he lay there, panting. "Follow my trail back. Ed's caught in a trap. It's bad," Allan gasped out.

Adrenaline surged through Doc, and he rushed to the door.

"Stay here," he ordered the exhausted werewolf.

"I am coming. I will slow you down, but you may need me," Nikolai insisted.

He nodded, and they ran out of the cabin and into the night. Using his nose, he followed Allan's trail, fighting against panic and forcing himself to keep to a pace Nikolai could match. The fear in the werewolf's scent made tracking him easier than normal. Especially since the wolf's scent covered Doc's land.

Nikolai managed to keep up reasonably well, and they both nearly skidded to a stop when they saw Ed.

The light blond werewolf had his front leg caught in what had to be a bear trap. Ed was lucky the thing hadn't taken his front leg clean off. He growled at the two men, lips pulled back to reveal long teeth.

Doc took a step forward, seeing red, but Nikolai put his hand on his chest to stop him, ignoring his angry snarl. "Look at his eyes."

Normally, Ed's eyes in wolf form were the same as his human eyes, sky blue. Now they looked like actual wolf eyes, dark brown.

"What did they do?" There was no question in his mind that the Andersons were behind this.

"Somehow, they blocked his humanity. He may be aware, but only the wolf has control. An injured werewolf could hurt you. I need to restrain him first."

"Go ahead."

Nikolai held his hands out, and blue motes filled the night, sinking into the ground. After a moment, vines twined out of the ground, growing quickly and encircling the wolf.

Ed fought, snarling and biting at them, but one wrapped up around his muzzle, and the vines trapped him to the ground.

The wolf glared at Nikolai, but couldn't move.

Doc stepped up to the trap and studied it. He knew how to open them, but Nikolai stopped him before he could try.

"Doc, there is a spell that steals humanity on this trap. Imagine what would happen if it stole yours."

He paled and stepped back.

"They are trying to hurt you, and they know what they're up against. They aren't aware you have a trained mage. Let me handle it for now."

"Thank you."

"Of course, now move."

Ed growled when Nikolai knelt near the trap. The Russian mage ignored the werewolf and held his hands over the trap. Blue motes sank into the spelled metal, and Nikolai muttered angrily in Russian.

After a short time, the trap snapped open and then disintegrated. Then Nikolai turned his attention to Ed.

"This is bad," he admitted.

"How bad?"

"It is a good thing both of us are here, or you would lose him, either to infection, or to the wild. Let him have some of your blood. It will stabilize his leg. It will be easier to combat the other spell if he is no longer in extreme pain."

He called his fangs back and, after removing his bracelet, sank his teeth into his wrist. He let the blood drip into Ed's muzzle. The vines loosened enough so that the wolf could lick the blood and swallow.

"That is probably enough," Nikolai said.

He nodded and licked the excess blood off of his wrist, which also helped to seal the wound, though it was closing quickly enough on its own. He put his bracelet back on and knelt next to Ed and Nikolai.

The mage muttered to himself for nearly half an hour, pouring magic into Ed. At some point, the wolf lost consciousness. "This is a nasty spell. It has the touch of demon magic to it, which is why it's so difficult to combat."

"Ash."

"Unless they have another pet demon."

"We're trying to prevent that."

"I know. There, it is gone. He will recover. He just needs to rest. Can you carry him back?" Nikolai banished the vines holding the wolf down.

"Yes."

"Good. I will check for other traps and meet you back at the cabin." Nikolai stood, though he leaned against a tree for a few moments before he was able to stand on his own. "This altitude…"

"Be careful, Nikolai."

"Yes, of course. Watch your step on the way back. This is still your land?" He gestured to the ground where they stood.

"Yes, it is."

"Hopefully, they would not set such traps on public land, but it is hard to say what they are capable of."

"Yeah," Doc replied. He knelt and gathered the light blond wolf into his arms, trying not to hurt him any further. Nikolai had done a decent job with the wound. The wolves healed nearly as quickly as Doc did, but something like this would take a while.

He walked carefully, all senses alert, as he carried Ed back to the cabin. Allan was curled up on the couch, wrapped in a blanket and looking both terrified and miserable, when Doc made it back to the cabin.

"Is he going to be okay?" Allan cried, his voice catching.

"Yes. Nikolai was able to reverse all of the spells, and we healed him enough to stabilize his wound."

"Those bastards," Allan growled.

"They're going to be sorry," he ground out.

"Damn straight they are." He followed Doc back to the bedroom and crawled into the bed next to where he laid Ed.

"I'm going to clean this wound. We'll clean it again and really bandage it when he shifts back," he said. "Get some rest, Allan. You look like hell."

"Feel like it. You're sure he's going to be okay?"

"There is a spell for that." Doc imitated Nikolai's accent, and Allan sort of laughed.

"Good. Hopefully there is also a spell for kicking the Andersons' asses."

"Yes, there is a spell for that, too," Nikolai said as he came into the room. "Many spells. I am battle mage. I believe I mentioned that. When we finally meet in combat, they will not know what hit them."

Chapter 12

Sofia

"What happened to your neck?!" I blurted when I saw Nikolai the next morning. He and a very subdued Doc met me outside my dorm room when I went down for breakfast.

"It is long story," he answered, cheeks coloring. "Later."

"I'm surprised to see you two."

"You're sick." Doc twisted his lips wryly. "And so are we. We need to talk, and we can't do it here, so I canceled my classes for the day, and you have a doctor's note if you need one for any of yours."

"I only have two today, and I'm caught up. Let's go." I wanted to ask what had happened, but I knew we couldn't talk about it until we were someplace safe.

I fell in beside Doc, Nikolai trailing behind us. I reached for his hand, but managed to remember at the last minute that I couldn't while we were around other people. At least, not yet. I shoved my hands in my pockets instead.

The parking lot was full of vehicles, but there weren't many people, so no one would see us leave together.

Nikolai opened the passenger side door of Doc's truck for me.

"Thanks." I grinned at him.

He smiled, looking pleased about something.

I glanced at Doc, who frowned slightly, watching us. I wondered what bothered him. Something had upset him the night before, too, but I hadn't had a chance to ask him what was up.

I pulled out my phone and texted Victoria, letting her know I would probably be back the next morning and not to worry. She replied with a winking smiling face and a thumbs up.

"We need to get Nikolai a phone," I stated, not sure how that would work.

"I already did," Doc replied. "I haven't had a chance to teach him to use it yet. We'll get his number programed into yours today sometime."

Once Doc had pulled out onto the road, I twisted around in my seat and repeated my earlier question. "What happened to your neck?"

"Eh, vampires. You know how they are."

My eyes widened, and I turned to Doc.

His cheeks were red, even over his darker skin, and he looked seriously embarrassed.

"Do I even want to know?" I didn't think Doc would try to hurt Nikolai unless the mage was actually attacking someone he cared about, and I didn't get the impression that the Russian was inclined toward random violence. Especially since being surrounded by werewolves and a half-vampire, he was physically outclassed.

Doc looked like he was going to say something, but then he shook his head and sighed.

"It is not his fault. I was trying to explain to them resonance. They required a demonstration."

I twisted back to study the mage. He shrugged and also looked embarrassed.

"I am afraid I took a bit of advantage of your boyfriend. My apologies."

My eyebrows rose as what he meant dawned on me. "Uh, sure. Apology accepted, I guess." I did not even know how I should actually respond to that revelation.

Doc glanced at me before returning his gaze to the road. He didn't say anything.

Maybe I was a little jealous. But jealous of what? I was quite certain I could imagine what had happened, especially with the fading bruises on both sides of Nikolai's neck. Doc wasn't usually rough, so the mage must really have provoked him. Did I even have cause to be jealous? I mean, I was dating three guys. It wasn't like they were hiding anything from me. I sighed. This was so complicated. Maybe I was just jealous that I hadn't been there?

"Do not be mad at Doc. It was my fault." Nikolai leaned forward until he was close to me.

"I'm not mad. I'm just...well...this is really complicated."

"Yes," the mage agreed.

Doc looked relieved, and that made me think for a minute. I knew Allan was interested in Doc in a more than brotherly fashion, and Nikolai had to have known what he was doing. Was there any way I could ask them to keep their hands off of each other when I wasn't around? Or even when I was around? It wasn't fair, especially when they shared their blood with Doc. And the thought kind of turned me on.

"You know." I smirked at Doc. "Whatever you guys want to do with each other is completely fine with me. I don't really feel like you need my permission, anyway, but seriously, enjoy yourselves. There's only one of me, and I'm not always around."

Doc's eyebrows rose, and he stared at me in surprise, perhaps a bit longer than was strictly safe while driving, before tearing his eyes off of me and focusing on the road.

"Just, you know, try to keep it in the pack."

I winked at him when he glanced at me again. He nodded ever so slightly back toward Nikolai.

Twisting around in my seat, I studied the mage. His face was a mask right now, and I wasn't sure what he was thinking, though I thought I saw a little relief. Probably that I wasn't mad at him. "That could include you. If the guys agree."

His mask broke, and his eyebrows rose. "I see." He opened his mouth as if he were going to say something else, before snapping it shut and nodding.

"We do," Doc said quietly.

I hesitated, surprised they had already discussed it without me. Of course, if Nikolai had been making out with one of my boyfriends, the subject had obviously come up.

"Good. Well, as interesting as this development is, it can't be why you pulled me out of class." I was worried about what possibly could have happened to concern everyone that much.

"Ed was hurt pretty badly last night," Doc stated. "While they were out running."

My heart clenched. "Is he okay?"

"He will be soon. He needs you," Nikolai said.

They filled me in on the details as we drove.

"Shit," I snarled when they finished. "Why didn't you call me?"

"He was fine last night. We thought today would be early enough to fill you in. He's not nearly as okay this morning."

I glared at Doc.

"Yeah, so we needed you to talk with Ed, and we all needed you with us so we could feel safe for a while," Doc wilted under my gaze. He turned off the main road down the narrow dirt driveway.

As soon as the truck was stopped, I jumped out and went into the cabin and headed back to Doc's bedroom. Light from the open window filled the room. Allan and Ed lay in the middle of the large bed. Allan was lying on top of the covers, dressed for the day, and pressed up against Ed. Under the blankets, Ed lay on his back, probably still not dressed, his left arm wrapped in bandages. He stared at the ceiling.

Allan looked over at me when I came in. "I'm so glad you're here."

Ed had to know I was there, but he didn't react.

Doc had told me that Ed was in a strange mental state, but I hadn't expected him to ignore me. I kicked off my shoes, crawled onto the bed on the other side of Ed, and pressed up against him.

"Hey, you."

He sighed in response. I glanced at Allan. Allan's eyes were wide, and it was clear he didn't know what to do.

"Ed, what's wrong?"

He didn't answer.

I didn't want to do the wrong thing and push him further into his strange frame of mind. He was usually so cheerful, like a giant blond puppy, even in human form. This was so different from normal, I didn't even know where to start.

"Allan, has he ever been like this before?"

He shook his head.

I put my arm across his chest and hugged him close, resting my head on his shoulder. It would have been more comfortable if he had put his arm around me, but he tensed instead.

"Ed, talk to me." Fear colored my voice, and that got him to turn toward me slightly.

He still looked vacant, but he sort of paid attention to me.

"Has he spoken at all since he woke up?"

"A little. He seemed pretty with it until this morning." Allan swallowed nervously.

I kissed Ed on the cheek and snuggled him closer.

Doc and Nikolai came into the room. Doc hung back, but Nikolai came over to us and studied Ed.

He put his hand on the werewolf's chest and pushed a little magic into him.

Ed shuddered, eyes going wide in fear.

"Sofia, maybe you do what I am. He will respond better to you."

Nikolai stepped away before I called my magic, standing back by Doc. Even so, as soon as I touched my magic, I could feel Nikolai as if he were standing next to me, hands on mine.

I gasped. "What the hell?"

"It is resonance," he muttered tightly.

"I didn't feel that when we traded languages."

"No. It takes once or twice for energies to sync." He sounded resigned.

I wanted to look at him, to try and figure this out, but Ed needed my attention, so I tried to tune Nikolai out. It helped that he was across the room, standing next to Doc. As soon as my thoughts turned to him, it was as if I could sense Doc, too.

Doc sank down into a chair, groaning softly. "Fuck." Obviously, he sensed the magical resonance, too.

"Yes," Nikolai agreed.

I glanced at Allan and got up on my knees, leaving one hand on Ed. Allan's eyes widened when I put my other hand on his shoulder and pushed magic into him.

"Whoa," he whispered.

My magic flowed through all of us, connecting us. It was erotic, as if all of them were connected with me, drawing Nikolai's magic into all of us, along with my own, but it was more than that. It pulled us together, joining us, burning through us. I used that connection and focused on the wild energy that belonged to Ed and tugged. He was buried deep, but once I found the way in, he clung to me and I drew him back to us.

Ed took a deep shuddering breath, and I clutched him to me as tears sprang to his eyes.

Doc came over and sat next to me, putting his hand on Ed's arm above the wound. Having all of us touch completed the pack, but not quite. Nikolai was missing. I had joined him to us, and we needed him now.

I looked over my shoulder at the mage.

His eyes were wide, and he looked like he wanted to refuse. We could all sense the acrid bite of his fear through the swirl of magic joining us.

Ed shifted under my hand, and I turned back to him. He stared at Nikolai as if he didn't quite know what to do.

"Ed," I whispered softly. "Talk to me."

He looked at me. "Sofia, I was so lost."

"You're here now. We found you. We'll always find you." Tears wet my cheeks.

"It was magic," Nikolai said. "Evil magic."

Ed winced when the Russian mage spoke, and the queasy unease he felt washed through us, but I wasn't sure what triggered it. Was it Nikolai, or the mention of magic?

Ed sighed. "This is quite the light show," he said, changing the subject. Maybe not ready to talk about it.

My lavender motes danced with Nikolai's dark blue and twirled around the room, darting in and out of us. Ed was right, it was quite the show.

It was beautiful. "What's happening?"

"You used your connections with Ed to bring him back," Nikolai answered, though the hesitation in his voice made me think that wasn't the full answer.

"You should come over here," I finally demanded. I couldn't take it any longer. I needed him to touch me, to touch us, to complete whatever we were doing.

The others agreed, even if it was just because they wanted to the incompleteness tearing at us to end.

"I cannot."

That fear again. It was stronger than Ed's. Did it have something to do with the mage who had nearly killed him?

Though it was one of the harder things I'd done recently, I broke contact with the others, got off the bed and went over to Nikolai.

He backed away when I reached for him.

"This is a bad idea."

"So is dating three guys, one who happens to be my teacher." I smiled at him. "What's one more bad idea?"

Nikolai arched an eyebrow. "I had wondered if that was considered acceptable."

"We're all adults," I said, dismissing the improperness. "It's not as bad as it could be." I was starting to tremble with the need to be physically touching my pack, not just touching them with magic.

"You're willing to share your magic with us, but not touch?"

Nikolai shook his head. "You called my magic. I did not stop you. Maybe I could not have." He shrugged.

I held out my hand. "Join us."

Both of his eyebrows rose, and he touched my wrist. The contact jolted through us, and I sucked in a breath, but the reason Nikolai had touched my wrist distracted me enough that I stayed focused on my task instead of throwing myself at Nikolai like I wanted to.

I was aroused to a degree that was getting painful, but the two wolf pawprints on my wrist that I had most certainly not gotten tattooed there were seriously distracting. One was an exact match in color to Nikolai's dark blue magic, and the other lavender like mine.

I gripped Nikolai's hand and flipped his arm over so I could see the underside of his wrist.

He had matching prints.

We met each other's eyes, and for a moment, the rest of the world faded away as the physical contact and our magical resonance drew us closer. I think the only reason I didn't kiss him then was because we both knew Ed needed us.

I tugged on Nikolai's hand, and he reluctantly followed me to the others. He stood behind me, hands on my shoulders while I settled back next to Ed and put my hands on the two wolves.

Doc touched me, and our magic flared again. His cool, yet intense energy joined us. Then Ed's puppy-like enthusiasm and Allan's more reserved energy flowed through the magic that connected us. The tug of the forest called. For a moment, all I wanted to do was run, feel the ground beneath my paws and the scents in my nose. Nikolai's energy was that of a raging snowstorm, Doc's a cool desert night, and mine, spring after a rain shower.

Once we were all full of the mingled energies, I released my magic.

The circle of energy we had built dissipated. I sagged down on the bed, suddenly exhausted.

Nikolai sank down on the floor, but kept his hand on my shoulder, and Doc stayed sitting, touching me and Ed.

None of us wanted to let go of the contact.

Ed finally broke the silence. "What the hell just happened?"

"I have no idea," I answered. "Nikolai?"

"I don't know."

"No?"

"Well, yes, I have an idea, but it would only be guessing."

"Guess away," Doc ordered. "You know more about any of this than the rest of us."

"Am I the only one with a couple of extra paw prints and a lot more color?" Allan stared at his wrist.

"No." I looked at my wrist again. Now I had five. Dark blue, lavender, sky blue, steel gray, and black. The color of mine and Nikolai's magic, and the color of the other guys' eyes.

Doc took off his bracelet and held out his wrist. His tattoo had changed to match mine.

Ed swore as he studied his wrist.

"Nikolai?" Allan asked.

I could sense the mage about to deny it, so I grabbed his hand off my shoulder and held it out for everyone to see. It matched as well. I ran my fingers lightly over his tattoo.

He gasped. "Perhaps you could…"

I let go of his wrist.

"Thank you." He didn't sound like he meant it, but I knew that's what he wanted.

"So, what did we just do?" Ed prompted.

"Sofia called our magic, or innate energies, and used them to draw you back, but then took it further and joined ourselves together in something akin to your pack bond. It would not have worked if there had been any true disagreement." Nikolai again sounded resigned.

"You don't sound particularly happy," Allan said.

"I was trying very hard not to intrude on your lives more than I had to," he replied. "Now you seem to be stuck with me."

"You said it yourself, Nikolai, if there had been any true disagreement, we wouldn't have been able to do what we did. You're part of our pack now," Allan insisted. "You're stuck with us."

"Thank you," he whispered softly. Though he sounded uncertain, he also sounded sincere.

"Guess that's what you get for letting Doc chew on your neck," Ed chided lightly.

I could sense Nikolai's embarrassment.

Doc laughed, and Allan grinned.

"Perhaps," Nikolai finally answered.

"Are you okay, Ed?"

"I think so. I just… Now I'm scared to change," he admitted.

"We'll be with you," I said before grinning mischievously. I leaned over and kissed him.

After a moment, he reached his uninjured arm around me, pinning me to his chest as he kissed me. He growled softly and rolled until he had me pinned to the bed.

I yelped in mock outrage before giggling.

His stomach rumbled louder than his pleased growl, and I laughed harder.

He sighed.

"You know, I don't know if anyone has had breakfast," I said.

"The pizza has worn off," Ed admitted. "Maybe I'll just eat you instead." He bit my neck.

I tried to yelp indignantly, but it came out as more of a gurgle as my brain decided it was done being restrained. I clawed at his back, bucking slightly under his weight. Distantly, I hoped I had spare clothing here, because between the magical energy turning me on earlier and Ed now, my panties were soaked. I didn't want to go around smelling of arousal all day.

Ed rumbled, pleased with himself.

I did cry out indignantly when he leaned back, sitting up and grinning at me.

"But I think maybe I should eat something. Feeling a little weak, after all." He crawled out of bed. I had wondered if he was dressed. Turned out, he was wearing pajama pants. They did nothing to hide his arousal.

Frustrated, I threw a pillow at him.

He laughed but continued to head to the kitchen.

"Werewolves and their stomachs," Doc laughed.

"Pot, kettle," I called up the old saying, fixing my gaze on Doc. "You just get to eat and have fun at the same time."

He opened his mouth as if he was going to deny it, but then realized he couldn't, so he just shrugged instead. "It's convenient."

"Eating is fun," Allan breathed on my neck. "Especially after you hunt it first," he whispered, voice low.

The primal joy in his voice tightened my stomach, and his breath on my neck sent tremors down my spine.

I turned to face him.

He kissed me gently on the lips before crawling backward off the bed. "He destroys the kitchen if I don't supervise."

"Are they trying to torture me?" I groaned, flopping back onto the bed.

"Maybe you're fun to torture." Doc's eyes shone with his smile.

"If you leave, too, I'm going to…" I didn't even know what to threaten.

"Going to what?" He stood up.

I just stared at him. He was really going to leave?

"Cry?"

He laughed. "We do need to discuss what we're going to do about the Andersons."

"I don't bloody want to think about Alex right now!"

The highly amused expression on Doc's face wasn't helping any. He headed for the kitchen. Nikolai had already vanished, leaving me alone in the bedroom, frustrated but also grateful that we had managed to call Ed back from whatever dark place the Anderson's magic had put him in.

Grumbling, I followed the guys into the kitchen. At least they could feed me.

Ed and Allan cooked while Doc sipped on tea, leaning against the wall.

"Where's Nikolai?"

"He went for a walk," Doc replied.

"Is he okay?"

"He's got a lot on his mind." Doc shrugged. "I think he'll be okay. We need to talk about a few things, though. The Andersons. Nikolai."

I sank down into my usual chair. "What are we going to do about the Andersons? Alex outright threatened us. If they find out Nikolai is a mage…" I trailed off.

"Yeah," Doc replied.

Ed and Allan filled the table with food. Ed sat next to me, and Allan took Doc's normal seat. They both sat closer than normal.

I leaned over until I touched shoulders first with Ed, and then with Allan.

"How do you feel about Nikolai?" Ed tilted his head to the side.

"Uh." What did I even say to that? Sure, I was attracted to him. He was easy on the eyes, nice to me and all, but the thing that was pulling at us was our magic resonance. Wasn't it?

"I mean, I like him. I guess. I know Doc likes him." I smirked at the blushing vampire, and shoved food in my mouth to avoid having to continue babbling.

"We need him to train you," Doc continued. "Sam said we would lose you to him if he did, though."

The thought of losing my pack brought tears to my eyes, and I couldn't talk around the sudden lump in my throat for a moment. "I would rather figure it out on my own," I managed to choke out, "than lose any of you."

"She said it was already too late," Doc added. His expression remained neutral, and I wasn't sure what he was thinking.

Ed and Allan both looked worried when they glanced at each other, then at me.

"Sam seems to say a lot of things," I grumbled. "I certainly don't feel like I've lost you." I twisted my arm until the tattoo on my wrist was exposed. "Besides. What does this mean, other than that we're all pack?"

"We can't ask him to train you and expect the two of you to not get involved with each other. Nikolai and Doc made that pretty clear yesterday," Allan said.

Though I was worried about what the guys might be suggesting, I couldn't help the sly smile that crossed my face. "I'm sorry I missed that."

Doc cleared his throat and stared at the ground.

"So, you just want to hand me over to him?" I said once the silence stretched.

"No!" they all declared together.

"Then what?"

"I guess we're asking you if you want to date him, too," Doc said when no one else spoke up. "Or maybe, more accurately, if you can talk him into training you, whatever happens between you two will be fine with us, as long as we get to keep you, as well."

"Oh." Though I had desperately wanted to kiss Nikolai earlier, I had dismissed it as the resonance. I still wanted to touch him, but it was easier to ignore, since he wasn't in the room. The guys were right, though, there was attraction between us. Even if it was just the magic. "I… What do you think?" I looked at Ed and then Allan.

"I would rather lose you to Nikolai than the Andersons," Allan admitted. "At least he'll teach you how to avoid becoming a host to a greater demon, but I'd rather not lose you at all."

Ed didn't answer, and I focused on him. He had his jaw clenched, and he stabbed at the eggs on his plate but didn't actually eat any. In fact, he hadn't touched much of his food compared to normal.

"Ed?"

"I agree with Allan," he added slowly. "We need Nikolai. We aren't giving you up. If you can convince him he has to share with us, then I guess it's okay with me." He stared at the table, his hands clenched.

"You're not okay with it," I stated, leaning against him.

"I just need to get used to the idea," Ed replied. "It was my idea to share you with Allan and Doc in the first place. I can let Nikolai in, too. Besides…" He grinned, looking closer to his normal cheerful self. "It looks like I don't have to try and convince you to get our pack tattoo." He ran his fingers lightly over my wrist.

I shivered, but returned his smile to him.

"What about you?" Allan took my hand. "How do you feel about the idea?"

"It's kind of sudden. Besides, maybe he just wants my boyfriend and not me." I wanted to laugh, but I didn't quite manage it.

Doc buried his face in his hand and sighed. "I don't think he's actually after either one of us."

"You sure about that?" Allan teased Doc.

Doc just sighed louder.

"I'll talk to Nikolai," I agreed finally. "We need to figure something out. I'm not positive this is really the answer, but if that's what we have to do, then we'll just have to decide what everyone is comfortable with."

"You know, it's not like we're asking you to date Alex," Allan said grinning at me. "Nikolai is nice. He seems to like you, and Doc says he's a good kisser, so it can't be all bad."

"I'm going to strangle you," Doc muttered through his hand.

This time, I did laugh.

Ed relaxed. "He's said he will fight for us, and he really has tried to keep his distance from you. It's not his fault, either. Let's just make the best of it and keep you safe from Alex. Besides, he's kind of growing on me." He went back to eating his breakfast, and Allan did the same.

I glanced at Doc. He studied me, and I couldn't tell what he was thinking.

"What?"

He shrugged. "I'm glad we found you."

"I've turned your entire lives upside down." I glanced at Ed's bandaged wrist, guilt twisting my stomach. That was my fault.

Doc set his tea on the table and came around behind me. He put his hands on my shoulders, massaging them gently for a second, before he leaned forward and kissed the top of my head. "Worth it."

"Yeah," Ed agreed around a mouthful of food.

Allan nodded his agreement.

"If you're sure," I murmured, wondering, again, if maybe I should just leave.

Doc tugged me out of my chair and pulled me against him. He brushed his fingers across my temple and tucked a strand of hair behind my ear before kissing me.

I lost myself in his embrace for a minute, enjoying his firm body pressed against mine, his mouth devouring mine.

"We're sure," Doc breathed when he leaned back.

Before I could decide if I was going to kiss him again or step away, Ed and Allan hugged me from behind, squishing me between the three of them. I rested my head on Doc's shoulder, content for the moment.

Chapter 13

Sofia

It didn't take me long to find Nikolai after I left the cabin. He sat, leaning against one of the aspens nearby, and looked out over the valley. I had thought I might talk to him later when he came back, but the guys had encouraged me to go find him and talk with him.

I still wasn't sure how I felt about this, but I didn't want to lose any of them, and clearly, at least some part of me had claimed Nikolai as my own.

"Hi." I switched to Russian. It was pretty damn cool that I could learn a language that fast.

He glanced at me before patting the ground next to him.

I sank down to the ground, sitting cross-legged next to him, not quite touching the mage.

"What's wrong, Nikolai?"

"Eh, it is nothing." He brought his attention to me, a bit of his blue magic shining in his otherwise dark eyes.

"It's not nothing. You're afraid. I can sense it."

"You can?"

"Yeah."

"Can you sense the others' emotions?"

"Only when the magic was actively connecting us all."

"Interesting." He stared at his hands.

"What's wrong?" I asked again.

He glanced at me, smiling sadly. "It all happened so very long ago, yet it is so very fresh to me."

"It must be hard."

Nikolai nodded, staring off into the distance. "Yes, but also, nothing stays the same, and it is just another form of change. A big one, but not without benefits." He smiled, glancing at me for a moment.

I grinned, his expression sending tingles through me and tightening my stomach. Maybe I was attracted to him beyond our magic.

"Besides, it seems like I missed some bad times that otherwise I would have experienced. I do miss those I considered friends." His face turned thoughtful for a moment. "It is possible Peter still lives."

I took his hand, and he tensed before taking a deep breath and obviously forcing himself to relax.

"I'm not that scary," I insisted. "Doc is way more terrifying than me." I winked when Nikolai glanced at me in shock.

"So far, I have not been stabbed in the back by a vampire. Female mages, on the other hand…" He smiled. "It's not fair to you. I am sorry." He touched his bruised neck.

"Nikolai, we need to figure this out."

His sad smile faded. "This?"

I clenched my free hand, uncomfortable. "Us."

"I am not trying to steal you away from your men."

"I know. You're just trying to steal my vampire away from me."

He sputtered, and I winked.

I took his hand and turned his wrist to expose the magical tattoo. He shivered when I ran my hand lightly over the top. "I seem to have claimed you."

"It seems so."

"I don't want to lose them." I stared at his wrist.

"Understandable."

"I need them," I insisted.

"Yes, you do." He tried to take his hand back, and I held on.

"I need you, too, Nikolai."

"You need me to teach you magic."

"Yes, but I also need you. Maybe it's because of our magic, but we've already tied ourselves together. Even if you chose not to show me how to use my powers, I still need you."

He didn't reply.

Concerned, I released his wrist and looked at him. He didn't take his arm back from me, but his lips were tight, as if he were annoyed or thinking.

I wanted to make a joke to break the tension, but I knew it wasn't a good time, so I stayed quiet, waiting on Nikolai.

Finally, he sighed and leaned back against the aspen. "I do not think myself so strong as to not try to get involved with you, should we continue as we are," he said. "I can stay long enough to see you safe from the Andersons, but then I should go."

"We talked. You're part of our pack. If you want me, you get me." That came out a little callous, but I wasn't sure how else to say it.

He frowned and glanced at me. "I would not expect them to share you."

"They would all rather lose me to you, than to the Andersons. They'd rather not lose me at all. The guys don't have too many boundaries with each other, but if you do, we can figure them out. They'll share if you will."

"And how do you feel about that idea?"

"I…"

My hesitation hurt him. He turned away, lips tightening again.

"I'm still getting used to dating three guys. I like it. I like you. They're okay with it, and I'm willing to give it a try, if you are."

"And what if I don't want to share?"

The way he asked the question made me think he was simply curious, as opposed to objecting, but the thought of having to give up part of my pack for my safety made my breath catch.

"Then we'll work through that, too," I finally replied.

"They must truly love you, if they're valuing your safety so highly, that they'd give you up." He looked at me again, expression closed.

"Please don't make them."

He nodded. "I would not wish that, either. I suppose we shall have to see how it works out then."

"Really?"

Nikolai sighed. "Sofia, I want you safe. I can teach you, and I should. The entire situation is difficult to take in, not just with you, but with everything." He gestured out toward the valley. "I am sitting in a country I had never even heard of a few days ago."

"I'm sorry."

"I am grateful to be out of the dimensional prison. Trust me."

"I do."

His eyes widened, and he looked about ready to bolt again before he nodded. "We shall have to trust each other."

"So, is that a yes?"

He nodded. "I have several spells I must show you. Like when we shared languages," he said, changing the subject.

"Okay."

"Do you have a safe place for us to work magic?"

"Yes." I stood and tugged on his hand until he was also on his feet, and then took him to my grove.

"This is quite impressive," he admitted once I had sealed us inside.

"I did it when Doc helped me access my magic on purpose the first time."

He touched the pines lightly, walking around the circle. I shivered. It was as if he touched me.

"You did well. See, you don't need me." He turned to face me.

"I think I do. Maybe if the Andersons weren't trying to capture me, but they are." I stepped forward and put my hands on his chest.

He set his hands over mine and sighed. "You're quite certain?"

"As certain as I can be."

"And the others are quite certain?"

I smiled. "Same answer. How about you?"

He cupped my face with one of his calloused hands and brushed his thumb across my temple. "I suppose we shall see what we can accomplish then."

Nikolai pulled at me with his magic.

I gasped as my body reacted as it had earlier, the desire so strong, it made me ache, and would have had me reaching for him…if we weren't now standing in the same ornate room as when we first met.

Chapter 14

Nikolai

Nikolai watched as Sofia looked around the room in wonder. Though she was far from naïve, there was an innocence about her that appealed to Nikolai. Maybe it was simply that she hadn't grown up fighting for her life like most everyone he had known up to this point had. Maybe it was just her. He was still trying to resist his attraction, though he wasn't sure why anymore. Perhaps he felt it was too fast. Maybe he simply hadn't recovered from Roza's betrayal. He had never been good at self-reflection. Though, he'd also never had much time for the luxury. Life was a nearly constant battle, fighting off the Tatars or battling the very elements as the Russian winters attempted to claim the lives battle had spared.

"You haven't gotten around to explaining this place," she said, switching back to English once she turned fully about and stood facing him again.

"We have only known each other a few days," Nikolai replied in the same language, though it mattered less here.

"True."

"It is, eh, a mental space for communicating with other mages. We may or may not speak same language. We may need to share spells. We are safe with your other men and the grove protecting us, so it is good spot for us to discuss magic."

"Other men?" That mischievous grin of hers was going to do him in.

"Eh, well." He held up his wrist and showed her the five pawprints on his arm. "As you said, you have claimed me."

Her expression fell. "Sorry."

Nikolai couldn't stand her feeling bad about it. He wasn't upset. Not really. He closed the distance between them and pulled her into a hug. "I am not angry."

"But you're not happy."

"I am happier than you think. I am simply not sure where I stand with anything or anyone. It makes me hesitant." That was probably the closest he could come to telling her how he felt when he still didn't understand his own feelings.

She leaned into his embrace, putting her arms around his back and holding him tightly. "We said it was okay."

He very suddenly wanted them back in their own minds, wanted to caress her with his hands, not just this mental projection.

Releasing her and stepping back, he cleared his throat. "So, the spells you need."

She focused on him intently. "Don't I need to know how to cast spells before you teach anything else to me?"

"You already know how." He shrugged. "You just need practice. Some focusing exercises. There is lots to learn, and these won't be hard for you. Simple spells. The first couple are probably some of the reasons mages got in trouble with the church." He grinned.

"Oh?"

"Yes, I never got the impression that the church liked independent women. Being in charge of your own body is very important. You have three boyfriends. I'm quite certain you don't want babies, too. There is a spell for that."

She raised her eyebrows. "I actually have a medical device for that, but I want to learn the spell."

Nikolai nodded, but before he could continue, she grabbed his wrist and traced the pawprints magically tattooed there.

Her touch sent shivers through him, and he sucked in a breath. "Sofia..."

"Stop excluding yourself." She glared at him.

"I did not wish to presume."

She ran her hand up his arm, stepped into him, and cupped her hand around his neck, tugging him down to her.

He didn't resist kissing her, and pulled her close. They explored each other's mouths for a time, and he let his hands wander over her body, caressing her sides, cupping her ass. She pressed into him, testing his resolve nearly to the breaking point.

Finally, Sofia released him. "Spells?" Her eyes sparkled with amusement.

"Ah, yes. There is also a spell to prevent disease. It is useful in outbreaks and for random trysts. Not that I feel you will have much time for random encounters with..." He hesitated, then gave in. "Four of us to keep you happy."

The smile that lit up her face was worth giving in. He brushed his fingers across her temple, pushing a strand of hair behind her ears.

"And the last for now is healing from a vampire bite. Most useful when your boyfriend is at least partially a vampire."

Sofia's face lit up. "You like vampires, don't you?"

"Eh, guilty. Peter and I were close." He shrugged. "We traveled together for many years, and it is not always easy to feed a vampire in a military camp. If the troops know the vampire is already fed, they aren't nervous about having one or two around. The mages kept the vampires fed, and the transference was useful also."

"Transference?"

"Vampires can temporarily borrow powers if they feed from mages, shifters, and other supernatural beings. Doc can do this, yes?"

Sofia nodded. "That's no longer common knowledge, by the way."

"I won't spread it around."

"Yeah, from what I understand, vampires got pretty reclusive and are lethally protective about their secrets."

"Understandably. They are quite powerful, but also exploitable. I will pretend I know nothing, should anyone ask." Nikolai touched his neck again. "So, the spells. I will show you." He shaped the first spell in his mind and then drew Sofia in so she could see it as well. There were lots of ways to teach spells. This was a useful way for shorter, quick to memorize spells that wouldn't require much practice to cast.

It didn't take long before she had the shape of all three and was able to replicate them in her own mind.

Satisfied, Nikolai drew them back into their bodies.

He blinked off the slight disorientation that always came with changing his mental perceptions and glanced around. The small grove she had created was quite remarkable.

Sofia met his gaze, holding him still without even touching him. He knew what she wanted. He still couldn't believe the others were okay with this.

Hoping his hands weren't shaking, he reached for her, pulling her to him, meeting her lips with his. Their magic mingled, arousing him further. He wasn't sure he'd ever experienced resonance this strong before. When she pressed against him, it drove everything else out of his mind.

Lips still pressed to his, she ran her hands up his chest.

Nikolai groaned, gripping her hips, pulling her against him. Modern pants were far tighter than he was used to, and it was getting very uncomfortable.

Sofia undid the top button of his flannel shirt. Doc had provided his clothing, and the vampire seemed fond of flannel. Of course, the way it felt against his skin as Sofia rubbed her hands over his chest before undoing the next button was endearing the fabric to him rapidly.

Her shirt didn't have buttons. He considered leaving it on, because it would interrupt her process on his clothing, but he wanted her skin against his.

Nikolai slid his hands up her hips. She groaned against his mouth, nibbling his lip and then kissing along his jaw. He hooked his fingers under her shirt and tugged.

Sofia took the hint and helped him pull her shirt off before going back to work on his.

He stared for a moment, taking in the view of the light purple clothing that covered her breasts. "I believe I like modern women's clothing," he declared. "Fewer laces."

She laughed, twisted her arms around behind her, and did something to make the garment fall away. She slid it off her arms.

Nikolai had seen plenty of naked women, and never failed to appreciate their individual beauty. He studied Sofia for a moment before running his fingers up her ribs, then circling around her breasts.

She groaned, pressing into his touch. After a minute to appreciate his attention, she went back to work on his shirt. She had the buttons undone now, and he had to release her so she could push it off his shoulders. That pressed them together, and he put his arms around her, pulling her close as he kissed her deeply.

Sofia traced a couple of the scars on his shoulders. They were from the same battle that had nearly taken his life. She dug her fingers into his back, and he rumbled in pleasure.

She kissed along his neck, nibbling at his throat.

"I think Doc has us all conditioned to like getting bit," she murmured. "How about you?"

"Yes," he managed to reply.

She found a spot that wasn't bruised and bit down.

He clutched at her back. "Sofia," he gasped.

"You're not going to tell me you want to stop for breakfast, too, are you?" she groaned breathlessly.

Not liking that idea at all, Nikolai tugged at her, pulling her to the soft moss-covered ground. "No. I will not abandon you for food." He smirked to let her know he was teasing.

"Good."

Chapter 15

Sofia

Nikolai's lips sent a burning shudder through my center, lighting me up from the inside. His pause at my collarbone only stoked the flames.

He hovered over me, still pinning me down with his hands on my arms. His strength was that of a warrior, as opposed to the supernatural strength of the others. He still had me beat, and I wouldn't have been able to budge him if I tried, without resorting to actually fighting him.

I moaned as he sucked on one of my breasts, his tongue working at my nipple. He dragged his hands down my arms and continued to kiss down my body. I wanted to touch him, but he held my wrists pressed into the soft moss, and my legs were pinned under him.

His teeth grazed my stomach lightly, and I arched my back, moaning. Nikolai release my wrists and caressed my waist, hands running lightly across my hips until they came to my pants. He popped open the button and slid the zipper down before hooking his fingers in the waistband and tugging my pants off.

I lifted my butt to help him, and he pulled them off. It took me a moment to realize he had snagged my underwear at the same time. I'd only been completely naked in front of one other guy, and while it hadn't been a horrible experience, it hadn't been amazing, either.

Nikolai stared at me, a smile curling his lips. I panted, desire waring with uncharacteristic shyness.

"You are lovely, Sofia."

I smiled back, letting his words caress me as his hands worked their way up my legs.

He leaned forward, his hair falling forward into his face and tickling my skin as he resumed his trek up my body with his mouth. He reached my mound. I put my hand on Nikolai's head, tangling my fingers in his dark brown hair, though I wasn't sure if I was trying to stop him or encourage him. This was all new for me.

Nikolai took one of his hands and gripped my wrist, pulling my hand away and pinning it to the ground again.

I squirmed slightly, testing his grip, teasing him a little. He looked up and met my eyes, looking a little concerned. Blue magic swirled through his eyes, enhancing the tender desire I saw there. I smiled, though I was nervous. Apparently, that was what he was looking for. He nibbled at my thigh, and I gasped, opening my legs in response. He used his free hand to slide my leg over his shoulder before clutching my hip and squeezing gently.

Nikolai licked me, his tongue parting my folds.

Gasping, I clutched at the ground as Nikolai's tongue skillfully worked at me. Pleasure built from my breasts to my core, the sensation overwhelming. Thrusting against him, I cried out again as he pushed a finger inside me, moving in sync with his tongue as my pleasure built. I trembled, so close it almost hurt.

"Nikolai!"

My release left me breathless as it shuddered through me.

I lay there trembling as Nikolai kissed his way back up my body, then lay next to me and held me while I shook.

"You are good?"

I nodded, as I couldn't quite form words. He held me, his skin warming mine, his hand igniting sparks along my back as he trailed his fingers across my skin.

Sated, but not quite satisfied, I trailed my fingers down Nikolai's defined stomach. His breath hitched as I worked my way lower. I reached the scar that crossed his body and ran my fingers lightly along it until it disappeared under the hem of his jeans.

He shuddered as I ran my hand softly over the length of him, his jeans an annoying barrier.

Nikolai groaned, his eyes shutting for a moment.

"I'm going to try something I've never done before," I said. "If you don't mind."

"You may do whatever you wish," he breathed out.

"You'll tell me if you don't like it?"

"Yes."

Grinning, I watched his eyes widen when I slowly undid the button on his jeans. I rolled up until I was sitting on my knees and slowly worked his zipper down. He gripped my thigh with his strong hand, callouses catching on my smooth skin as he slid his hand up my hip. Delicate shivers of pleasure traveled up my back, and I took a moment to savor his touch.

Before I lost my nerve, I refocused on Nikolai. He lifted his hips when I slid my fingers between his pants and his hips, and I tugged at his jeans until I pulled them off. Tracing my fingers up his muscular calves and thighs, I admired what a lifetime of intense physical activity had done to him. He moaned softly as I again brushed my hand over his hard length, this time without his pants as a barrier.

"Sofia," he gasped and clutched at my thigh as I leaned forward and gently ran my tongue along his soft skin. He groaned as I took him into my mouth, the taste a little salty but not unpleasant. Nikolai shuddered, his breath coming faster as I ran my tongue over his tip before taking as much of him into my mouth as I could and wrapping my hand around the rest of him. He panted as I found a rhythm with my hand and mouth, his hips thrusting, fingers digging into my shoulder.

"I am close," Nikolai groaned, voice husky.

I let him slip from my mouth, and continued to rub with my hand, he thrust harder against me, breath coming in short gasps. He grabbed my wrist, and I let go of him. He shuddered, coming on his stomach.

Laying back on the soft moss covering the ground, I pressed up against him while he got his breathing under control.

He ran his hand over my shoulder and turned to kiss me.

I could taste myself on his lips, and I hesitated for a moment, before deciding I didn't care. He cupped my neck, and I opened my mouth, letting his tongue explore, before I did the same to him.

Eventually, he pulled away. "How did I get so lucky?"

"Maybe it's us who got lucky."

"No, definitely me." He smiled. "We should maybe get back, though," he said a little reluctantly.

"We need showers." I sighed, not really wanting to put clothes back on while I wasn't clean, but also not wanting to wander around naked. That might be a little much.

Nikolai's eyes glinted with amusement. "There is a spell for that. I will teach you."

His words warmed me. I finally had a teacher. Now if he could just show me everything I needed to know before the Andersons caught up to me, everything would work out fine.

Beyond that, I was looking forward to getting to know the Russian more. He was very good with his tongue, among other things.

Smiling, I watched as he shaped his magic, memorizing the spell, but also enjoying the grace of his movements and looking forward to the next time we would get to explore each other more.

∞ ∞ ∞

I sank down on the couch and stared at my hands. Doc found me a few minutes later. He sat next to me and put his arm around me. I pressed into his embrace.

"Is he going to help us?"

Needing some form of reassurance that everything was going to be all right, I curled into his chest. He hooked my legs with his free hand and pulled them over his legs so I could snuggle into him.

"Yes," I replied.

"Good." He clutched me close, taking a deep breath. "Enjoy yourself?" he asked, his voice low.

I groaned, not exactly having forgotten how good his sense of smell was, but I wasn't used to thinking in those terms.

"No?"

"Yes. It's just an adjustment. I haven't even gotten used to having the three of you yet, and now I have four."

He kissed the top of my head. "It will be an adjustment for all of us, but I think it will work out just fine."

I tilted my head back, and he kissed me, even though the scent of Nikolai had to be all over me. Doc didn't seem to mind as his mouth devoured mine.

We both looked up when Nikolai came in the front door.

"Must we send her back to school tomorrow?" The Russian mage sat in the armchair he seemed to prefer, his eyes consuming the two of us. His expression sent tingles down my spine to gather low in my core.

Doc tightened his arms around me, and his breath quickened. Apparently, I wasn't the only one affected by the heat in Nikolai's gaze.

If I'd had any doubts that Nikolai would be willing to share me, they were gone. At least with Doc, but then, he had admitted he had a thing for vampires, anyway.

"We all need to get back tomorrow," Doc grumbled. "But we can keep her tonight."

"Do I get a say in that?" I teased.

"Only if you're going to say yes," Nikolai replied, eyes twinkling.

"I've got news for you, Nik," I teased. "Modern women don't take orders well."

He chuckled. "No mage takes orders well, no matter what century they were born in."

Doc nibbled on my neck, and I tilted my head back to give him better access.

"I can't imagine you're hungry," Nikolai said through a laugh.

"For once, not terribly," Doc replied, though he continued to tease me, his lips traveling along my neck, biting gently.

Moaning, I clutched his shirt. "Jealous?" I had to ask.

"Perhaps," Nikolai answered, though he probably knew I was teasing him.

"Of which one of us?" My snicker turned into a cry of pleasure when Doc bit me just hard enough to draw blood. If that was supposed to be a reprimand, it didn't work. Nikolai replied, but I didn't hear what he said as Doc's tongue caressed my neck, driving other thoughts from my mind.

He relented after that. Kissing me on the mouth again, a faint coppery taste on his lips, before he went back to simply holding me.

"Before I am completely distracted…" Nikolai cleared his throat. "I do have a question."

I glanced at the mage. Blue motes sparkled in his otherwise dark brown eyes. I wondered if that always happened when mages were aroused.

"Yes?" Doc shifted his attention to Nikolai.

I hoped whatever he wanted to ask wasn't going to be emotionally difficult to deal with. I was already tapped out for the day.

"Do you know how to shoot a gun?"

The question was so far away from what I had expected him to ask that I stared at him in surprise. He was a mage, what did he need a gun for?

"Yes," Doc answered.

"Do you have any?"

"Several. Why?"

"I am used to fighting with various weapons, but these modern firearms I've not dealt with. I wish to practice shielding in case it becomes necessary. Is there a place we can do this?"

"Yeah. It's a bit of a hike from here, but there's a natural backdrop not far into the national forest. We can practice there."

"Excellent. As for the Andersons, if you won't allow me to kill them, the best thing we can do right now is keep her safe long enough for me to teach her sufficiently, so she is no longer useful to them."

"What if they try to expose us?" That was one of my bigger fears.

Doc's arms tightened around me. "Then they'll learn the hard way they should not have, and then we'll disappear for a while, if we can't talk our way out of any repercussions. Hopefully, the older Andersons are sufficiently afraid of me, and they'll keep Alex in check."

"What did you do to them?"

Doc clenched his jaw. "I'd really rather not talk about it."

I pressed into him. "Okay."

Doc tensed, and I glanced up at him. He tilted his head, as if listening, brow furrowed.

"What?" Nikolai stood and faced the door, as if ready to defend us.

"Sam's car."

I didn't want to move, and Doc didn't act like he wanted me to either, so I stayed put.

Nikolai answered the door when Sam knocked.

"I need your help." She didn't offer any other greetings, though she did look confused when she saw me on Doc's lap.

"What's wrong, Sam?"

"The fae are screaming about death metal blocking them from their land. Who else knows how to get to the portal?"

Doc shook his head. "I don't know."

"If the Andersons are determined to use Sofia, they may have attempted to trap some of the fae to use in the binding," Nikolai cautioned. "They are useful for such things. Their demon could have found the entrance to the fae lands. The demon realm and the fae realm have much in common."

Sam rounded on Nikolai. "And how do you know all that?"

He glanced at Doc, who shook his head.

"Perhaps it is best if you trust that I know what I speak of."

She glared.

Ed and Allan burst into the cabin, both shirtless and covered in sweat.

I licked my lips as I enjoyed the view, despite Sam's grim words.

"What's wrong?" Ed glanced between all of us while Allan kept an eye on Sam.

Ed, looking for reassurance, Allan, keeping his eye on the potential threat.

"Sam said the fae are in trouble and wanted our help," Doc answered.

"Oh. Well, let's go," Ed replied.

"It is most assuredly a trap." Nikolai crossed his arms and glared at Sam.

I glanced up at Doc. His eyes narrowed.

"For the fae," Sam replied.

"For us," Nikolai clarified. "And the fae. Is the expression, two birds with one stone?"

"So, you've joined their happy little pack then?" Sam glared at Nikolai.

The Russian didn't answer.

"Well, if you're not going to help them…"

Nikolai waved his hand dismissively. "Of course I will help them. I am simply pointing out that it is likely to be a trap. We must be prepared."

I swung my legs off of Doc's lap and stood up. He did the same. "Excuse me for a minute," he said, and headed into his bedroom. I guessed to get weapons.

"Sofia, you will stay close to me?" Nikolai made his order sound like a question, and I smirked. Maybe he did have practice dealing with women.

Going over to his side, I watched Sam's eyebrows raise as I slid my hand into Nikolai's callused one.

She finally looked at Ed and Allan, and if anything, her eyebrows rose even further.

"What happened to your arm?" She gestured toward the bandages on Ed's forearm.

"Allan and I were wrestling. He bit me a little harder than normal. I'll be fine in another day or two." The lie came easily, so he must have rehearsed an excuse.

"Need to remind him who is older every once in a while," Allan said lightly.

Sam didn't quite look convinced, but she let it drop.

Doc returned, wearing a flannel shirt over his T-shirt, and his cowboy hat. "We'll follow you there."

"Okay. Sofia, do you want to ride with me?" Sam looked at me.

Nikolai tightened his hand, but relaxed when I shook my head. "I'm good riding with the guys. We can squeeze in the back seat."

She gave us all another curious look before shrugging. "All right. Let's go."

Chapter 16

Sofia

"It is most assuredly a trap," Nikolai insisted once we were all in the pickup.

I had squeezed into the back seat with Ed and Allan. Allan had his arm around me, and I leaned into him while Ed held my hand.

"Yeah, but does Sam know it?" Doc's voice was grim.

"I cannot decide." Nikolai shrugged. "It is no matter. We will be prepared."

"Is it just me or is anyone else a little worried about our mage feeling a bit overconfident?" Allan muttered.

Nikolai twisted around to look at us and grinned. "I think we are about to find out."

"You don't have to look so happy about it," Allan grumbled without any real annoyance.

"I am bored, and a good fight always relieves the boredom."

"If you're bored already, then maybe we need to lock you in Sofia's grove with her more frequently," Ed quipped.

Nikolai's brows raised, but his grin widened. "I would not complain." He winked and turned back around.

My cheeks heated, and I buried my face in Allan's chest. Ed squeezed my hand.

After that, we drove for a while in silence until Doc turned off into the parking lot for the trailhead. Sam was already there.

"The last time we were here, there weren't any other cars, either. Is this not a popular trailhead?" I slid out of the truck on Ed's side, and he kept a hold of my hand. I leaned into him, and he turned and pressed his lips to my head, inhaling after he kissed me.

Sam watched us, confusion clear on her face. I did my best to ignore her while I pressed against Ed.

"It's far enough away from the valley that it's not super popular. It's also a weekday. There are a lot of closer trailheads," Allan answered.

"Smells like snow." Nikolai studied our surroundings.

The air did smell crisp and had a distinct chill to it. The morning coolness had lingered today, especially at this higher elevation.

"Stay close," Doc ordered as he headed for the trail.

Sam trailed behind him, and suddenly, I didn't trust her there. She was leading us to a trap, if she knew it or not, and she didn't seem terribly worried. Sam knew the danger the Andersons posed. Maybe she had been outside of their notice before, but it was possible her loose association with the guys had changed that.

I glanced at Nikolai. He may have been having similar thoughts, because he fell in behind her, walking almost too close. Ed tugged on my hand until I was walking behind Nikolai, and then he let go, dropping back a little until he and Allan were trailing us. Not as far as normal, but far enough back that they could keep an eye on everything more easily.

Nikolai subtly cast a few spells, and I wasn't sure Sam noticed. I didn't sense him do it through magic, only noticed because I saw him move his hands. Even the color of his magic was hidden.

He glanced at me and winked. He was definitely teaching me that later.

Though the surroundings were still beautiful and the pine forest we walked through smelled divine, the hike was not nearly as enjoyable as the last time I had been here. I knew I wouldn't be much use in a fight, and that scared me. I didn't want to hinder the guys, but I also knew it wouldn't have been wise to leave me alone, either. Splitting up might have been what they were hoping for. Either that, or they thought they were well enough prepared for the guys, that taking them on all at once didn't worry the enemy mages.

Of course, they had Ash. He could level the playing field a lot if properly commanded. Alex didn't seem to be very good at that yet, but it was hard to tell if that was because he was lazy, or he actually didn't know he was leaving commands open to interpretation.

In a short time, we reached the turn off the trail. Before, I couldn't tell there was another path. Now, it had been heavily trampled, the trees damaged, and the underbrush disturbed. Even I could tell something had crashed through there without a care to the noise it, or they, made and the damage they left.

Ed growled as we stared at the damage.

Nikolai and Doc shared a glance before the mage waved Doc back and stepped slowly into the woods.

Doc fell back to stand next to me, and we both watched Sam while also trying to pay attention to everything else.

Ed and Allan watched our backs.

Though we were prepared to be attacked, it still shocked me when Doc grabbed my arms and shoved me behind a tree, sheltering me with his body as he pulled me low to the ground.

I heard a sharp crack, and dirt sprayed from the ground where Doc and I had been standing.

Ed grabbed Sam and dragged her off the path. Allan had already disappeared into the woods. Nikolai came over to us, crouching, but studying the surrounding forest.

"Trap," Nikolai stated, smiling slightly. "And it looks like I get to practice against firearms after all."

The dirt around us erupted in an orange and green light show. Unless they had other mages with similar magical signatures, that would be Alex and Ash.

"You are surrounded," a male voice shouted. I thought it sounded familiar, but it wasn't someone I actually knew. Maybe someone from when I had escaped Alex's home not long ago.

"If you hand Sofia over to us, we'll let you live."

Sam looked startled, but not completely surprised when I looked over at her to see how she was taking all this. We warned her it was a trap, so maybe that was all it was, but I couldn't help but feel she had sold us out for her own safety.

Nikolai squeezed my shoulder before shaking his head. "It is weak attack. Trying to intimidate us." He shrugged. "It is not working."

I managed to smile. "If I was alone, I'd be intimidated."

"But you're not," Doc pointed out.

"No!" Ed yelled out for all of us.

"Have you located their positions yet?" Nikolai whispered, and glanced at Doc, who nodded.

Sam was watching us closely, though she probably couldn't hear what we said if we stayed quiet. I didn't like her expression at all. Ed still crouched by her side, and I wasn't sure where Allan had disappeared to, but I knew he wouldn't be far. I hoped Ed kept an eye on Sam and not just to keep her safe.

Nikolai was used to working with vampires, and his familiarity with their powers would certainly be an asset here.

Doc leaned close and whispered their locations, and the mage nodded.

"You and Sofia stay here and cast this shield. I will scout." Nikolai pushed a bit of magic into me, and I caught the shape of the spell from it.

"Support Sofia," he ordered Doc, before he held his hand over his head and sprinkled blue motes on himself. Moments later, he vanished.

Sam gasped. "That's not supposed to be possible."

Ignoring her, I formed the spell like Nikolai had shown me. Doc fed Nikolai's magic into me, and we expanded the shield until it surrounded us, Ed, and Sam. I hoped Allan knew what he was doing.

"He's taught you quite a bit already," she murmured.

"Not really the time," I muttered through gritted teeth. Maintaining the spell wasn't actually as hard as I was acting, but I didn't want her to be able to judge my capabilities. I also didn't want her to know Doc was feeding Nikolai's magic to me, though she could see his signature in the spell. Hopefully, she couldn't tell where I was getting it from, or if she knew about Doc's bracelet reservoir, maybe she thought it was from that.

My skin tingled where Doc touched me, still shielding me with his body while he fed magic to me. As it melded with my own, my nerves tingled, and power coursed through me, connecting me to my surroundings and my pack. My awareness of Doc increased, his cool desert energy mingling with the raging storm of Nikolai's. With a moment's concentration, I could feel the mage's location, and then Ed and Allan entered my awareness.

Beyond the bond we had formed, I got a sense of Doc's awareness of everyone, and then Ed and Allan's senses. Nikolai's were enhanced through some of the magic he had cast, but remained much closer to my levels.

"Focus," Doc whispered in my ear.

His breath on my skin brought me solidly back to myself, but I was left with the knowledge I had gained from the others. I knew where our attackers were. There were five of them. Alex and Ash, and three men I didn't recognize. All mages. Only one smelled of gunpowder, and he was the one Allan stalked.

Ash and Alex came into view and studied the shield I had cast. Ash's gaze found Doc, though his expression remained neutral.

"Yeah, take that down." Alex gave a negligent wave toward my shield.

Ash pulled his attention away from Doc and raised his hands. Orange light built around them before he cast pure energy at the shield.

I poured more of my energy into it, and while the shield flexed under the assault, it didn't break.

Both Ash and Alex looked surprised.

I bared my teeth at them and focused on maintaining the shield while Ash tried to overload me. He would win, eventually, but it was going to take a lot longer than they had probably anticipated.

Alex blended his green energy into Ash's assault.

Sweat beaded on my forehead and ran down my back.

"You've got this," Doc whispered.

I drew on my own reserves and the magic Doc had taken from Nikolai through his blood and strengthened the shield before it could waver.

My arms trembled. Doc held me.

The gun fired, and a man screamed, but I could sense that Allan was okay. The bullet impacted my shield, and the only thing that let me keep it up against that much concentrated force was Doc's support. He was starting to run out of borrowed magic, though, and we were going to need Nikolai soon.

Fortunately, the mage stepped into the clearing behind Ash and Alex.

The demon continued to concentrate on the shield, but Alex had to stop and throw up his own shield as Nikolai pelted him with blue energy. I wasn't sure what spell Nikolai cast, but the shield Alex used shattered, and Nikolai hit him again, and Alex crumpled to the ground.

Nikolai studied Ash.

Ash ignored the mage for a moment, before speaking in Nikolai's dialect of Russian. "I was merely instructed to take out the shield. However, it would be unwise for anyone to observe that loophole. I will not defend myself unless I'm truly in danger."

"What'd he say?" Sam looked over at us.

I shrugged, though I understood perfectly well.

Nikolai brought his hand back and formed a glowing blue spear. He launched it at the demon.

Ash dodged, dropping his attack on the shield long enough to put up a token resistance to Nikolai's attacks.

He blocked the second, but the third struck home, and the demon collapsed to the ground.

Allan returned, eyes wide, but otherwise unharmed.

"The others are dead or unconscious," Nikolai informed us. He kicked Alex. "What should we do with him?"

"How long will he be out?" Doc asked.

I dropped the shield, sagging in relief. Doc pulled me to my feet and held me.

Ed and Sam also stood.

"A few hours."

"That's enough time to find their fae traps and get out of here."

"You truly want to leave him alive?" Nikolai looked shocked.

"I'm not certain killing him would solve anything," Doc replied.

"It would send message." Nikolai shrugged. "Very well."

"Wait, you'd just kill him?" Sam gasped.

"This is war. They started it, unless I'm mistaken. Always kill the enemy mages, or just fight them again. Unless they surrender."

She stared at him, horrified.

I was too tired to judge him, especially since I had no way of knowing what it was like to grow up like he had. I was just grateful he was here.

"Well done." Nikolai came over to me and put an arm around me, though he didn't try to take me from Doc. I hugged him back.

"Let's get these fae traps and get out of here then," Ed suggested.

Allan hung back, and I pulled away from Doc. I didn't need our pack bond to know something bothered him.

"What's up?" I put my arm around him and held him against me while we trailed behind the others. Still alert for danger, but thinking we were probably out of it for now.

He remained silent for a moment before his words came out in a rush. "I, uh, killed that guy who was shooting at us. Just snapped his neck. It was so easy. I was so worried about protecting the rest of you. I've never killed anyone before." He trembled.

Wrapping my arms around Allan, I let him feel my gratitude that he was there to protect us and my love for him.

Allan sighed, breathing in my scent, distracting himself from what he had done. "Mmmm, you smell like all of us."

"You did good, Allan. You did what you had to. They were going to kill all of you. Nik can probably take care of the bodies." I kissed him gently, then pulled on his hand, keeping it in mine when we found the others gathered around several iron pots. They were really simple, just round pots that you might make soup in. Inside lay quite a few of the tiny fae.

"Are they dead?" I clutched Allan's hand.

"Maybe," Nikolai replied sadly. He knelt by the traps, and the whole area glowed blue for a moment. I watched closely, trying to absorb what he did.

"There are no additional spells beyond the ones to attract and capture the fae." Holding his hand over the first of the traps, he whispered softly before lifting his hand slowly. The fae were drawn out on a bed of blue magic. He set them gently on the ground before moving to the next pot and repeating the procedure.

Once he was finished, he glared at the pots. "These, I will destroy."

He didn't wait for anyone's objection, just picked them up, tossed them into the air, and blasted them with magic.

They disintegrated, and he hit the air with a light breeze, blowing the metal contaminants away from the fae portal.

Once he finished, the forest lit up with sparkles as the other tiny fae descended on their brethren and carried them away.

A couple remained.

Nikolai held out his hand, palm up, as if used to dealing with fae.

The tiny creature landed on his palm, bowed their thanks, and then took to the air again.

Once we were alone, Nikolai headed back to the trail, and we followed.

"Can you do something about the bodies?" I asked.

"Yes." He knew what I referred to and headed off to handle the deceased mages. Ed went with him. The rest of us trudged back down the path. Even Doc looked exhausted.

We said goodbye to Sam at the parking lot and climbed into Doc's pickup, waiting for Ed and Nikolai to catch up. They finally joined us.

"I still cannot tell if Sam was involved or not," Nikolai grumbled once we were headed back to Doc's place.

The shadows stretched, and it would be late by the time we got back.

"I can't tell, either, but they know about you now. That won't go over well," Doc replied.

"No."

"You're sure we can't keep her up at the cabin with us?" Ed pulled me against him, nuzzling my hair.

"It might be good idea," Nikolai agreed.

"We'll talk about it. We also have to worry about Victoria's safety," Doc reminded us.

"We could bring her up, too," Ed suggested hesitantly.

"Regardless, she's not going anywhere tonight." The possessive tone in Doc's voice sent tingles through me, and I squirmed in pleasure.

∞ ∞ ∞

Allan still felt awful about killing that mage, so Doc pulled him onto the couch and put an arm around him, comforting him. I sat on the other side and lay in his lap, one hand stretched to Doc's thigh, and the rest of me pressed into Allan. The werewolf leaned into Doc and rested his hands on my arm and hip. Doc held my hand with his free one.

We didn't speak, just let the physical contact keep us connected while Nikolai helped Ed in the kitchen.

"Food will be done in about thirty," Ed declared when he came into the living room, followed by Nikolai. He sat down on the loveseat, and Nikolai sank into the armchair.

"Nikolai, Sam was very surprised when you turned yourself invisible. She said that was supposed to be impossible. Do you know what she was talking about?" Now that everything had settled down for a while, I thought we should talk about the day a little.

"Perhaps she thought I teleported? Invisibility is my favorite spell." He grinned. "I perfected it to steal pastries."

I raised my eyebrows. "Really?"

He ducked his head for a moment, grin widening. "Yes. I was four. The baker was a werewolf. Very sensitive nose. It took six months before I perfected the spell so I wouldn't get caught.

It has proven very valuable. It is easy for me, but most people have a hard time with it."

"How old are you, Nikolai?" Doc asked after a bit.

"I am old. Twenty-five." He smiled.

Ed snorted. "Not that old."

"Not now, no," Nikolai agreed. "Practically ancient for someone who's been fighting in battle since he was ten." He shrugged. "I am lucky to have survived."

"Ten?" I blurted.

"Different times. Powerful mage in a family of powerful mages. I learned the sword as soon as I could hold it. Magic almost since I was born. If we weren't fighting the Tatars, we were fighting the elements."

The oven timer chimed, interrupting us.

I reluctantly got off of Allan's lap, and we all headed into the kitchen. Even if he still felt like crap, not much would keep a werewolf from dinner. I helped Doc bring over food, and we dug in. No one spoke much, and by the time everyone had finished, my eyelids were drooping.

"Why don't you three go to bed," Nikolai suggested. "Doc and I can clean up and keep an eye on things for a while. It may be best if someone keeps watch tonight."

I shivered, unnerved by the necessity. Nikolai was right, though. We were safer here, with established protections and whatever Nikolai had added to the house, but we weren't safe.

It didn't take long for us to get ready for bed. I curled up between the two werewolves, and, knowing Nikolai and Doc kept watch, fell deeply asleep.

Chapter 17

Nikolai

"Can we keep her safe?" Doc sank down onto the couch and Nikolai sat next to him, pulling his leg up on the cushion and turning so he could face him.

Nikolai shook his head. "It is hard to say. In my time, yes. We would simply take the Andersons out. Then she would be safe. Now? Well, I don't truly exist on any records. I could still do it." He shrugged. "I would need help though, and it is dangerous. Best bet is to keep training her. She has to go to classes, though, and that takes up time. One of us should be with her all the time, but I am not sure how that's possible." He wished he had a better answer, but he didn't know enough about this time to really come up with a good solution.

"We can ask Victoria if she minds if you sleep at the dorm," Doc suggested.

"It would be better to keep her here, but that could work."

"Victoria has some protection against the mages. Sam made a shield spell for her."

"I noticed. It will not protect against physical attack, though." Nikolai sighed and leaned back against the couch. "It is very complicated. Things were much simpler when you could simply attack the enemy."

"Do you miss home?"

He shrugged. "I barely know enough about this world to say if I miss home or not. I miss some of the people. I don't know that I miss dealing with the, eh, politics, I guess you could say." He did miss the familiarity, but the companionship he had found with Sofia and the others was making up for a lot of his loss.

They sat in comfortable silence for a while before Nikolai held out his arm. "You must be starving."

Doc glanced at Nikolai, raising an eyebrow.

"You used a lot of energy helping Sofia today. Seems to follow."

Doc nodded and took Nikolai's arm. "Are you sure you're not exhausted?"

"No. I am fine. Remember, I am used to fighting entire battles with magic and sword. Despite this altitude, I'm not tired."

"Thanks."

Nikolai wasn't in the mood to start anything with Doc, and he was fairly certain the vampire wasn't interested at the moment, either, so he tried to ignore the pleasure when Doc bit down on his wrist. He leaned on the back of the couch and stared at the wall, concentrating on keeping his breathing even. Peter, his vampire partner, had never quite been able to explain how vampires controlled what the person they fed from felt, but he'd had quite a range that he could inflict on people, from outright pain, to a more neutral pleasure that only masked any potential discomfort to varying degrees of pleasure, depending on what the situation called for. Doc didn't seem to have as much control in that area, and despite his best intentions, he was still panting and hard when the vampire finally released him. Modern pants were simply too tight. He shifted in discomfort.

"Sorry," Doc apologized.

It took a minute for him to catch his breath, then he shook his head. "It is fine. Get some rest. You can take over in a while."

Doc nodded and curled up on the couch, while Nikolai got up and found the tablet Doc had given him. He curled up on the other end of the couch and settled in to learn more about this world he found himself in.

The wards would alert him with plenty of notice if something was going on. He could have gone to sleep as well, but he decided it was safer if one of them were awake.

After a few hours of catching up on history, Nikolai got up and went to the kitchen to make some tea and stretch his legs. He wandered around the cabin while the tea steeped, and even that didn't wake Doc. He had thought to wake the other man up in a few hours so he could get some rest. Doc was exhausted, though, so he left him alone and returned to his spot on the couch.

At some point in the middle of the night, Doc shifted around on the couch until he was actually laying down, with his head on Nikolai's thigh and his legs curled so he fit. He didn't think Doc woke up and chose to cuddle with him, so much as he had gotten used to sleeping with the werewolves, and now Sofia, and had felt alone.

Nikolai ran his fingers through Doc's long hair, and marveled that the others had accepted him so easily into their pack.

Sofia had a lot to do with it, he was certain. He studied the pawprints she had added to his wrist for a moment, before he went back to playing with Doc's hair, amazed that she also had accepted him so quickly. True, she needed him, but it was more than that, he was sure. Or hoped.

Doc's light breathing changed, and the vampire tensed.

"It's still the middle of the night," Nikolai whispered. "All's quiet." He slid his finger along Doc's temple, brushing the vampire's hair out of his face. "You can go back to sleep."

"I thought the idea was for us to take turns," he replied softly.

"You need the rest more than I do, I think."

Doc didn't reply. He also didn't move, so Nikolai continued to play with his hair. "Tell me about where you are from," he asked once it became clear Doc wasn't immediately going back to sleep.

"I'm not sure I'm really from anywhere," Doc mused after a while. "I was born in Arizona, though it wasn't a state when I was born. We moved around a lot when I was younger, traveled all over the Southwest. California, Nevada, Arizona, New Mexico. I didn't make it up to Colorado until much later. Lots of desert. Lots of cactus." Doc spoke slowly, as if he were reliving memories while he shared a few hints of his early life.

"First time we spent more than a few months in any one location, was at a cattle ranch in California. My father had injured himself, and they graciously allowed us to stay while he recovered. The cowboys taught me to ride, work cows. We ended up staying for nearly a year before the cowboys started asking questions about me. That's when we moved on. We continued to move around until my father died. Then I started spending a little more time in one spot, mostly cowboying. Occasionally hunting down rogue vampires or werecreatures."

Nikolai's hand stilled. He had never considered that Doc might be a hunter. He spoke slowly. "I suppose you've killed many vampires?"

"Only a couple. Only ones that were noticeably preying on humans. More weres. I was not quite so dedicated to the cause as my parents were. I only got involved when there was a real problem."

He went back to running his fingers through Doc's hair. "How did you end up with Allan and Ed?"

"Their parents were killed by werewolves while they were out camping. They ended up in the foster care system, which is a bad place for a couple of new werewolves to end up. Somehow, they evaded detection, but it was getting tough for them. They ran across me not long after I moved to the area. Long story short, I was able to get them out."

"And then you found Sofia," Nikolai added.

Doc smiled. "Yes. She has certainly turned our lives upside down."

He traced his fingers lightly along Doc's jaw and down his neck.

The man shut his eyes and tilted his neck, enjoying the attention.

"What do you want for yourself, Nikolai? Now that you're here," Doc asked after a few minutes of silence.

The mage stilled his hand, resting it on Doc's shoulder, and thought. "I don't know. There is so much to learn before I can answer. I suppose in the short term, I want to help keep her safe. See where I fit in to this modern world. Figure out how I fit in here."

Doc put his hand on Nikolai's and ran his fingers lightly across his knuckles. "We're glad to have you."

"You are. Sofia is. I'm having a harder time reading Allan and Ed."

"They are glad to have you, as well. They just have to get used to you, and the whole situation with the Andersons is going to make everything more difficult than it really needs to be."

"And Sofia wants all of us."

Doc dragged his fingers over the back of Nikolai's hand until he could touch the mage's wrist, then he traced the colorful wolf paws marked there. "She wants all of us, and we all want her."

"Yes," he whispered, Doc's gentle touch sending shivers down his spine. "We do." His breath quickened as Doc continued to run his fingers softly over Nikolai's hand.

Doc stilled his hand. "Sorry."

"No need to apologize. I should think it obvious I do not mind."

"I suppose I'm not very good at any sort of relationship," Doc said, voice contemplative.

"Seems to me, you're doing fine."

"Allan and Ed were grateful for anyone who even remotely understood them. Sofia, I have no idea how we attracted her."

"Stop. You and the werewolves are quite likeable. Also, attractive. Of course, Sofia was drawn to all of you. She can be herself with you, and you make her feel safe. I can see no reason why she wouldn't want to be with any of you. Or, in this case, all of you. Just because modern times are not friendly to your kind, or any of us really, doesn't mean you won't find someone who loves you."

"What about you?"

"What about me?" Nikolai asked.

"You don't seem to mind vampires."

Nikolai chuckled. "As Sofia has already figured out, I like vampires. Peter, he was my best friend for long time, and the others that fought with us, I was friendly with, as well."

Doc turned onto his back so that he could look up at him.

Nikolai brushed some of the hair out of his face. "Though I do get the impression you're not used to having men interested in you."

The vampire blushed. "I'm not used to having anyone interested in me. At least, anyone it was safe to get close to."

The mage smiled and leaned forward, his shoulder length hair brushing against Doc's face, his lips just barely brushing the other man's. "I'm safe," he whispered, and waited, letting Doc make the decision.

After a moment, Doc put his hand behind Nikolai's neck and pressed their lips together.

Doc opened his mouth when he ran his tongue over the vampire's lips. He explored Doc's mouth with his tongue, his heartrate quickening, breath coming faster. The vampire responded in kind, fingers twining in Nikolai's hair. They explored each other's mouths for a few minutes, before Doc released him. Nikolai straightened, grinning, breathing heavily. Doc returned his smile, eyes shining. He liked seeing the touch of his blue magic shining in Doc's eyes, though he wouldn't have minded Sofia's lavender dancing there, as well.

"Get some more rest," Nikolai ordered. "I will take a nap in the morning."

Doc rolled back onto his side, pressing a little more firmly into the mage. His breathing finally quieted, and Nikolai went back to reading about this strange future he had found himself in. Though, he reflected, his current circumstances had some distinct benefits, and he looked forward to thoroughly exploring them.

Chapter 18

Allan

Allan woke with his back against Sofia's front, one of her arms curled around his chest, holding him tightly. Ed was pressed into her back, curled around her. Though he wanted to stay, his stomach growled, and he knew he would regret ignoring that. He generally liked being a werewolf, and he rarely minded how much he had to eat to stay fed, but at times like this, he wished he could comfortably sleep in a little.

Ed stirred when Allan got up.

Sofia pressed more firmly into Ed, still asleep. She was used to waking up in Doc's arms, and Allan didn't want her to wake up alone. When Ed opened his eyes a crack, Allan whispered, "Stay with Sofia. Doc and I can make breakfast."

Ed's lips curled into a smile, and he snuggled Sofia closer.

Allan went out into the living room, thinking he would find Doc awake. He hesitated when he saw Doc asleep, using Nikolai's lap as a pillow. The mage had one hand tangled in Doc's hair. The other supported his chin as he stared out the big window.

The sheer comfortable intimacy that scene evoked bothered Allan far more than seeing the two of them kiss had. If Doc was going to sleep, why hadn't he just come to bed? Allan snapped his jaw shut when Nikolai stiffened slightly and turned, sensing his presence somehow.

Nikolai tilted his head, obviously not understanding Allan's confused expression. Allan truly wasn't sure if he understood his own reaction or not, either. He just knew he couldn't deal with the mage right then. Instead of heading to the kitchen, he went out the front door, shutting it a little harder than necessary behind him.

He didn't have the super sensitive hearing that Doc did, but it was pretty good, and he heard Doc startle awake, despite the shut door.

"What happened?"

He could picture his friend looking around confused, long hair in his face. He never used to wear it down so much, but Sofia liked it down. Allan did, too.

"I am not sure. Allan is upset about something," Nikolai answered.

Whatever Doc replied, Allan was finally out of hearing distance. He headed into the woods, wondering why he was so upset.

He had barely come to terms with having to share Sofia with the mage. He hadn't considered that he might have to share his best friend, as well. Allan really hadn't been bothered by watching Doc and Nikolai make out with each other. He'd certainly been turned on. But this?

"Fuck." He kicked at a tree with his bare foot, just hard enough to sting a little.

"Allan, what's wrong?"

He jumped, spinning around. Doc rarely snuck up on the werewolves.

"I…" His heart clenched.

Doc's hair hung around his face, messy from sleep. He was also barefoot, and his shirt was half tucked into his jeans. He was hot as hell, and Allan didn't know what to do about it. At the same time, Sofia was with more than one of them…was it really that different if Allan had those sorts of feelings for both Doc and Sofia?

Doc frowned, as if trying to make sense of what he could read from Allan. He now had a pretty good idea of what Sofia had been going through when she realized both the werewolves and Doc could essentially read her emotions from her body's reactions.

He turned to walk away. He couldn't deal with this right now. He didn't know how.

Before he could get more than a step, Doc grabbed his arm and turned him until they faced each other. He tried to pull away, but he might as well have tried to budge a mountain. He couldn't remember a time when Doc had used his full strength on one of them.

"What's wrong?"

Allan tried to pull away.

"If you really want me to let go, I will," Doc said.

Did he want Doc to let go? No. He wanted Doc to pull him into a hug. Wanted him to kiss Allan like he had kissed Nikolai. He sniffed the air. The mage's scent was all over Doc. He growled slightly.

"If you don't talk to me, I can't fix it."

"I don't know how to answer you," he bit out.

Doc dropped his hand and shoved his hands into his pockets, eyes roaming over him.

The intensity of his gaze twisted Allan up even more inside.

"I think I was prepared to lose Sofia to Nikolai," he finally admitted. "I wasn't prepared to lose you, too."

Doc's eyes widened, and he ducked his head, hair falling forward around his hunched shoulders. "You haven't lost either of us, Allan."

"No, Sofia and I haven't had as much time to explore our relationship as you two have. And that's okay. We have time, and I don't feel like I've lost her, but you…" Allan shook his head. "I never really had you to begin with, I guess. I mean, I was happy with the way things were between us, but I can smell Nikolai all over you, and it's pissing me off." He shrugged, realizing his words didn't quite make sense.

Doc took a deep breath. "I'm sorry, Allan." He looked up and met his eyes. "This is new for me, too. All of it. I know we talked about figuring you and I out once Sofia was safe, but maybe we should figure it out now."

"What's to figure out? Don't you think if you were interested in me, you would have said something before now?"

He turned away, though the memory of the one time he had kissed Doc surfaced, and he hugged himself, not sure why he was so upset. He had Sofia. He did not mind sharing Sofia. His pack brother, though…

He didn't hear Doc move, but suddenly he was there, putting his arms around him and hugging him from behind.

"Allan, I didn't know before that you were interested in me. I've always thought of you as a brother, and it never occurred to me until recently that you might want more. It also didn't occur to me that I might be willing. I'm not used to getting close to people like that. I can only hide what I am for so long, and it's just not safe to reveal ourselves. I have next to no experience actually being in relationships. I honestly think Nikolai is the only one who does. Sofia, probably a little. I'm sorry I'm not good at this. Please tell me what you want?"

Sighing, and feeling like he might actually cry, he leaned back against Doc and turned his head so he could bury his face in the vampire's hair. He inhaled Doc's scent, mingled with Sofia and Nikolai's. Ed and his own lingered as well.

"I don't know," he finally answered. "How am I supposed to know what I want? I have Sofia, shouldn't that be enough?"

Doc laughed gently. "You would think, wouldn't you? Maybe the answer is that we all have each other. Maybe we have to concentrate on bringing Sofia and Nikolai into our pack so tightly that we're all as close as you, Ed, and I were. Maybe that means we get different things from each other. Or…" He hesitated when Allan tensed. "Maybe this is a bad idea, and we shouldn't even try."

"Do you really believe that?" He shuddered at the thought.

"No. I think we weren't ready for Nikolai. But he's here, and we need him."

"You like him."

"I…" Doc hesitated. "Yes, I do."

Allan sighed.

"That doesn't mean I don't like you, Allan."

He didn't reply. He wondered if he was being unreasonable. A lot of things had changed in a short amount of time. Maybe he just needed to focus on Sofia for a while. He inhaled Doc's scent, mingled with the others' again. That was what pack smelled like. Even Nikolai. Sofia wanted and needed him. That had to be enough for Allan. That Doc also wanted Nikolai was tweaking him out, though.

Something in the vampire's energy changed. He spread his hands out on Allan's stomach, and his breath hitched in response.

"You know," Doc whispered, sliding his hand up Allan's chest until he cupped his chin. His other hand he kept against his stomach, pressing the werewolf back against himself, his grip suddenly as rock hard as earlier when he'd stopped Allan from running. Damn, he was strong. "The only thing I don't want to lose more than Sofia, is you." He hesitated, then said, "And Ed, of course."

Allan's breath came fast, and his heart raced. He was afraid for a moment, completely trapped by Doc's iron grip, not used to being so completely helpless. Doc tilted Allan's neck like he was going to bite, but instead, he kissed him on the neck.

He melted, still a little afraid, but more from this being new territory than actual fear of what the vampire might do to him. He panted as Doc nibbled his way up his neck. "What do you want, Allan?" Doc breathed against his neck.

He turned his head, and Doc released his hold on his chin. "I think I want Sofia and you." Turning his head had put his face a breath from Doc's. He smelled a hint of blood on Doc's breath and guessed it was probably Nikolai's.

Doc pressed his lips to Allan's.

He growled, biting at Doc's lip. Doc opened his mouth and Allan ran his tongue along Doc's teeth, surprised to find them elongated into fangs. He really was turned on, not just trying to make him feel better.

He turned to face Doc and pushed him backward until Doc was pressed against a tree. Then he cupped Doc's face and explored his mouth. Doc's hands roamed down his back, digging into his ass and pressing them together.

Allan panted, breaking off to catch his breath.

Doc's eyes were completely black, shining with lust and a hint of blue from Nikolai's magic.

Allan licked his lips, tasting a hint of the mage there. This time, he wasn't nearly as bothered by the evidence of the other man's presence. "We should probably make sure Sofia is okay with all of this," he stammered.

"She is." Doc dragged his hands up his back.

"You're sure?"

"She already told Nikolai and I whatever we, as in all of us, got up to with or without her was fine with her."

"Really? When did this conversation occur?" He gasped as Doc dug his fingers into his back.

"After I bruised the shit out of Nikolai's neck."

Allan laughed. "That was so hot."

Doc bit him gently on his shoulder, not drawing blood.

Allan groaned, shutting his eyes. "I was going to suggest that we go back," he whispered. "You're making it awfully hard."

Doc chuckled, the sound vibrating through Allan's chest. "Want me to stop?"

Leaning forward, he kissed Doc's neck before biting down.

Gasping, Doc clenched his hands against his back hard enough to leave bruises.

"No, I don't want you to stop."

Doc froze. Not quite the response Allan had expected.

"What?"

"I'm suddenly worried that leaving Nikolai alone in the kitchen wasn't the best idea."

"Why?" He bit back a growl at the interruption.

"Because the smoke alarm is going off."

He burst out laughing, resting his head on Doc's shoulder. "I'll meet you there."

"There is a spell for that," Doc drawled in a Russian accent. "But we should go." He kissed Allan one more time, relatively chastely, and then released the werewolf from his strong arms. Doc didn't seem to be in much of a hurry, and Allan walked next to him. Doc surprised him again by taking his hand and squeezing, though he let go before they got back to the cabin.

Chapter 19

Sofia

I woke up slowly, feeling warm and safe wrapped in one of the werewolves' arms. His arms tightened around me when my breathing changed.

"Morning," I whispered.

"Hi, beautiful." Ed held me. He buried his nose in my hair and inhaled.

I rolled over so I could wrap my arms around him, tucked my head under his chin, and hooked a leg around his.

He rumbled deep in his throat and pressed into me.

Feeling his hard length against me ignited a fire in my nerves. My stomach tightened, and I moaned, no longer content just to cuddle. I dug my fingers into his back, glad he wasn't wearing a shirt, before dragging them along his firm muscles.

Ed nibbled at my shoulder, sucking gently and then nipping at me, and I thrust against him, wrapping my leg more tightly around his. I only wore a long T-shirt and underwear, and the shirt rode up with my movement.

"Sofia," Ed whispered.

"Yes?" I managed to gasp out.

"You're amazing." He grabbed the hem of my shirt and tugged.

I raised my hands so he could take it off, then he rolled us so I was on my back beneath him. His warm hands wandered over my curves before cupping my breasts, rubbing gently, lips sucking at one of my nipples.

Wrapping both of my legs around his waist, I quivered as he thrust against me, heart racing, breath coming fast.

"I think you're still wearing too much." His voice was a low growl. He dragged his hands down my sides and hooked them in my panties, tugging until I unlocked my legs from around him so he could pull them off.

The heat in his eyes as his gaze traveled up my body made my stomach tighten, and I groaned, wanting his hands back on me. He nudged my knees apart and knelt between my legs, studying me.

"Ed, you can touch me wherever, but just touch me," I panted, desperate.

His eyes lit up. It was so nice to see him looking so alive after he had felt so vacant the day before.

Leaning forward, he pressed his lips to my stomach, kissing me, trailing lower, gripping my hips with his hands as he kissed slowly down to my folds.

I cried out as he blew gently on my moist folds, the sensation intense as I clutched the sheets. His tongue followed the breath of air, licking until he found my sensitive nub, and I thrust against him, gasping.

"Good?"

"Yeah, don't stop."

He obliged, licking and sucking as I writhed under him. He held my hips as I bucked when he pressed his tongue into me, before licking back out.

An ache built in my core, tingling to my breasts, begging for release. Ed continued to work, and I thrust against him, breath coming fast, moaning with every stroke of his tongue.

"Ed!" I gasped, as my release shuddered through me.

He continued to lap at my folds as I cried out, body rocking with my orgasm.

The fire alarm went off, startling both of us. We both froze, and moments later, we heard cursing in Russian from the kitchen.

Ed and I looked at each other, eyes wide, before we both giggled, and he collapsed on top of me. "Who let him in the kitchen unsupervised?"

"Where are Doc and Allan?" I laughed.

"Outside. Though I'm sure they're on their way back by now."

I felt a tingle of magic as Nikolai did something to make the fire alarm stop. It ignited me again. Ed gave me an interested look, before sighing and rolling off of me.

"I could wake up like that every morning," he groaned happily.

"Me, too." Waking up in one of their arms would never get old, and I was glad Ed had stayed with me this morning, though it was usually Doc who held me until I woke.

He went into the bathroom for a few minutes, and I pulled the comforter over myself while I waited for my turn.

I heard the front door and then voices in the kitchen. Ed left the bathroom, still not dressed other than his sleeping pants, but he looked like he had washed his face and cleaned up a little.

He grinned at me. "I'm going to go supervise."

"I'll be quick." I finally remembered it was a school day and glanced at the clock. It was early, but if we didn't leave soon, Doc and I were both going to miss class.

The others apparently came to that same realization, because they were already eating, and Doc headed for the bedroom as soon as I was in the kitchen.

Whatever Nikolai had set on fire, he had still managed bacon, eggs, and toast just fine. Maybe bacon grease?

"Thanks for cooking," I said.

Ed and Allan mumbled agreement.

"You're welcome," he answered, smiling and looking pleased.

We hurried through breakfast, and Nikolai elected to stay behind and sleep. Apparently, he had been up all night.

Once we were ready, we piled into Doc's truck. I sat in back with Allan and leaned against him. Doc drove a little faster than normal, and we pulled into the parking lot with about fifteen minutes to spare before we both had to be at his class.

I hugged Allan and Ed, wished I could hug Doc, and walked next to him as we headed to our classroom.

Ash caught up to us at some point, looking no worse for getting nailed with Nikolai's magic yesterday.

He glared at us. However, he walked on my other side the whole way to class as if we were friends. His situation sucked. I really hoped I didn't find myself in it soon.

"They may have figured out Alex is an idiot," he muttered before shoving past us into the classroom and sinking down into his normal seat.

Doc and I shared a worried glance. Doc put his hand on Ash's shoulder and squeezed gently as he walked to the front of the room. The anguish on the demon's face gutted me.

Paying attention to Doc's stories of the American west proved nearly impossible for the first time that semester as worry ate away at me. My stomach roiled, and I regretted breakfast. If someone competent were in charge of Ash, we might be in real trouble.

Doc and I shared a heated look before I left for my next class. Hopefully, no one besides Ash noticed. He had, for once, waited for me and was studying me as I walked toward him.

"What?" I asked gently when I was close.

Shrugging, he fell in next to me, and we headed for the stairs.

I didn't try to talk to him again, and he didn't follow when I split off for my next class.

Alex didn't make an appearance that day, for which I was grateful, and by the end of the day, I was exhausted. Allan and Ed both found me and walked me to my dorm before they headed back up to their cabin. Allan passed on a hug and a kiss from Doc as well, and I headed to my room, anxious to talk to Victoria.

I considered taking the elevator but made myself take the stairs, even though I was tired. My feet dragged as I went down the hallway and scanned my fob on my door.

I pushed the door open and trudged inside, dropping my bag by the door before looking up and freezing.

Victoria stared, eyes wide, a hand clamped over her mouth, and a gun pointed to her head.

I froze, not sure what to do. I was sure there was a spell I could use, if only I knew it. I wished Nikolai were here. My chest clenched, and fear made my hands shake. We had been prepared for magical attacks, but not this. Apparently, Nikolai hadn't been the only one with the thought that firearms might be more persuasive than magical spells.

The man that held the gun to Victoria's head was one of the Andersons' men. I had seen him before, but I didn't know his name.

"Just put your hands in front of you," he ordered, voice low.

I did as instructed, keeping eye contact with Victoria, trying to apologize without speaking.

"Now turn around, and keep your hands where I can see them."

I slowly turned, keeping my hands out to the side, breath short, heart racing, trying not to panic, trying to think. I didn't know anything useful. The shield spell might not be enough with the gun right against Victoria's head, and that was all I could do.

Victoria gasped, and I looked over my shoulder in time to see her crumple to the ground.

Before I could react, the Andersons' man had the gun pressed against my back. "Don't try anything. I doubt you can stop a bullet."

"What did you do to her?" I cried out.

"No longer your concern." He grabbed one of my arms and twisted my hand up behind me before casting something akin to Nikolai's invisibility spell and marching us out of the dorm room.

Tears sprang to my eyes, and I whimpered. I didn't even know if my roommate was still alive.

As soon as we were outside, hot magic burned into my back and I crumpled, my vision going black before I could cry out.

Chapter 20

Sofia

I didn't recognize the room I woke in, but the gray quarried stone walls and flat slate ceiling said dungeon to me. Or at least, non-flammable, and therefore, possibly a good place to practice spells. Bare electric blubs lit the space. Also easily replaced should something happen to destroy them.

Trying to lift my arms produced predictable results. I was tied down, lying on something cold and hard that might have been stone, or a really hard wood. My heart raced, and I whimpered.

Cloth rustling and the scrape of a shoe on stone caught my attention, and I turned my face toward the sound. Ash walked over to me from a wooden bench sitting along one wall.

His brow furrowed, and his mouth turned down as he stood next to me. The table I was tied to was about hip height on him.

"I'm sorry, Sofia." He ran a warm hand across my forehead.

Tears sprang to my eyes, and he wiped them away. If I thought that my guys knew I had been taken, I wouldn't be as worried. This time, the Andersons had taken out Victoria. No one would know I was missing until the morning or later, since I didn't have a class with Doc today.

"You can't do anything?"

He shook his head. "Unfortunately, you'll understand why soon."

My breathing came faster, and I tugged at the ropes holding me. This couldn't really be happening.

Ash didn't say anything else, just put a hand on my shoulder while I tugged at the ropes holding me.

Wood scraped across stone, and I looked over, half expecting to see Alex coming in a door. Instead, four people walked in. Three men and a woman. I had never seen the woman before. She had silver gray hair and avarice gleaming in her slate blue eyes. She wore a long black dress and moved with stately precision as she came to stand by my head. The woman gestured to Ash and, though he tightened his jaw, he moved to my feet.

I wanted to scream, tried, but no sound came out.

"No need to make any sound," she said, voice cool. She touched my shoulders, and my body relaxed, though I tried to fight my bonds again.

I screamed in my mind instead, trying to struggle, trying to get my body to respond to me.

Either she saw some of the panic I felt in my eyes, or she knew what I was going through, because she smirked at me. "You'll get used to it. Well, the demon will anyway. You'll be gone. After tonight, you won't have a care in the world."

I had to do something. But what?

The three men, one I thought I recognized from one of my fights with the Andersons, and two I wasn't sure if I'd seen before, took places around me. One stood by Ash, and the others by my sides.

Heart racing, mind screaming in fear, I tried to fight, tried to do something. I made a desperate grab for my magic, and for a moment it fluttered in my grasp despite my panic. I formed the shield spell Nikolai had taught me, but before I could manage, the woman put her hand on my chest. Heat and pain seared through me, and I screamed in my mind, though my body didn't move.

"Enough of that," she hissed.

I tried again before the pain even receded, but this time, I felt nothing, no magical response, no ability to move my body, nothing. No, not nothing. Buried deep, beneath whatever the woman had done to me, I found my connection to my guys. The bond I had forged just a short time ago. I could access that.

Still able to see and hear what was going on around me, I saw the mages and Ash join hands. Their magic flowed, silver, amber, green, magenta, light blue, into a circle surrounding me, the colors melding. The woman chanted, though I didn't recognize the language.

The magic penetrated me, and I couldn't stop it. It shoved at me, pushing me away, pushing me deeper, trying to shove me out of my body.

Still struggling, though I knew I wasn't going to be able to fight them, I resisted. Pain built until it burned through me as if molten metal had replaced my body, and still I fought. They pushed me, but instead of being pushed out of my body, I sank further down into the pack bond.

I could sense when the guys realized something was wrong. It was like I sat there with them in the cabin, screaming though they didn't hear me. All four of them bolted upright and shared a horrified look. Ed grabbed for his phone. Doc raced for his truck. The others followed.

For a time, I lost the sense of them, trying to fight the mages. My guys were coming. Maybe they would be here in time.

Blinding pain worse than anything I had yet experienced threatened to jolt me out of my body, and I clung desperately to the thread of connection with my guys.

They had reached my dorm. Nikolai pounded on the door.

Doc gripped the handle and twisted. I could hear it snap as the door opened.

Victoria lay on the ground, and Nikolai went to her side while the guys checked the room for me.

The mage pushed some magic into Victoria, and she groaned. She lived!

Fire lanced through me, and I screamed. All of the guys jerked, looking at each other. I could taste the sour flavor of their panic. They didn't know what to do.

I got the sense that Nikolai ordered Allan and Ed to take Victoria back to the cabin.

They didn't want to go. Nikolai explained something.

My connection with them faded as I was again shoved away. I scrabbled at the threads of energy that connected us, knowing somehow that it was the only thing keeping me from being destroyed.

I struggled against the mages trying to force me from my body. I was slipping. Alone again. The threads tying me to my body frayed. Pain shattered through me as the threads snapped one by one, slowly releasing me from my physical form. I had hoped they would reach me in time. It looked like I was lost.

My grip on the pack bond failed, I slid, blackness about to claim me.

Wilderness wrapped around me. The crisp mountain breeze turned into a raging torrent and pulled me away from the brink. The pine littered forest tickled my paws as I ran, scented the air, stalked deer…

Ed, and then moments later, Allan, wrapped their energies around me, gripping me tight, holding me close, filling me with their love and need for me.

I clung to them.

Their presence anchored me to myself and then let me reach for Doc and Nikolai again.

They were still trying to get to me on time.

The three of us watched, experiencing things as Doc and Nikolai did. Doc slammed on the brakes, almost losing control of his truck and barely remembering to put it in park and turn it off, before they jumped out. The only reason it even crossed his mind was that they would need it to get away.

My attention shifted to Nikolai. He was desperately angry. Terrified of losing me. They all were.

The Andersons had placed guards around their large manor house.

Nikolai didn't even hesitate. He hit them hard. I could see the shape of the spells he cast since I was riding along and knew I'd be able to cast them if I ever escaped.

The results were devastatingly fast. The guards never even had a chance to defend themselves, as Nikolai's spell lanced through their shields and sank into their bodies, stopping their hearts.

"Modern shields," I heard him think in disgust.

The resistance inside the house was more organized, and still they fell to Doc and Nikolai's fury. A few of the guards pulled guns.

Doc raced forward, a blur to Nikolai's senses, and the men with guns fell, blood spraying as Doc used his long knife efficiently, no motions wasted. One got off a shot that Doc didn't even bother to dodge.

We all felt the burn as the bullet ripped through him, but also the immediate relief as his body began healing the wound.

They pushed deeper into the house, and I lost track of them as fury invaded my mind.

I cried out again. Ed and Allan held me tight, trying to shelter me from the foreign rage burning through me.

"How dare you!"

The being shrieked. It couldn't direct its rage outward for some reason that wasn't immediately clear to any of us. As soon as it sensed my presence, it turned on me.

If I had been alone, I wouldn't have survived. As it was, the three of us barely stood against the onslaught of foreign energy.

"It's not their fault!" Nikolai joined us, supporting us.

The presence hissed. "Whose fault is it?"

We all sensed Nikolai's guilt, as if he were responsible, and the being turned on him. Before it could retaliate, Nikolai dragged us all into his perception. We watched as Doc sank his blade into the chest of one of the mages.

Another cast a spell at Doc, but Nikolai blocked it. He couldn't do much beyond basic defense while he concentrated on us, but Ash was already out of the fight, and Doc had the others handled.

The woman with the white hair was gone. I could sense from Nikolai's memories she had escaped when they had barged in.

"Theirs."

"There is not room for all of us in here!" The being screamed and shoved at us.

Nikolai held fast. "This is not your body. You can't have it. We want to release you. We just have to figure out how."

"I will release myself." The being tried to do something. The lance of pain that speared all of us forced the guys out of my mind and me into blackness.

Chapter 21

Doc

Nikolai staggered just as Doc gutted the last mage. He spun, watching as Nikolai sagged against the table Sofia lay on.

"Did we lose her?"

"No." The mage muttered something in Russian before shaking his head. "I don't believe so," he finally replied. "But we were too late to prevent the demon from being forced to possess her. We will still lose her, if we can't unbind it. Honestly, I am not sure how she's still there at all. I know something of these things. Usually the host mind is gone by now."

"You don't know how to reverse it do you?"

Nikolai shook his head sadly. "I have always found it is much easier to simply ask for assistance and offer payment. I never saw the point in binding a powerful creature. I have never worked with demons, though." He pointed at the wide golden cuffs now on Sofia's wrists. They were similar to the ones binding Ash.

"We need to get out of here."

"Carry Sofia. We're not out of the fight yet."

Doc cut away her bonds and picked her up. She hung limp in his arms, lifeless except for her labored breathing and erratic heartrate.

He followed Nikolai, trying not to think about losing Sofia, as they left the basement and hurried up the stairs to the main part of the house.

"I will create a distraction," Nikolai said, pausing at the top of the stairs. "Then maybe we can get out without more fighting. It would be safer."

He glanced up and down the hallway and nodded. They were alone, but probably not for long. They had killed a lot of people on the way in, but the Andersons probably still had a few in reserve.

Nikolai held his hands together and muttered in Russian for a moment, before spreading his hands wide. A wisp of energy rose into the air. A long minute later, an explosion ripped in another part of the house.

Both of them winced as the concussion pressed against them.

"Let's go," Nikolai ordered.

Either they hadn't been willing to lose more of their people, or the diversion worked, because they made it outside and back to Doc' truck with no resistance.

Doc put Sofia in the back seat, and Nikolai climbed in with her. He started the truck and headed back to the cabin. He was careful to observe the speed limit, hoping no one would notice them. As good as the explosion was for a diversion, unless the Andersons had some sort of shield up, others would have noticed it and reported in.

It was nearing dawn when they finally reached the cabin. He never did see any signs of emergency vehicles, so maybe the Andersons did have some shielding up.

Doc carried Sofia inside, with Nikolai staring anxiously at her the entire time.

"Put her on the floor."

Allan, Ed, and Victoria were all unconscious. She was on the couch. Ed and Allan lay on the floor as if they had collapsed.

"What happened to them?" Doc could hear them breathing, but the thought of losing them too clenched his heart.

"Probably when the demon tried to escape. I was prepared, had shields. Ed and Allan would not have had any protection."

Nikolai put his hand on Allan's chest and then Ed's. "They will wake shortly." He checked on Victoria. "This is only a sleeping spell. She will also be fine shortly." Then he sank down next to Sofia.

"What do we do?"

He sank down on the floor next to Nikolai. The mage put his arm around his shoulders and leaned against him for a moment.

"I don't know. First step, we see if the demon will cooperate. It will make all of this much easier."

Not expecting comfort from someone else, but grateful to have it, Doc put his arm around Nikolai's waist and leaned against the mage, trying to fight off soul crushing weariness. He had finally found someone, and he hadn't been able to do enough to protect her. He guessed by the anguished expression on Nikolai's face, the mage felt similar.

Victoria sucked in a breath and bolted upright.

Both Nikolai and Doc turned.

She stared at them for a moment, wide-eyed, before she looked around the cabin. Her eyes landed on Ed and Allan where they lay stretched out on the floor, and finally they landed on Sofia.

"Is she going to be okay?"

Nikolai shrugged and turned his attention back to Sofia. Doc could hear his breath hitch, and knew he was holding back quite a bit at the moment.

Victoria scrambled over to them and sat down on his other side, tears streaming down her face. He wasn't sure if she would welcome him touching her or not. He put his other arm around her, anyway. She could move away if she didn't want to be held.

After a moment, Victoria scooted closer and leaned against him. "What do we do?" She sniffed and rubbed at her face.

"Don't know," he muttered, trying to hold his anger in check. "Wait and see what happens when she wakes up. Go from there."

"Did they…get a demon?"

"Yes," Nikolai grunted, biting the word off angrily.

"They had a gun." Victoria trembled. Doc tightened his hold on her. "There wasn't anything either of us could do."

"We shouldn't have left her alone," he replied. That mistake would haunt him, even if they did rescue her from this. "We shouldn't have left you alone."

"You can't follow us everywhere. Eventually, they would have done something."

"There are a lot of things we could have, maybe should have done," Nikolai said. "There is no point in looking back."

Though he knew Nikolai was right, he doubted the mage followed his own advice.

Tires crunched on gravel, and he tensed. Victoria and Nikolai glanced at him.

"I hear a car, don't recognize it."

Nikolai stood, went over to the window, and glanced out. He felt the mage's absence keenly, even though he was only a few feet away.

"No idea what kind of car it is," Nikolai cautioned. "It's black. Not a truck."

Victoria tensed, fear coloring her scent.

"It's Ash," Doc declared, not sure how he knew, but certain he was right.

Nikolai glanced back at him, eyebrow raised. "You can sense demons now?"

"Ever since…" He snapped his mouth shut. Victoria still didn't know all their secrets, and it was better if she didn't. "I see Ash a lot."

Normally, Nikolai's knowing smile might have made him blush, but he didn't have the energy at the moment to react to the mage's gibe.

Victoria glanced between them, brow furrowed. "I would like to ask again, isn't he a bad guy? Like, powerful demon, could kill us all? You don't seem worried."

Nikolai shrugged. "He likes Doc. He won't do anything to us unless directly ordered to."

"What if he was ordered to? And how exactly does he like Doc?"

"Then we'll defend ourselves," he answered. "He probably wouldn't drive up in a car if he was going to try and kill us. He knows at least three of us can hear it a fair ways off. Not exactly stealthy." He ignored the other question, not sure how to answer it.

Nikolai opened the door before Ash could knock, and the demon came inside. He didn't say anything, his blue and white eyes fixed on Doc for a moment before shifting to Sofia. He moved to sit cross-legged on the other side of them and stared at Sofia.

Nikolai sat next to him, across from Victoria.

"Is this not weird to anyone else?" she finally pleaded.

Doc still had his arm around her, and he squeezed gently. "Why are you here, Ash?"

"I was ordered to bring her back once she had killed all of you. Until she does, or they get tired of waiting and call me, we can stay here."

"Why do they think she'll kill all of us?" he asked.

"Sometimes, when a demon is first bound, especially a powerful greater demon, they can still do a little magic. Usually, they try to kill anyone near them. As the demon doesn't have full possession of this body, she's unlikely to be able to do much. The Andersons do not know they failed to push Sofia out. I'll stay until they call me and order me to return, or you want me to leave."

"Turn your phone off," Doc ordered.

Ash shook his head. "I tried that. I can no longer neglect to keep my phone charged, turn it on silent, turn it off, or ignore it." He grimaced.

Doc held out his hand.

Ash tilted his head slightly, but after a moment, pulled his phone out and handed it to him.

Smirking a little, Doc tightened his grip around the phone, crushing it.

Victoria gasped, but to her credit, didn't pull away.

Ash's eyebrows rose, and then the demon smiled, before his expression fell. "That will work for a while."

"Do you have any other orders we need to know about?"

Ash shook his head.

He put the remains of the phone on the table and brushed his hand off on his jeans.

Allan groaned, and everyone turned their attention to him. He clutched his head, before slowly sitting upright. After a moment, he looked around, eyes going wide as he saw Ed still unconscious and everyone else gathered around Sofia.

He scrambled forward on hands and knees, stopping next to her.

"We were too late, weren't we?"

"Yes," Ash answered for everyone else. "Mostly."

"What do you mean? Why are you here?" Allan growled at Ash.

"I'm here because maybe I can help them." Ash gestured at Sofia. "And because I'm supposed to bring her back, eventually."

Allan shook his head. "This is so fucked up," he muttered.

Ed woke after another few minutes and came over to join them, sad puppy dog eyes resting on everyone for a moment before he completed the circle they had formed around Sofia's body. He didn't say anything. He did glare at Ash, but the demon ignored him.

Nikolai stared intently at the demon. "Ash, do you know how to release the bindings?"

"We all know how." He winced, as if talking about it pained him. "But if I think about it too much, the magic punishes me. If I actually try, or were to try to tell someone else, well…" He gestured at Sofia.

Nikolai sighed. "If only I had access to my library."

Ed straightened and looked at Nikolai. "What about the Anderson's library?"

"Please do not discuss your plans around me," Ash grumbled.

Everyone fell silent.

Doc heard Sofia's breathing change, and he focused his attention back on her. He took his arm from Victoria's shoulders in case he needed to restrain Sofia as she straightened.

Her eyes fluttered open, and his heart clenched. Her normally gray eyes were golden, and no hint of her lavender magic shone in them.

She looked around at them before they settled on Ash. Screaming in anger, she launched herself at the demon.

Ash held up his hands, protecting himself like a boxer. Doc scrambled to his feet and grabbed Sofia, pulling her off of the demon.

She turned on him, swinging.

He caught her arm as gently as he could and held her until she stopped struggling.

As soon as she did, he released her and stepped back.

She staggered, looking around the room, wide-eyed. "I know this place, but I've never been here before."

Ash stood up and went over to her.

She snarled and took another swing at him. Doc snatched her arm and pulled her back against his chest. He guessed eventually he wouldn't be able to hold her back, once the demon really had control, but for now, it wasn't any more difficult than restraining any other human.

She kicked his shin. He ignored the brief pain.

"You're going to hurt yourself."

"When I have control of this body, then I will hurt all of you," she snarled.

"They didn't do this," Victoria cried out. "We're trying to help."

Sofia turned her now golden eyes on Victoria. "I know," she fumed and jerked away from him. He let her go this time, and she sank to the ground.

He settled back next to Victoria, keeping a wary eye on Sofia.

No one knew what to say.

Finally, Nikolai broke the silence. "How should we address you?" He spoke respectfully.

Her attention jerked to the mage, and she pursed her lips. "This body was called Sofia?"

Nikolai nodded.

"Perhaps you should stick with that." She clenched her fists and then stared at her wrists. The golden cuffs that imprisoned her glinted in the early morning light from the big window.

"I have some things to tell you, that will help should you choose to listen. Most I learned the hard way," Ash said.

She glared at him. "You helped them do this."

Ed growled.

"I had no choice. You will have no choice once your powers meld with Sofia's." Ash pulled his long sleeves up and showed his own cuffs. Unlike Sofia's arms, which weren't damaged, his arms were red and cracked where the cuffs dug into his skin.

"Talk," the demon inhabiting Sofia growled.

"You seem to know that these people aren't responsible." He gestured at the others.

"Yes, we've spoken already." She waved her hand dismissively. "Carry on."

Ash looked confused at that. "You have?"

"Tell me what I need to know," she ground out.

"My apologies. They weren't able to completely push Sofia out of her body. Which is unusual. Normally, as I understand it, your powers would integrate with that body right away. You would probably fight the restraints, and the magic would cause you a great deal of harm, but you would recover and eventually stop fighting."

She glared at him. "So, you've given up?"

"I fought every day for three hundred years. I still try it occasionally. It never goes well." He shrugged as if it didn't matter, but Doc could see the pain in his eyes. "If it weren't for Sofia, I would let you learn the hard way. However, she will experience everything you do, I believe."

The demon nodded. "It is likely. She seems like she's listening now. Ah, yes, she's now quite upset. Her yelling is giving me a headache." She touched her temples. "Strange sensation."

"So, if you don't fight them, you won't damage Sofia."

"You expect me to give up? I do not wish for an existence of servitude," she snarled.

"No. I'm suggesting you do your best to keep Sofia in her body as long as you can. It will limit your usefulness to the Andersons until your magic fully integrates. I don't believe it can while Sofia is present. We won't tell them it's because of Sofia. We'll tell them it's because the integration takes time. Maybe they," he gestured toward Doc and Nikolai, "can figure out how to unbind you before she's gone."

The demon frowned and looked at Nikolai. "You know how to bind demons?" She did not sound happy about that.

Nikolai shook his head. "It is very specialized magic. I know something of bindings and unbindings, but how to fix this?" He shrugged. "I am trying to find a solution. May I?" He gestured toward her wrists.

Glaring at him the entire time, she held out her arm.

Nikolai's hands glowed with his dark blue magic signature for a moment while he studied the restraints. He pushed magic into them. Magic flared, flinging Nikolai backward.

Doc didn't use his full speed that often, and he almost didn't react fast enough to save Nikolai from being flung through the large glass window, but he managed to get across the room to catch the mage before he got hurt.

"Thanks." Nikolai straightened, and he held on to him maybe a moment longer than necessary before letting go.

Victoria's eyes were huge when he happened to glance at her, but she didn't ask questions.

"I will not try that again," Nikolai laughed nervously. "I believe I have the information I need, however."

"Are you okay?" Doc asked.

"Yes, am fine."

The demon was clutching her head, but Ash didn't look terribly concerned, so Doc hoped that meant she and Sofia were okay.

Ed and Allan's gazes darted around, clearly not sure who they should be worried about or focusing on.

"So, there's a chance we can save Sofia?" Victoria finally whispered.

The demon laughed bitterly and shook her head. "If you do it fast."

"How fast?" Victoria replied.

"I don't know. I can barely sense her after that little explosion of pain," the demon replied.

Ed lunged forward, grabbed the demon's shoulders, and stared into her eyes, as if he could physically see Sofia. The demon tried to jerk away, but he held tight.

"We can't lose her," Ed cried out as he continued to search her face.

She finally jerked away, and Allan grabbed Ed around the waist and pulled him back.

"Ash, would you mind stepping out of hearing range for a time?" Nikolai asked.

Ash nodded and left the cabin.

"She tied herself to us." Nikolai held out his arm and showed the magical tattoo they all had. "It may be why the Andersons couldn't push her out. Ed, you and Allan should take turns staying with her through the pack bond as much as you can. Doc, too. Keep her anchored to us. I will see what I can learn from the Andersons' library."

"How will you do that?" Victoria asked.

"I can sneak a pastry out from under a werewolf's nose. The Andersons shouldn't be an issue." His smile was a touch sad.

The demon studied her wrist, but the golden cuff covered Sofia's tattoo.

"What about Sofia's parents?" Victoria's eyes widened.

He swore. "They will be a problem."

"Doc, you, Ed, and Allan keep our visitor from drawing too much attention to herself. We need to keep her parents from finding out, as well. If we succeed, then it won't be issue. If we fail…" The mage shrugged. "I'm all for unleashing holy hell on the Andersons. We will tell her parents then."

"Doc will have to manage her parents," Ed pointed out. "As far as they know, she's only dating him."

Nikolai wasn't completely in the loop on Sofia's parents, and he tilted his head. He understood it wasn't going to be an easy situation though. "Enjoy that," he said to Doc, sarcasm heavy in his voice.

Doc raised his eyebrows. Nikolai wasn't normally sarcastic.

"What if I don't wish to cooperate?" The demon crossed her arms and glared at the others.

"Then we will do what we can without your help, and hope it's enough," Doc growled out.

"If you unbind me, and I decide to keep this vessel?" The smirk on her face was so unlike Sofia that Doc's anger flared. He would never have been able to react this way toward Sofia, but he wanted to punch the demon.

"Somehow, I think you'd rather go home." He glared at her.

"And what if you figure it out too late, will my cooperation still buy my freedom?"

Because he was watching, he could see the uncertainty under the arrogant tilt to her chin.

"Yes."

She considered for a moment before shrugging. "Then I suppose I will cooperate, for now."

His shoulders unknotted. If she was agreeing, she probably had hope that they could succeed.

"Act fast." She turned away from Doc's angry stare and headed for the kitchen, looking around curiously as she did so. "Someone make me something to eat. This vessel is starving."

Doc glanced at Ed and Allan. They stared after the demon, almost identical expressions of anguish on their faces.

"Now," she commanded.

Growling, Ed and Allan stalked into the kitchen.

Nikolai came over and put his arm around Doc, leaning against him.

"Fuck," he muttered, returning the pressure.

"Indeed," Nikolai answered.

Victoria raised her eyebrows at them before following the others into the kitchen.

Chapter 22

Nikolai

Ash stayed until it was clear the demon inhabiting Sofia wasn't about to kill all of them, and then he left. He promised to tell the Andersons the demon wasn't fully integrated yet, and that there was no real point in stealing her back until she was more useful to them. He offered to give Victoria a ride back to the college, but rather understandably, she declined. Doc ended up running her back to the dorms while Nikolai, along with Ed and Allan, tried to instruct Sofia's inhabitant on what she needed to do to pretend to be Sofia.

The demon constantly waved them off, saying she didn't care, or that she had the knowledge needed. Nikolai thought she was mostly uncomfortable with how little she knew about the world and how little power she currently had. If the demon had been able to fully integrate with Sofia's body, she wouldn't be so powerless until the Andersons commanded her anyway, and he suspected she had thought of that. Hopefully, her promise to give them time to release her held.

While Ed and Allan tried to explain the modern world, Nikolai sat in the armchair he preferred and let his mind travel along the threads of the bond they had formed. He needed to contact Sofia, see if she was okay.

The demon sensed what he was doing and leveled a stare at him. He met her gaze and clenched his jaw, not wanting to fight with her, but knowing they needed to keep Sofia close and make sure she didn't give up.

Finally, the demon nodded and turned her attention back to Ed and Allan, or rather, turned back to pretending to ignore them.

Nikolai sank down into his mind.

"Sofia."

She had crafted the space in her mind she had carved out to hide in to look like her grove.

Sofia's eyes widened when she saw him. She sprang up and threw herself in his arms.

He held her tightly, breathing in her scent. "I'm so sorry, Sofia."

"Why?"

"We didn't protect you."

"You tried."

"Them knowing about me may have forced their hand."

"You'll save me." Her eyes glistened, and his heart broke a little more.

"I'll try."

"What do I do?" Her voice cracked, and she pressed against him.

"Stay strong. Stay here. Hide from the Andersons. Don't let the demon shove you out."

"Okay. Will you stay with me for a while?"

"A little while. Ed, Allan, and Doc will be here as much as they can. I need to figure out how to reverse the magic. It will be quite complicated."

"You'll figure it out."

Her faith in him twisted like a knife in his back. He was very good at battle. This side of magic was not something he had spent a lot of time with. Which might be why Roza succeeded in trapping him in an interdimensional prison in the first place. She certainly hadn't learned that magic from him.

"I will," he assured her, wishing he felt as confident as he tried to sound.

He held Sofia for a time, trying to lend her strength and anchor her more closely, but finally, he had to let go. "I will return as soon as I can. I'll send the others back sooner."

She gave him a sad smile, though it didn't reach her eyes. She kissed him gently on the lips and stepped back.

It startled him to be back solidly in his own mind, and he found himself alone in the living room.

After a moment of panic, the rest of his senses caught up to his eyes, and he heard them in the kitchen and smelled cooking. Was it that late? A quick glance at the window showed that he had stayed with Sofia for quite a long time.

The others looked up when he entered the kitchen. Sofia's now gold colored eyes gave him an interested look, before the demon realized that was counter to her current image, and she turned back to the table. She sat stiffly, giving the food a disgusted look.

He recalled having read that on their own plane, demons tended to feast upon energy. She would have to adapt. At least for now.

Doc hadn't sat at the table, and Nikolai studied the vampire. He was tense, angry, and probably hungry. He leaned against the cabinets and sipped at some tea, glaring in the demon's general direction but not quite looking at her.

Ed and Allan ate and shot worried looks at the demon, and then at Doc, and then at each other.

He sat at the table and helped himself to the food.

"We have to go back tomorrow. It's Friday. We'll have the weekend to work on stuff," Doc said, interrupting the strained silence.

"You want us to go to school. Seriously?" Ed turned an incredulous stare on Doc.

"Yes. We're not going to solve this tomorrow. Nikolai can shadow our guest here, and we can try to pretend like everything is normal."

Nikolai laughed, he couldn't help it. "You want the mage from fourteen fifty, who can barely navigate the present, to make sure our demon friend doesn't do anything weird?"

Doc's lips twitched, but he didn't quite smile. "I guess."

"I suppose going to this college is part of my agreement to help you rescue Sofia?"

"Yes," Doc replied.

"Very well. This vessel is exhausted. Wake me in the morning." She got up and left the room.

Doc followed long enough to see where she went before returning. "Guess she remembers enough to know she usually sleeps in my room." His shoulders sagged.

"I'll crash with Ed," Allan offered sadly.

Doc nodded. "Go run or something. You should get some exercise in. Tomorrow will be a long day."

The werewolves left, and Nikolai helped Doc clean up. He tried to think of anything he could remember that might be helpful, but he came to the conclusion that the only truly helpful thing he could do was sneak around at the Andersons and see if he could find the answers there.

Doc stopped him, hands on his shoulders, once they were done cleaning the kitchen.

"We can do this, right?"

"Yes. If I can find the right information."

"I wish I couldn't tell that you aren't nearly as confident as you sound," Doc sighed.

He half smiled, stepped forward, and rested his head on Doc's shoulder. The vampire wrapped his arms around him and held him tight. "Me as well."

∞ ∞ ∞

The wolves returned a couple of hours later. Doc and Nikolai were on the couch. Doc grading papers, while he surfed the internet on the tablet, using Doc's thigh as a pillow. He was currently looking for any inspiration in old myths or legends that might be helpful. The internet was a pretty great source of information, but it was pretty general and so far, he wasn't having a lot of luck.

"There is plenty on exorcisms." He snorted as the wolves came in. "But that is largely a religious thing. Also, we are not trying to banish the demon to hell. We are simply trying to free her so she can return home. Does this hell even exist? Do they really think demons are from hell? They're not servants of the devil this article references. They're simply beings from another plane." He grumbled in frustration and put the tablet on his chest. He glanced at the werewolves. Allan came over and sat on the floor, leaning against Doc's legs. Doc reached down and touched his shoulder absently.

Ed stared, eyes narrowed.

"What?" Nikolai finally asked.

That drew Doc's attention away from his grading, and he looked up, tilting his head when he saw Ed studying them.

"So, what, are you two a thing now, too?"

"A thing?" Nikolai wracked his brain for an explanation. While he had all of Sofia's language skills, sometimes the idioms still didn't quite make sense to him.

Doc sighed. "Ed…"

"I'm going to bed." He spun away down the hallway to his room and slammed his door.

"I don't think I can deal with him tonight," Doc groaned.

"You don't need to," Allan replied. "He's just tired and freaked out. It's not like none of us ever cuddle on the couch. I'll tell him to stop being a jerk." Allan stood up, stared at Doc for a moment, then leaned forward and kissed him.

Nikolai watched idly, still using Doc as a pillow, as Doc returned the kiss.

The werewolf stepped back and then went after his brother.

Doc put his tablet on the end table and leaned back on the couch.

"You and Allan seem to have worked things out."

"I guess," Doc replied tiredly.

Nikolai stood. "We're all exhausted."

Doc nodded but didn't follow when Nikolai took a few steps toward his room. "Where are you going to sleep?"

"Couch, I suppose."

Nikolai held out his hand.

After an uneasy glance toward Ed's bedroom, Doc stood and slid his smooth hand into Nikolai's calloused one and followed him to his borrowed bedroom.

Nikolai released Doc's hand and held his out in front of him. Blue motes filled the space, moving to the edges of the room.

"There, now we can talk, and no one can hear."

Doc arched an eyebrow. "Do we need to talk?"

"You, my friend, need blood. I need your fangs in my neck."

His other eyebrow rose before his eyes darkened, turning predatory. "I hardly call that talking."

Nikolai's pulse raced at the look Doc was currently giving him. "What do you call it?"

He stalked forward. "The guys call it starting shit." His lips curled into a hint of a smile. "And if I didn't need blood, I'm not sure I'd have the energy."

Nikolai nodded. "I am not trying to forget about Sofia." He felt he needed to clarify. "But we also must continue our lives."

"I'm over a hundred years old," Doc whispered. "This is something I'm well aware of."

"Also, you do not usually let yourself get close to anyone." His heart skipped a beat when Doc slid his hands up Nikolai's arms.

"No. Doesn't mean it has never happened."

Nikolai stepped into Doc, and the vampire kissed him. He parted his lips, letting Doc explore his mouth, before he did the same, running his tongue along Doc's fangs, digging his hands into the vampire's back.

He wanted more, but he also knew it wasn't a particularly good time to push Doc's boundaries. They both wanted comfort and some form of reassurance, and right now, this would do.

Doc pushed him back until his legs hit the bed and he had to sit. Doc straddled him, knees on the bed, lips locked on his.

He leaned back, needing to breathe. His blood pounded in his veins, and his jeans grew far too tight.

"Perhaps, you could give me a moment to change into some sleeping pants. These jeans are very tight," he managed to gasp out.

Doc's eyes glinted with amusement, and he let Nikolai up, backing away a couple of steps to give him space.

Feeling a little shaky, he went and leaned on the dresser. He dug out a clean pair of flannel pants and tossed them to Doc.

He changed, though the heat of Doc's gaze on his back burned into him. When he turned around, Doc was sitting on the bed, changed into sleeping pants, staring at him, clearly as aroused as Nikolai. He hadn't even heard him move. He studied the other man's muscled chest, noting the thin scars crossing it

"You heal quickly enough, I wouldn't think you would scar."

"Depends on how much blood I've had. I've been well fed recently. Getting shot wasn't going to be a problem. Sometimes, not so much." He tilted his head. "Change your mind?"

"Ah, no. Was just looking."

"The ones on my back are from a werewolf. Much harder to heal."

That got Nikolai's interest. He twirled his finger, asking Doc to turn. He obliged, standing and putting his back to the mage.

He came over and traced the thin lines that crossed most of Doc's back. "They healed fairly well."

"Nearly killed me."

"Fortunately, it did not." He brushed Doc's hair out of the way, then touched his hair tie with magic, liking his hair down.

Doc's breath caught as his hair fell free. "That's Sofia's trick."

"I'm sorry," he replied, his own voice catching. "I won't do it again."

"No. It just surprised me."

He rested his forehead against Doc's shoulder, hands on his arms. "So many things we should have done."

"Nikolai," Doc whispered. "I'm not sure we could have done much more. Maybe we should have tried to get help from other mages, but in this time, we have to be so careful. As you've noted, it hinders us. What else could we have done?"

"Not left her alone."

Doc stiffened for a minute before nodding. "That is one thing we should have done. She should have been safe in her dorm."

"We'll get her back." He dragged his hands down Doc's bare arms, callouses catching on his smooth skin.

Doc's breathing quickened again, and he turned, bringing Nikolai to him and sinking back onto the bed, pulling the mage with him.

He pressed his lips to Doc's, and the other man devoured his lips, biting, though not hard enough to draw blood. They kissed, exploring each other, Nikolai resting on his forearms, fingers curled in Doc's hair.

Doc traced his muscular back with his fingers, igniting his nerves. He pressed into Doc

"If you keep that up," he gasped when he came up for air, "you may shake my resolve to not push your boundaries tonight."

Doc's lips curled again, not quite smiling, but clearly pleased with himself. He grabbed the mage and turned them both so quickly, Nikolai barely had a moment to register he was now underneath Doc before he was pressing his fangs lightly into his neck.

"We wouldn't want to test your self-control," Doc murmured against his neck.

"It is not so good in these situations," he admitted, gasping out the words as Doc applied more pressure. The vampire pressed into him, and he thrust against the other man, grinding into him.

Doc growled what might have been a warning before sinking his teeth into Nikolai's neck.

For a moment, Doc let him experience nothing but the icy pain of his bite, then he hit the mage with pleasure. The contrast undid him. He clawed at Doc's back, crying out his release and thrusting against Doc while the vampire took his blood. Doc shuddered, licking Nikolai's neck to stop the bleeding and sending tremors through the mage's body. He collapsed on top of him, and they lay there, both trembling for a few minutes, until their bodies calmed.

Finally, Doc groaned and rolled off the mage, lying next to him in the relatively small bed.

"I need a shower," Doc muttered.

He grinned, pleased. "There is a spell for that." He waved his hand, and blue magic touched both of them.

Doc yelped in surprise as the magic washed over him.

It wasn't as satisfying as actually bathing, but keeping clean on military campaigns was difficult, and he didn't prefer to be dirty when he didn't have to be.

"Thanks," Doc said looking down at himself.

"Of course. I don't like to be dirty. It is not always easy to get a shower."

They shifted around until they were actually under the covers, and Doc rolled on his side.

He traced the rapidly fading scratches he'd left on Doc's back before curling up around other man.

"You don't mind?"

"I'm so used to sleeping with Ed and Allan that it feels weird to sleep alone. I don't mind."

"Good."

Chapter 23

Sofia

The guys worked out a rotation so that I wasn't alone in my mental prison very often. It was the only thing that kept me sane. If I wanted to, I could look out and see the world through my eyes, but it was as a passenger and it freaked me out.

After a while, I stopped looking.

The demon inhabiting me did its best to ignore me, and for about a week, the only thing it had to do was pretend to be me.

Then the Andersons decided they wanted to have a look at their new toy.

The demon's alarm roused me from my stupor and turned my attention from the warm energy Ed had wrapped me in. He and Allan weren't quite as good as Nikolai was at being able to project themselves into my mind through our shared pack bond. I could share emotions with them, but we couldn't actually talk.

To Nikolai, it was simply like the mental space he created when we shared spells.

Ed slipped away when I looked out into the world. Nikolai stood next to us, and Ash faced us. The view was disorienting because I couldn't control my body, or do anything, and my range of vision was much smaller than normal. I didn't like it, but I wanted to know what had worried the demon.

"The Andersons want you to come now," Ash ordered.

It was a Friday, I thought. We were on campus still. Maybe ready to go back to the cabin. The demon had flat out refused to sleep at the dorm. I didn't think Victoria minded not having me there, so we were going back and forth with the guys every night.

"I do not wish to go to the Andersons," the demon said. I shivered at the sound of my voice.

"You don't have a choice. They've given me control over you in this matter."

"You! You're a lesser…" Nikolai slapped a hand over my mouth, and the demon fell silent.

I flinched away from her anger. The knowledge that a lesser demon would rarely interact with a greater demon on its plane, let alone command one, leaked from it to me. In fact, I actually gained quite a bit of knowledge about their plane without intentionally trying. It would have been more interesting if I wasn't a prisoner in my own mind, but it did give me something to think about.

"Come." Ash sounded resigned.

The demon's horror as my body responded to Ash's command without either of us being willing chased me deeper into my small prison.

I wasn't sure how long I cowered before I felt a presence focused on me.

I should be angry with you.

"With me?" I studied the being standing before me. This must be how the demon saw itself. It—she?—had vaguely feminine curves on a humanoid body, but she was a being of pure golden energy instead of flesh.

It is your fault I am here.

"How is it my fault?"

You allowed yourself to remain untrained.

"That wasn't really my choice."

The demon's attention shifted outward for a minute before it came back to me.

Do you really think your men can free me?

"I hope so. If anyone can figure it out, they will."

I will try very hard not to shove you out. It is difficult.

"I'm sorry."

She seemed to accept this. *I do not know what they will require of me, but with you here, I do not know that I can accomplish it. Stay hidden. Hopefully, the lesser demon is not commanded to speak of your presence.*

"He's had a lot of practice using his words wisely."

The longer I am in your body, the harder it will be to leave it intact when I depart.

I shivered. "Let's hope this doesn't take long."

I do not like it here. I do not like being commanded. Your pack is pleasant enough, but obviously, they do not want me here, either.

"I don't think they'd have any problem with you at all if you weren't in my body."

The demon laughed. *They do seem fairly accepting. They even tolerate the lesser demon.*

"It's not his fault he has to do what the Andersons say."

No. She changed the subject. *Your mage is close. I do not know what they intend, but I expect it will be painful. Perhaps he can shield you.*

"Painful?"

I doubt I can do whatever it is they require of me. Your body is not fully mine, so my capabilities are limited.

I shuddered, fear tingling through me.

We have arrived. Be cautious.

She vanished, and shortly after, Nikolai replaced her. I melted into his arms.

"I was going to look for their library," he explained. "But your demon has good point. You will need protection."

"She's talking to you?" I didn't let go of him, burying my face in his chest.

"She knows I'm here and asked me to help."

"Invisible?" I guessed.

"Yes. I found a safe spot to hide. I will stay with you."

He held me, and we both listened while the woman with the white hair who had led the ritual to bind the demon to me spoke. Her name turned out to be Melinda Anderson. She was Alex's grandmother, though she didn't look much over forty, and she wanted the demon to demonstrate some magic.

At first, the demon simply refused.

Nikolai certainly saved my life as he shielded me from the worst of the pain the backlash of her refusal brought down on us.

Nikolai held me and shielded us as hot fire raced through my body and stabbed at my brain. He kept me anchored, kept me from fleeing. It still hurt, but it wasn't as unbearable as it would have been without him.

He experienced everything I did, wincing as pain seared our nerves.

"You should leave." I desperately didn't want him to leave me to this alone, yet I also didn't want him hurt.

"It is tolerable," he replied, and refused to let go.

I had no idea how long the torture lasted. It came and went. I suspected the demon offered several refusals before they finally commanded her to perform some sort of magic.

This time, the pain was different. My entire body was being stretched, filled, new pathways burned through me.

The demon and I both screamed as magic poured out of us. My body collapsed to the hard ground, nerves screaming in pain, completely spent.

"I told you," I heard Ash saying. "You can't force the integration. Sometimes it takes a while. If you burn her out before the demon is fully in control, she'll never heal, and she'll be useless to you."

"How long will it take?" Melinda snapped.

"It will take as long as it takes. Not usually more than a month."

Nikolai was listening as well, and he swore. "He's buying us time, but more would be better."

"Fine. You will stay with her constantly. Bring her to me as soon as the process is complete. We have work to do," Melinda snarled at them, and I got the sense that she left.

I had no energy, and neither did my body. Someone picked me up from the ground.

"And where do you think you're going?"

That was Alex's voice.

I growled, and Nikolai tensed next to me.

"I was instructed to stay with her. Not to leave her lying on the ground. I will take her somewhere more comfortable."

"Fine, take her back to them. It will torture them to see her like this, and maybe the two of you can learn some of their secrets. They're such idiots, I'm sure they'll allow you to stay around."

Nikolai held me close, kissing me, before stepping away. "I must go for now. One of us will return soon."

∞ ∞ ∞

For a time, I lost myself again, clinging to the guys, not aware of much else. The demon mostly left me alone, though she did check in on me every now and again to make sure I was still there.

Ed spent the most time with me over the next week. Though they both had to go to classes, he had managed to perfect hanging out with me while still doing life things.

It was so tempting to simply let go, but the guys forced me to hang on.

They forced me to have hope.

They forced the demon to have hope.

Ash followed us everywhere as commanded, and the guys tolerated him living with them. On some level, I got used to having him around, though I mostly tried to hide from the world as life went on around me.

I missed the first mountain snow. The guys were right though, it snowed before Halloween.

What is Halloween? The demon's voice jerked me out of a light daze in one of my rare times when I was alone.

For a minute I couldn't remember. Couldn't remember anything. What did it matter? Why was I here?

Sofia!

The demon had never used my name before, but that brought me back to myself.

"Uh, Halloween? It's a holiday, or like, a fun day for people to dress up in costumes, party, things like that. It used to be a harvest celebration, among other things. We've turned it into a party, though."

Alex is forcing me to go with him to the college Halloween social. This sounds annoying. I suspect he wants to annoy your men, and maybe try to get information.

I shuddered at the thought of having to go with Alex. The thought of him touching me in any way made me shrink away from the conversation with the demon.

I would have cried if I had actual eyes to cry with. It wasn't so much that I really wanted to go to the Halloween party, but that I was missing going with my guys.

Even if all I could do was be around him, I could hang out with Doc. I could get Ed and Allan and maybe Nikolai to dance with me a little. We would all have costumes. I wondered what the guys would dress up as.

Instead I was slowly slipping away.

Fuck.

What do I do? The demon sounded lost.

"I guess just find a costume. The guys can help you out if Alex doesn't have something horrible in mind. And do what they say, because otherwise, it will hurt." I collapsed into a chair that I formed in my mental prison, just so I could collapse into it.

She faded away.

∞ ∞ ∞

"Sofia!" Doc yelled my name.

I looked up from the ground I stared at and didn't recognize my surroundings for a moment. It was my grove, but the moss carpet had withered, and the trees no longer connected. Several were rotten, and a few had fallen. Brown pine needles littered the ground.

The effort of looking up cost me, and I almost didn't reply.

Doc looked around frantically, yelling my name again.

"Here," I gasped, though my voice made next to no sound.

He heard me and finally focused on me. Doc rushed to my side and pulled me into his arms. His arms nearly passed through my body.

After another moment, Nikolai appeared and warmth from the werewolves wrapped around me. Nikolai pressed his arms around me, sandwiching me between him and Doc and the warm wilderness Ed and Allan brought with them.

I wasn't sure how long they held me, but eventually, everyone began to feel more substantial, and some of my strength returned as the guys shared their energy with me.

The others left, but Doc stayed, and I clung to him, shuddering.

"Sofia, you have to hang on."

"I'm trying." The frustration at not being able to actually cry overwhelmed my fear for a moment.

He gathered me close and pressed his lips to mine.

Neither he nor Nikolai had done more than hold me since I'd been imprisoned, and I hadn't asked, not wanting the reminder of what I was missing.

This time, I needed the reminder so badly, that I would have bruised his lips had this been our real bodies. I nearly attacked him with my need.

Doc held me tightly, kissing me until I finally returned to as close to normal as I thought I could manage.

He brushed my short hair back from my face and rested his forehead against mine. He looked a little faded, but I was a lot better.

If you give her too much of your energy, vampire, you're going to hurt the Russian when you feed on him later.

We both straightened. The demon stood on the edge of my grove. It also looked a little improved, or less rotted, anyway.

"We'll do what we need to. Sofia needs the energy."

Have you informed her of our other issue?

"Not yet."

"What's wrong?" My stomach sank. "I mean, besides the obvious."

"We are trying to keep your parents from knowing what's going on. At least for a while longer," Doc explained.

I nodded. I knew about that and agreed.

"It's almost Thanksgiving break, and they're expecting you to go home."

If I were fully in my body, I knew my heart would be racing and adrenaline would be making my limbs tremble. As it was, a brief imitation of that reaction pulsed through me, as if my mind remembered what my body would respond with.

Then another thought hit me.

"Wait, what happened to Halloween?"

"Other than that, we all barely refrained from killing Alex in front of a lot of witnesses, not much," Doc grumbled.

"But, wasn't Halloween like, tomorrow or something?"

"Sofia," he replied sadly, "Halloween was a few weeks ago."

"But we just talked about it!" I glanced at the demon. Though she was in her pure energy form, she still somehow conveyed sadness.

Doc held me, and I sagged against him. He nuzzled my hair in a very Ed-like move. "Nikolai thinks he's close," Doc whispered. "Hang in there."

"So, what do we do about Thanksgiving?"

"We've got a couple of options. One, just tell your parents. None of us are real happy about that idea for so many reasons, especially since Nikolai is increasingly convinced that he can fix this. He's looking for one more piece of information."

"How?"

"He's putting his invisibility spell to good use in the Andersons' library."

Despite how awful I felt, I grinned, leaning my cheek against Doc's chest. He kept his grip on me tight.

"I can fool a werewolf, I can fool idiot modern mages." Doc mimicked Nikolai's accent. It twisted me up inside.

"Okay, so what are our other options?"

"Fake that you're desperately ill and can't come back. That risks your parents coming to see you, and doctor's visits, and other awkward questions, like why can't your mage boyfriend just heal you. We don't think it's a great option, either."

"I'm assuming you have a more viable option?"

"Yes, just trying to give you everything we came up with so you can choose."

"Okay."

"Our demon friend here has offered another alternative. Right now, everyone is trying to keep the two of you separate from each other."

For good reasons.

"She thinks that if you join more closely with her, allowing you to actually interact with the world to some degree, the two of you will be able to fool your parents long enough to get through Thanksgiving."

"Why haven't we done this before now?" Being able to interact again sounded amazing. As it was, I was rapidly slipping away.

Because, once we do this, there's no going back, and soon, our powers will fully merge. We've been trying to avoid this very thing we're proposing. Once the Andersons sense I have fully merged with your body, then they will command me to use our powers and there will be no point in not telling your parents, as all will be lost.

"Oh."

"The Andersons have already..." He hesitated a moment, finding the right word. "Approached me, about going back to Nebraska with you. They're not interested in losing their prize, and until the demon settles in fully, you're useless to them."

I smiled, and the demon's enjoyment of being useless warmed me as the sensation coursed through my connection with her.

"That must have been an interesting conversation."

Doc sighed. "Ash is the only reason Alex and the other mage they sent with him are still alive. He restrained me. Barely. Probably only because I knew it really was a bad idea to kill them."

I raised my eyebrows and pressed myself closer to him.

"So, what does the pack get out of it?"

"Their silence on what we are."

"Oh. Damn. So, they want you and me to fool my parents for a little while longer, so they don't have to worry about my parents going to the authorities?"

Doc nodded. "But more importantly, we get a little more time to figure this out. Unfortunately, if Nikolai hasn't solved the issue before we return, the game will be over."

"Fuck."

"He's freaking out about it in his very understated way. I've had to force him to sleep for the last week, otherwise, he'd be a complete wreck." Doc sighed.

You should ask him what forcing the mage to sleep is like. The demon sounded sly.

I glanced up at Doc. His face turned redder than I had ever seen, and he cleared his throat.

"I can guess." I laughed. "I really am missing out on all the fun."

Doc shook his head. "We're all losing our minds."

"Well, we'll just have to make up for lost time when I get back. How are Ed and Allan? I don't really get to talk to them."

"Ed is a wreck. Allan is only marginally better. I don't think Ed has shifted since he was injured, and we can't talk him into it. Allan still runs, but not as much. I'd tell you we were all fine, but you wouldn't believe me." He tightened his grip on me. He laughed bitterly. "And it would be the biggest lie I've ever told."

"Okay, so as soon as we're on the road back to Nebraska, the demon and I try to integrate without fully integrating so I can interact enough to fool my parents? And we hope Nikolai fixes this before the Andersons find out."

"Yes."

"Okay."

You must know, even if the mage frees me in time, I do not know how this will affect you, Sofia. It will change you. Also, it will make it harder for me to leave your body intact. I warned you of this already.

"It's worth the risk. It's the only thing we can do."

Very well. Be warned. I do not share well. It will be difficult for both of us.

"This is already difficult."

She nodded in agreement.

"Okay, I need to go. Hang in there, Sofia." Doc kissed me again before releasing me and fading away.

Your vampire is lucky your mage knows healing spells.

"I'm surprised Ed and Allan aren't helping out." They usually shared blood with him, too.

Your werewolves have exhausted themselves sharing their energy with you, as has your vampire. You see your mage less because he is trying to stay rested so he can perform the necessary healings on himself and the werewolves, and of course, soon he will be performing a complicated piece of magic he has never done before under extremely stressful circumstances. It is wise of him to conserve himself. He does not like it.

"How long before we do this?"

Tomorrow, by your days.

"Okay. I'm looking forward to another real taste of the world. I hope it won't be the last."

This is also my hope. I wish to go home.

The demon left me, and I sank back down to the ground to wait.

Chapter 24

Doc

The demon was right, Doc came closer to actually hurting Nikolai than either of them cared to admit after giving Sofia so much energy. He barely felt recovered as he lay there, holding Nikolai while the mage slept. He stared at the ceiling and tried to convince himself that the next week wasn't going to be a complete disaster.

Nikolai snored lightly, head resting on Doc's shoulder. He didn't normally snore.

Someone knocked lightly on the door.

"Come in," Doc whispered just loud enough for a werewolf to hear.

Allan pushed open the door.

Nikolai didn't stir.

"Are you two okay?" Allan's eyes trailed over Nikolai's muscled back.

Doc gestured for Allan to come over, but didn't move, not wanting to disturb the mage.

"We're fine."

Allan sank down on the bed, and Doc held his arm out, inviting Allan to lay down with them. He squeezed onto the small bed and pressed his back into Doc's side. "We're going to fix this, right?"

"Yeah, Allan. Nikolai will find the last bit of information he needs. I'll keep her safe this week."

"You sure you can deal with her dad for a week?"

Doc groaned. "Don't remind me."

"Room for one more?" Ed whispered from the doorway, sounding uncertain but desperate to not be alone.

Without comment, Allan shifted until he was basically sprawled on top of Doc and pressed against Nikolai. Ed took the spot Allan had just occupied, and Doc counted himself lucky that he could still breathe.

Doc laughed quietly. "And I thought it was hard to fit three in a queen-sized bed."

"I'm looking forward to moving us back into your room," Ed admitted. "Pack should sleep together."

Nikolai didn't budge, and Doc worried he had injured the mage despite the healing spells he'd cast before passing out.

They finally all drifted off, and even Doc managed to get some sleep, despite the worries that kept his mind spinning.

∞ ∞ ∞

"Did I miss something?" Nikolai woke first the next morning.

Doc's eyes snapped open, but he was weighed down and couldn't move. It took him a minute to remember he was literally buried under werewolves. He took a few calming breaths.

"No."

"Ah, good." The mage ran his hand lightly over Allan's back, and the werewolf's eyes fluttered open.

Allan glanced at Doc before seeming to realize it was Nikolai rubbing his back. He shut his eyes again and lay there.

"That looks cozy."

Doc glanced over at the doorway. Ash and the demon stood there.

"I had wondered why breakfast was delayed."

Doc turned his attention to the ceiling and rolled his eyes. The demon really was easier to deal with inside Sofia's head. She made more of an effort to play nice there for some reason.

Or maybe it was just because Ash was present. Him having some form of command over her pissed her off to no end, and she took every opportunity to let everyone know she considered them all beneath her. And he used to think Nikolai was bad about acting like royalty.

Ed grumbled and got up. Allan did as soon as Ed was out of his way, and they all headed to the kitchen.

"Are you all right?" Nikolai pushed himself up on his arms and looked down on Doc.

"A little squished, but otherwise okay."

Nikolai smiled. "Not what I meant."

"It's going to be a very long week."

"How long can you go without blood?"

"If I'm not exerting myself, several days to a week before it gets uncomfortable."

"Take more of mine. You are still tired. I can see it in your eyes. I'll rest today and get one of the werewolves to borrow Ash's car and drop me off near the Andersons' place tonight."

"Are you sure, Nikolai? I can't imagine the last few weeks have been easy on you. Even with your healing spells."

"It is okay. I have all week to recover."

He took Nikolai's wrist and bit gently, trying not to overpower the mage with pleasure. Though from Nikolai's general lack of reaction, either Doc had figured out how to tone it down a lot more, or the mage really was exhausted. Energy coursed through Doc.

"Do you need anything?"

"No. I'll sleep. Eat later." Nikolai pulled the blankets over his shoulder. "Doc, keep her safe for us."

"I'll do my best."

Doc had already packed a duffle bag for the week, and he'd asked Victoria to help the demon pack something for Sofia. Her stuff was already in his truck. He hit the bathroom to clean up and joined the others in the kitchen.

"Hey, Doc. It's supposed to snow again. You know that, right?"

"I looked. Shouldn't be too bad." He grabbed some of the powder he used to make his protein drinks and, not trusting Sofia's parents to have decent tea, threw some of that in his bag as well.

The demon stood. "Are you ready?"

"Yeah."

He hugged Ed and Allan tightly and gave Ash a quick hug, too. The lesser demon really was trying. "Keep an eye on Nikolai," he ordered Ed and Allan.

"I'll take care of him for you," Allan winked.

Doc cocked an eyebrow and shook his head.

Ed laughed.

Sofia followed Doc out of the house and got in his truck. He fired up the diesel and headed toward the first mountain pass he had to get through before they could swing up into Wyoming and take the interstate down to Sofia's current hometown in Nebraska.

Fortunately, the roads weren't too bad. It hadn't snowed in almost a week, even in the highest peaks, so the first part of the trip went reasonably quickly. They didn't speak. The demon flipped through the radio stations as Doc headed out of the mountains.

The wind kicked up once he hit Wyoming and his first stop for fuel. It was one of the older fuel stops, where the diesel pumps were set up for semis and he had to go pay inside.

When he returned to the truck, Sofia, her eyes now the normal gray with purple highlights from her magic, let herself out of the passenger side and threw herself into his arms.

He crushed her against his chest, inhaling her scent. She smelled like herself again. The demon's sharp petrichor scent still colored it, but she was obviously at least partially back in charge of her body.

"Sofia," he murmured, a few tears pricking at his eyes.

"Almost in the flesh," she replied.

"Well, if you're feeling good enough to joke..." He kissed her, not caring that they might have an audience at the gas station.

She clung, kissing him like she needed his touch more than oxygen, and left him breathless when she finally did come up for air.

Someone cleared their throat. Doc ignored the person filling their truck at the other pump and held the door for Sofia so she could get out of the bitter wind. He filled his truck, keeping alert for trouble. He didn't run across as many issues as he used to for his skin color and long hair, but it still happened now and again.

As soon as the truck was full, he went back inside for his receipt and then they were back on the road. The only thing keeping him from gripping her hand was the wind buffeting the pickup.

"I wish we could have brought everyone." Sofia sounded sad.

Doc glanced at her. "This is going to work."

"Yeah." She frowned. "I'm just glad I get a chance to see the world again."

He clenched his jaw, not about to argue with her at the moment. She had every right to be worried.

"I do not share well." She removed her hand from his arm and grumbled. Clearly, the demon had reasserted control over Sofia's body.

"It's her body."

"I know." Instead of angry, she sounded petulant, and Doc smiled to hear the demon pout, even though it wasn't a laughing matter.

"Kissing humans is weird," she grumbled.

Doc's eyebrows rose. "I see."

"Yes, very strange. Don't do it again."

"My apologies. Sofia wasn't objecting."

"No, and she's positively throwing a tantrum right now." The demon crossed Sofia's arms over her chest.

"And you're not?" Doc had somewhat gotten used to her, but he wanted Sofia back. The mere half hour had not been nearly enough. Maybe this week would be worth it, if he got to spend time with Sofia in the real world.

"Demons don't throw tantrums." Amusement colored her tone, and he could sense Sofia behind some of her words and inflection.

As much as he wanted Sofia back, he hoped they didn't merge too quickly, or they really would lose her for good.

"What is she saying?'

The demon laughed. "That you are an excellent kisser, and I should just get used to it. Oh, now she's embarrassed. Why? I would think it obvious she enjoys kissing you. Humans are very strange."

Doc just shook his head.

∞ ∞ ∞

The demon relinquished control of Sofia when they got near her house. The nine-hour drive was long, but Doc was fairly certain that he was shortly going to wish he were back behind the wheel. It would have been easier in so many ways if either Ed or Allan had been able to come along or go instead.

"This isn't going to be fun," Sofia sighed.

"No. But let's just try to make the best of it. If they ask about your eyes, blame it on a side effect of magic."

"My eyes?"

"They've got some gold in them now from the demon's presence."

"Oh." She sighed, and her shoulders sagged. "Good to know."

"If they ask what I do for a living, I work at the college as an administrator. It's close to the truth."

"What, you don't want me to tell them I'm dating my teacher?" She grinned at him.

"No," he replied emphatically, even though she was teasing him.

"Yeah, me neither."

Being winter, everything was brown, dormant for the season. Snow covered patches of ground, and the gray skies promised more on the way. The weather forecast had steadily been worsening, and Doc wasn't real excited about getting stuck here in a snow storm, but they were starting to talk in feet instead of inches.

The town they had pulled into looked very much like a small town spurred to life by the oil fields, a lot of single-family housing made from manufactured homes. Quick to go up for workers and their families who needed housing. It looked nice enough. The town had been around long enough to have an elementary school and some shops for essentials in the small downtown area they had passed through to reach Sofia's place.

This was also obviously a cow town, as Doc thought of them. Sofia's place backed up to a field, and cows grazed in the distance. The house was manufactured. The two-acre lot had a barn and some other outbuildings on the far end.

Several pickups sat parked off the dirt driveway, and Doc pulled in near them. He let the truck run for a minute while he clenched the steering wheel.

Sofia put her hand on his and squeezed. "We'll survive this."

"The Andersons are easier to deal with. At least I can kill them."

After not hearing the sound for forever, Sofia's laugh lifted his spirits enough to fortify himself so he could deal with her dad.

He shut off the truck, and they both got out. Sofia's mother came out of the house and wrapped her arms around Sofia.

"It's so good to see you, honey."

"You, too, Mom."

Sofia sounded like she might cry, and Doc knew she expected this to be the last time she saw her parents. He had to believe Nikolai would come through for them. The mage was close.

Her mother came around and gave Doc a quick hug.

"Hello, Doc."

"Hi, Mrs. Collins."

"Please, call me Beth. Come inside. Thank you for driving her down here. You must be exhausted."

Doc nodded, grabbed both of their bags, and followed them inside.

Sofia went over and hugged her dad, but the look she gave him was full of warning instead of affection. Doc winced internally at that.

"Who else is here?" Sofia glanced around.

"Rick and Donna and their kids. Their pipes burst in the last storm, and they're staying with us until it can get repaired. George is here too for a few days. His heat is out. Half the town had issues with the last storm, and it's taking a while to get everyone fixed up. We're in for another storm, if you couldn't tell." Sofia's mom glanced at Doc, who nodded. They both knew.

"They're all out with George's cows right now, getting ready for the storm."

"Here." Sofia's dad held out his hand, and Doc hesitantly handed over their bags.

He took them and went down a hallway. A minute later, he headed outside.

"It's going to be a little crowded," her mom continued. "We figured you and Doc could share your room. The guest rooms are taken."

Sofia raised her eyebrows. "That's awfully progressive of you."

Doc could hear a hint of the demon in her phrasing, but he didn't think Beth noticed.

Beth shrugged. "You're both adults. If you don't want to share, we can figure something else out."

"No, that's fine," Sofia replied.

"Come in, why don't you show Doc around. We already ate, but there's leftovers in the fridge." Beth gestured for them to enter.

They had a coat rack in the front entry way, and he took Sofia's coat and hung it before taking off his. He hesitated by the coats, inhaling and trying not to be too obvious about it. Over the scent of oil, grease, cow, and hay, he caught a scent he was well familiar with. Werewolf. *Great*. They really should have tried to put this off until Christmas.

His phone chimed, and he pulled it out after he hung up his jacket. He left his boots on when no one else took off theirs and followed them into the house. The text was a group text from Nikolai. One of the guys must have taught him how or done it for him. Sofia wasn't on the chat. His chest tightened, but he understood why.

Nikolai: Make it safely?

Doc: Yes, we're here.

Allan: Kill anyone yet?

Doc: We literally just got here. Give it time.

Ed: LOL

Nikolai: Would be easier to deal with her parents in the future if you refrain.

Doc: I'll do my best. One of Dan's oil field friends is a werewolf. They have a few people staying with them. Haven't met them yet. Could get interesting.

Ed: Keep us posted.

Doc: Will do.

Sofia glanced at him, so he handed her the phone. She scrolled through the messages, eyes shining with amusement.

"Tell them I said hi." She returned his phone.

"Cell reception isn't great around here," Beth cautioned. "It's good at the house, but drops off pretty fast. We do have a landline if you need it."

"Thank you," Doc replied. "Just friends of ours checking to see if we made it safely."

"Ed and Allan?" Beth reminded him that she knew the werewolves, though not necessarily that they were werewolves.

"Yes, and Nik," Sofia said. "Victoria also texted me."

"How is Victoria?"

"Doing good. Enjoying her family time this week," Sofia answered.

"Who's Nik?"

"A friend from out of town who's visiting," Doc answered.

"Oh, I didn't realize we were dragging you away from company." Beth sounded concerned.

"No. He's in town for a while. Ed and Allan can keep him entertained for a few days. He came to visit all of us." It was close enough to the truth.

"Oh, well, thank him for me, for sharing his time with you."

"I will."

Sofia's amused smile almost made Doc blush. He managed to keep his expression neutral despite her mirth.

He sent another quick message and put his phone in his pocket.

Beth continued to give the tour. The house was nice, two guest rooms, Sofia's room, and the master bedroom. The guests all had to share a bathroom, and the living room would be crowded with everyone in it. The tour didn't take long, and they ended up back in the kitchen.

Beth insisted on fixing Sofia food and acted disappointed when Doc didn't want anything. That, more than anything else, was going to be the hardest part of the whole week, Doc thought. He didn't eat solid food and had no good way to explain why.

Just as Sofia was finishing her dinner, the front door opened and several people came inside, bringing the strong scent of cow and hay with them.

Sofia glanced at Doc. He just clenched his jaw and shrugged. Here was hoping the werewolf didn't know what a vampire smelled like. Or that Doc's scent was sufficiently disguised by only being half vampire, and constantly around werewolves that the werewolf couldn't figure out what he was.

"Oh, they're back. Let's go introduce everyone."

Doc trailed along behind Sofia, and mentally crossed his fingers.

A pair of young boys who looked very similar in features saw Sofia and ran forward to hug her. She smiled and returned their hugs, though Doc could imagine the demon was annoyed with the physical contact. A younger boy hung back and smiled shyly. Sofia hugged him, too.

Dan had returned with them. The living room was very crowded with everyone standing around.

"Doc, this is Rick, Donna, and their kids, Matt, Eric, and Bobby. And this is George. Everyone, this is Sofia's boyfriend. George and Rick work with me on the oil fields and they live a few houses down."

"Howdy," Doc drawled. He had always found the country boy charm usually distracted people enough that they thought more about it than anything else they might think unusual about him.

The kids all gave him uncertain looks, but Donna smiled brightly and shook his hand. She looked to be in her mid-thirties, with short brown hair, brown eyes, and a friendly expression. Her grip was strong, and she probably spent as much time outside with the animals as she did inside. She carried the faint scent of horse and he suspected she used to rodeo, if she didn't still ride.

Rick, predictably, tried to crush his hand. He was a big guy, dark eyes, dark hair, and a heavy tan from hours in the sun. Doc thought this was one of the people Sofia had mentioned had native blood, and he could see some of it in the man's high cheekbones and darker skin.

He ignored the hand crushing, returning just enough pressure to keep the grip even.

"Nice to meet you," Rick offered cautiously.

Doc nodded.

George was the werewolf. His nostrils flared when he tried to crush Doc's hand. He returned the same amount of pressure, like he had with Rick. George's eyes widened as he had exerted considerably more force than Rick would have been able to.

It was probably not smart, but Doc had bigger things to worry about at the moment and didn't care. He could have crushed the other man's hand. Especially with as well fed as he was recently. Hopefully, it wouldn't come to that.

George didn't say anything, just released Doc's hand and continued to study Doc curiously. At least no one looked openly hostile.

Though he had never really been in a situation like this before, he had some expectations and was pretty shocked when they didn't immediately ask him about himself. They all went into the living room, and instead, started asking Sofia about college.

That was just fine with Doc.

Chapter 25

Sofia

It was so freaking amazing to be back in my body. Even the demon acted a little more comfortable. Instead of having me as a small itch in the back of her mind, it was more of a melding and more harmonious. Of course, soon we would be literally inseparable. That wasn't so exciting.

I watched the others react to Doc and noticed the extra attention George paid him. Now that I knew what to look for, the barely domesticated look in his eyes and the way he scented the air when he shook Doc's hand screamed werewolf.

Doc's fixed attention on him just confirmed what I expected. If he wasn't a wolf, he was something else supernatural.

We all found places to sit in the living room. I grabbed an armchair, and Doc sank down onto the floor next to me. My parents claimed a loveseat, and Rick and Donna grabbed the couch, with their younger son, Bobby, sitting between them.

Matt and Eric, twins, headed off to their room, and George grabbed a chair out of the kitchen.

The wind chose that moment to pick up in front of the storm coming in. Doc and George both tilted their heads, listening, before bringing their attention back to everyone in the room. I wasn't even sure they noticed they did it.

Between the awkwardness of the situation and the demon's presence, I was hyper aware of things going on around me. I was also pretty sure my senses were heightened, because my parents didn't notice the wind until a few minutes later when it started gusting.

"Is everything secure?" Mom asked Dad.

"Yeah, I checked a few things after the last storm, and the tarps over the hay are still secure. The barn is shut up, and I don't think there's anything left to blow around after the wind storm a few weeks ago," Dad answered.

The wind picked up fast, and we all fell silent, listening.

I thought I smelled snow and got up to look outside. The snow wasn't supposed to start until much later, according to the last forecast I heard on the radio.

"It's already snowing. So much for the forecast." I went back to my seat.

"George, do you want to stay a few more days?" Mom offered. "It'll be the couch, but you have a bit of a drive ahead of you."

He stared at Doc. "Sure, thanks, Beth. As long as you don't mind me staying for the holiday. Not sure anyone will be going anywhere tomorrow or the next day."

"We almost told you to stay home," Mom said to me into the silence that followed. "But then it looked like the storm would hold off. If I had known how close it was going to be, I'd have made you stay in Colorado."

I glanced at Doc, and he sighed quietly. We both wished we were back in Colorado. Or maybe not. He smiled at me and winked, probably meaning that at least he got to hang out with me again.

My phone chimed that it had a text.

"So, Sofia, how's Colorado treating you?" Donna glanced between me and Doc for a moment.

Oh, how to answer that question. Hopefully, George wouldn't be able to smell any of my lies.

The demon was keeping herself buried deep right now.

I checked my phone while I answered.

Ed: How's it going?

"Colorado is great. Sunnyglade is great. The school is really good, and I like all my classes. I've made a few friends." I had no idea if my parents had mentioned the magic mafia to anyone or not, so I avoided talking about it.

Sofia: So far, we're surviving. No one has killed anyone yet. Pretty sure George is a werewolf.

Ed: That could be interesting. He isn't glaring daggers at Doc?

Interesting was an understatement.

Sofia: No. Snow has started. Wind is really howling.

Ed: We're supposed to get hit by that same storm later tomorrow. Or a related one anyway. Snow for a few days off and on.

Sofia: Be careful.

Ed: You too.

He sent a little heart icon. My cheeks heated as I put my phone back in my picket.

Doc glanced at me.

"Ed."

He smiled.

"I guess they're going to get hit with some snow, too."

Doc frowned, but nodded.

"Tell us about your friends," George asked.

My eyes widened slightly, though I tried to keep my nervousness in check. The demon exerted a little control, and my heart calmed. I mentally sent her a touch of gratitude. George didn't need to know I was nervous about talking about my friends.

"Victoria is my roommate. We get pizza most every Friday, and we go hiking and hang out. Ed and Allan are friends of Doc's, and they hike with us. Sometimes we all study together. Things like that." I left Nikolai out of it, in case they had forgotten about him.

"And how did you two meet?" Donna asked.

"Um, actually Ed introduced us. He and Allan, his brother, were helping us move in, and we just kind of clicked." I hoped that was a good enough answer.

Dad was watching George. George was still staring at Doc. Somehow, I thought Dad knew George was a werewolf. Him being here probably wasn't an accident, even with the story about his heat being out at his house.

"It's getting late, Bobby. Why don't you go to bed?" Donna said to her son.

"I don't want to, Mom."

"Bobby, go to bed."

"Matt and Eric are still up."

Rick sighed and got up. "Come on."

Bobby's eyes widened, and he shrunk back into the couch as if he could hide under the cushions.

Rick held out his hand, and Bobby took it and slid off the couch, looking resigned.

I didn't think he was afraid of his father, not the way he clung to Rick's hand. I wondered what was up.

With my heightened sense, I could hear the older boys argue with their father about going to bed, but shortly, Rick had returned and it sounded like the kids had settled down.

No one else spoke for a while, and the wind continued to howl. I really wanted to go to bed, though with George in the house, Doc and I wouldn't be able to really talk. I wasn't sure we needed to. I just wanted to be held.

"Are you a student, too?" George sounded like he knew Doc wasn't.

"No. I work at the college. Admin stuff. Nothing exciting."

"Where are you from?" Rick glanced at George then back at Doc, as if highly interested in Doc's reply. Far more than the question probably warranted.

"Arizona. Phoenix area."

"So, Doc as in like a doctor?" Donna took up the questioning.

I saw Doc's hands twitch where they rested on his knees. He wasn't happy about that question.

"No, it's a nickname. Ed gave it to me. He likes westerns and said I reminded him of Doc Holliday for some reason. It stuck." He sounded tired, or maybe resigned.

"Oh."

He didn't offer his name, though my parents knew it.

"So, you're good with a gun? Because I'm guessing you're not deathly ill or actually a doctor." Donna grinned. She'd obviously seen the movie once or twice herself.

"I'm not bad with a gun." Doc shrugged. "I think it was that, and my accent, and he'd never actually met a real cowboy before he ran across me."

Rick seized on the real cowboy thing and started questioning Doc about cows and his experience.

I knew enough to know Rick was really grilling Doc, but he didn't seem to mind these questions as much.

"What is your name, then?" Rick threw that out there at the end of the extensive cow conversation.

I was watching Doc more than Rick, and I saw his hands twitch again. He was outwardly calm, but I'd seen that coiled, ready to spring expression more than once. His jaw clenched slightly, but he answered smoothly. "Roy Cassidy."

Rick blinked, just staring at Doc for a moment before he slowly turned to look at George.

The name didn't seem to mean anything to George. He was giving Rick a curious look.

"Really?" Rick finally said, turning back to Doc.

Doc sighed quietly. I only heard because I was paying attention and sitting right next to him.

"Last I checked," he replied.

"That Roy Cassidy?"

"Probably." This time he just sounded resigned.

"You're sure?"

This time Doc actually laughed tiredly. "I am the only half Navajo Roy Cassidy that I know of. Admittedly, I don't know everyone."

"What?" George's gaze darted back and forth between Doc and Rick.

I wanted to do something to protect Doc, if I needed to, but I couldn't access my magic. He was on his own, and it pissed me off.

"He's a vampire hunter."

"Not really," Doc objected.

"That's not what I've heard."

"How?" George's voice lowered to not quite a growl. "You're not a mage like you've told Sofia."

"I'm not?" Doc held up his hand and the dark blue motes of Nikolai's magic formed into a spinning sphere above his hand.

Everyone stared at the open display of magic.

George continued to glare, but he backed down a little.

Rick shook his head. "Aren't you a little old for Sofia?"

Doc shrugged. "Maybe." The sphere of magic sank back into his hand.

That question was going to lead into even more awkward ones, so I cleared my throat. "I think that's probably my decision. Anyway, I think he's more of a werewolf hunter than a vampire hunter. There aren't too many vampires around from what I understand."

Doc glanced at me, arching an eyebrow, before flicking his gaze toward George. "Really?" he mouthed.

Why the hell had I said that?

The demon chuckled.

I groaned.

Doc shook his head, probably guessing what had happened. He glanced back at George, who definitely had his hackles up now.

"Is that why you reek of werewolf?" George did growl now.

"I don't know, George. Why do you?"

Dad, Mom, and Donna's eyes were about as wide as I had ever seen them. Wind gusted, making the house shudder. The tension in the room swirled like the snow outside, filling the space and threatening to drown us all.

The lights flickered with the storm, but no one reacted.

George growled and surged to his feet.

Doc simply watched, arms loose, ready to spring if he needed to. He could be up and across the room before even a werewolf could get to us.

Did you have to? I growled at the demon.

Give me some credit, Sofia. We were trying to distract them from the Doc's a vampire line of questioning. They're distracted.

I'm not sure that helped.

He'll be fine.

George glared for another moment before stomping toward the door. A breath of cold air and then the front door slammed.

"It's storming," Mom exclaimed. "He can't go out there in this. He didn't even put on a jacket." She could see the entry way from where she sat.

"He'll be fine," Doc replied.

"Is that true, what Rick said?" Dad sounded mild, but I could hear an undercurrent of something in his voice that I didn't quite understand.

"Not exactly. My parents were quite dedicated to the cause. I'm a cowboy. The only supernatural beings I've ever killed were preying on humans, and the authorities weren't going to be able to handle them."

Rick shook his head. "I guess I've only heard rumors."

Doc shrugged. "You know how rumors go."

They all looked at me for a minute. I just shrugged. Clearly, I had known. What did they want me to say?

"You know, it's really late. No one is going anywhere. We should get to bed," Mom said after another long, uncomfortable silence.

Everyone was ready to escape the awkward conversation, and it took very little convincing to get everyone to head off to bed.

Rick grabbed a jacket and went after George.

Doc rose smoothly to his feet and offered me a hand. Simply because I wasn't going to do anything to undermine him at that moment, I slid mine into his and let him help me to my feet.

I hugged my parents, though Dad barely took his eyes off of Doc, before I dragged Doc off to my room.

"I'm so sorry," I whispered, knowing he would hear.

Doc came up behind me and put his arms around me, holding me tight, making me feel safe.

"There are worse questions they could have asked. Worse rumors Rick could have heard. Besides, it wasn't your fault." He nuzzled my neck.

"Mmm," I murmured.

"Let's get some rest. It's going to be a long few days."

I shivered as his breath tickled my neck.

You're not allowed to kiss him. It's gross.

You nearly started a damn fight. Shut up and let me enjoy my body while I still can.

Your mage will come through for us.

If you sounded more certain, I'd have more consideration.

Ignoring the demon's protests, I turned and pressed my lips to Doc's. He gripped me tightly, strong hands painfully tight as he clung to me.

Ugh!

You're starting to sound more like me.

Unfortunately.

I didn't let her protests distract me, and we kissed until I needed air.

Doc's eyes shone in the light from my bedside lamp. He brushed his fingers through my hair and hugged me to him.

I could only hope that Nikolai really would come through for us. We were running out of time fast.

Chapter 26

Sofia

The brain fog was real the next morning. Doc was already awake when I finally crawled out of a deep sleep. As was his normal custom, he had stayed in bed and held me until I woke.

Tears sprang to my eyes, and he tightened his arms around me, as if he could tell I was crying.

"He'll figure it out."

I took a couple of deep breaths and nodded. "I know."

He kissed my shoulder.

The demon had muttered last night when Doc pulled me into his arms to sleep, but she didn't say anything about his kiss. That worried me a little. She was playing nice right now, but I knew if Nikolai didn't come through for us, she wouldn't let me keep control of my body much longer.

If she even let me stay at all.

If I even could.

Those cheerful thoughts made me want to pull the covers over my head and hide, but my bladder and my stomach both chased me out of Doc's warm embrace.

The wind still howled, and a quick look out my window revealed blowing snow and almost no visibility.

"That's quite the blizzard."

Doc looked over my shoulder, hands resting lightly on my arms. "Wonderful."

"No kidding." I let the curtains fall back to help keep the warmth in and headed for the bag Victoria had packed for me.

By the time I was finished in the bathroom, Doc was in the kitchen. He'd found the tea kettle had tea steeping for both of us.

"I knew there was a reason I liked you," I mumbled as he handed me the mug.

Mom came into the kitchen a few minutes later. "Want breakfast?"

"Yes please." Mom made the best breakfast.

"I'm okay with tea," Doc answered. "I'd offer to help, but I'm a terrible cook."

"Not a problem. Thought you were a coffee drinker?" Mom glanced at the empty coffee pot before looking at me.

"Yeah, since Alex drugged my latte, I'm having a hard time with coffee."

"Oh." Her expression fell and she glanced at Doc, a great deal of gratitude in her expression.

My parents knew he, Ed, and Allan had saved me. She liked Doc a lot more than my dad did, so at least one of my parents didn't hate my boyfriend. Of course, if they knew I had three more, they'd flip. It might not be an issue for much longer, anyway. If Nikolai didn't save me, no one would be left to care.

Doc moved away from the oven, and Mom took over. Shortly, the smells of bacon had the rest of the house stirring.

I cradled my Earl Grey at the table while Doc leaned against the wall, out of the way, like he did most every morning and sipped his tea.

The storm raged outside. The house shuddered now and again with some of the stronger gusts. George and Rick were talking about the cows when they found their way into the kitchen. Rick glanced at Doc, noting his presence but otherwise not paying much attention to him. George glared.

Doc ignored him.

The weather was more pressing than my boyfriend though, and pretty soon, they were back to discussing contingency plans for the snow. The forecast was steadily deteriorating as the front pulled moisture out of another storm system that had unexpectedly worsened. Nebraska, Wyoming, and the Front Range in Colorado, along with parts of Kansas, were getting battered by fifty plus mile an hour winds and varying amounts of snow.

Matt and Eric came in and sat at the table. Rick got the kids food and helped Mom until Donna arrived. She sank down in Rick's chair when he pulled it out for her, and he served her, too. She looked exhausted. Being in someone else's house with three kids, especially over the holidays, had to be grueling.

I shoved food in my mouth once it was on the table, and Doc made me another cup of tea without me even having to ask.

Dad showed up after a while, and we rotated seats so everyone could eat. He made Mom eat before he did.

George didn't take his eyes off of Doc for more than a few minutes at a time, but my boyfriend continued holding up the wall in the corner and staying out of the way.

"Where's Bobby?" I had expected him to join us before long, but Matt and Eric had been put to work cleaning up, and the younger kid hadn't come to eat yet.

"He said he was coming," Matt grumbled.

Even I could hear the lie in his voice. I glanced over at Doc. He frowned at the kids.

"Rick, go get Bobby and get him in here," Donna sighed. "Please."

He patted her shoulders and left the kitchen, only to return a minute later frowning.

"Matt, Eric, where is Bobby?"

"Maybe the bathroom?"

"I checked, son. Where's your brother?"

"We don't know. He said he was coming," Matt whined.

Donna buried her face in her hands. "What did you say to him?"

"Nothing," Eric bit out.

"You two have got to be nice to your brother, or at least not mean to him. Picking on him is not helping anything."

"We didn't do anything!" Matt crossed his arms and sat down in one of the chairs, lips pursed.

George, Rick, and Dad left the kitchen while the boys pouted.

"Finish cleaning up!" Donna snapped and left the kitchen.

Mom gestured to me, and I followed her into the living room. Doc trailed along behind us.

"What's going on with the boys?" Mom sat down next to Donna and put her arm around the other woman's shoulders.

"They caught him playing dolls with the neighbor's girl a month ago. They have said everything and anything they possibly can to him since then to push him around. I don't know why. They played with dolls with neighbor girls at that age, too." She sank back into the couch and wiped at her eyes. "I'd like to strangle both of them."

Dad and his friends stomped back into the living room. "He's not in the house."

"What!" Donna bolted up. "Where is he?"

I heard Doc sigh. I glanced at him. He had his eyes shut and brow furrowed. After a quick moment, he blinked a couple of times, before looking up. I guessed he had used his vampire senses to look for Bobby and didn't want anyone to see his eyes darken, though it wasn't real easy to tell unless you were close, since they were already so dark.

George went to the door and looked outside before shaking his head. "I'll go look, but I'm not going to find him by scent."

"I'll find him." Doc squeezed my shoulder before leaving my side and heading for the door. I followed.

He slipped on his boots while the others stared at him.

"How exactly are you going to do that?" George blocked his way, arms crossed.

Doc ignored him, pulling on a jacket.

George grabbed for Doc's arm.

Even though I was expecting it, I jumped when Doc slammed George's face into a wall. George struggled for a moment, but Doc had twisted the man's arm up behind his back in an arm lock, and he did it faster than anyone could have seen.

He leaned close, pressing against George's back, and I could imagine that the other man's heart raced. Even if George wasn't actually scared, the wolf in him would probably react to another predator that close.

"Stay here. I'll find him." Doc's voice was low, dangerous. I shivered, and I trusted the man with my life.

George nodded, face pinched in pain.

Doc released George and stepped back, keeping his eye on the werewolf. George rolled his shoulder, glaring at Doc.

The demon purred, enjoying the violence amongst us. I tried to ignore her.

"Hey," I called before Doc could leave the house.

He glanced at me, lips curled slightly into a smile. He'd enjoyed that.

"Be careful."

"I will. Not my first blizzard." He leaned down and kissed me chastely before heading out into the storm.

The chill he left behind was only partially due to the blast of cold air when he opened the front door.

"I don't care what anyone says, that is not a mage," George growled, eyes turning to me as if I was going to tell Doc's secrets now that he was out of the house.

I shrugged. "He does magic. Seems like a mage thing to me."

"He's stronger than I am. How do you explain that?"

Turning and heading back to the armchair in the living room that I liked, I shrugged again. "There's spells for that sort of thing."

George rubbed his shoulder as he followed me into the living room. "Is he really a vampire hunter?"

I shook my head. "No. His parents were. I think they taught him everything they knew, but he's not really the type to go out hunt someone down just because they're a vampire, or a were. He'll defend anyone he thinks he needs to, but he's not going to look for trouble."

I curled up in the armchair and hoped no one else would ask awkward questions I didn't want to answer.

Mom and Rick focused on Donna. Tears streaked her eyes and she clutched her hands into fists while they tried to comfort her. Matt and Eric had been banished to the bedroom, and George paced by the front door. Dad flipped on the TV. Though the reception flickered with the storm, most of the local coverage was about the closures due to blowing snow.

I pulled out my phone and held it, in case Doc tried to get a hold of me. I knew reception was bad here, but maybe he could get a text through.

Time crawled, but finally my phone dinged.

Doc: Found him. He's okay.

Sofia: Great!

"Donna, Doc found Bobby. He said he's okay."

Donna started sobbing.

It was still about another half an hour before the front door banged open, and Doc stumbled in. I jumped to my feet and just barely beat Donna and Rick to the door.

George shut it behind them, closing off the draft of cold air and swirl of snow that followed Doc inside. He had Bobby wrapped in his own jacket and clutched to his chest. Snow coated both of them.

Rick took Bobby from Doc.

"Bobby, are you okay?" Donna managed through her sobs.

The kid nodded, and Rick set him down and handed Doc's jacket back to him.

"Where did you go?"

"I tried to go to the barn, but got lost." He cried, too.

"He needs to get warmed up," Doc ordered. He shook the snow off of himself before wrapping his arms tight around himself, shoulders hunched.

"You need to get warmed up, too," I ordered, and wrapped my arms around him. Deliberately placing myself between him and George just in case the werewolf thought he might try to take advantage of the situation. Doc shivered in my arms, but I guessed he would warm up quickly as he didn't seem worried.

Dad handed Doc a thick blanket, and I pulled him into the living room and shoved him into the armchair, before sitting in his lap. He wrapped the blanket around us and soon his tremors subsided.

I rested my head against his chest and let him borrow my warmth while everyone fussed over Bobby.

His story slowly came out. His older brothers had been tormenting him again, so he'd decided to go to the barn. That wouldn't have been so bad. Chilly, but the farm dogs were in there along with some livestock, and he would have been able to stay warm and get away from his tormentors for a while. The blizzard had disoriented him, and once he realized he was lost, he had found some shelter out of the wind and tried to keep warm. He was mildly hypothermic, but they were slowly getting him warmed up.

"You okay?" I whispered.

"Yes." He tightened his arms around me.

Once it was clear Bobby was okay, Rick turned his attention to us.

"Doc, we can't thank you enough."

My boyfriend tensed, not comfortable with the attention. He nodded. "You're welcome."

"Are you warming up?"

"Yes. I'll be fine before long."

"Need anything?"

Doc shook his head.

Rick went back to helping with Bobby. They finally decided he was warm enough to try a warm bath and herded him off to the bathroom.

George sat down on the couch and stared at us. We both ignored him as much as we could.

Dad helped Mom in the kitchen, making lunch for everyone.

"Have you heard from anyone?" Doc asked after a while.

"No. They've been strangely silent." Ed, especially, had been texting a lot since they knew the demon had given me my body back for a while.

"Hmm."

I drifted off in Doc's arms, warm and comfortable, only to be startled awake moments later.

"Sofia."

"What!" I jerked upright, looking around.

Doc still held me cradled in his arms

"I'm going to help them go check the stock. The storm has let up somewhat."

I grumbled, warm and comfortable.

He laughed. "Sorry."

"I'll probably survive this."

He kissed me on the top of my head, and I crawled out of his arms.

"I'll come. I think my coveralls are still here." I glanced at Dad to make sure he didn't have any objections, but he nodded. The more hands the better.

I hurried to my room and found my warm clothing. I might actually bring some of it back to Colorado with me. Especially since we would have space in Doc's truck. Of course, it might not matter, anyway.

"We need to check that gully in the south pasture," Dad was saying when I returned. "The cows like to go in there during storms, but they get stuck. We'll probably have to pull a few out. We can throw some hay and check the horses. Cut open the stock tanks and hope they get enough water before they freeze again."

Doc nodded. Someone had found him coveralls, and he had bundled up along with the rest of us. I didn't actually know how much the cold bothered him, but clearly not badly or he would have been in worse shape earlier.

Dad fired up the old farm truck. The bed was full of hay and we all squished into the cab. If we got the farm truck stuck in one of the pastures, it wouldn't be the end of the world and at least the stock would have hay.

I sat on Doc's lap. They made Matt and Eric come along, and they had squeezed in next to Rick. We were all in the back. Dad and George rode up front. With as much wind as we had, the snow was patchy. Some areas were deep, some bare. The service road we used to get out to some of the cow pastures looked clear.

We made it about halfway to the field before the truck got stuck in a drift across the two track road.

Dad put it in reverse, but the wheels spun. "Damn it," he muttered.

George grumbled and got out. He glanced at Doc before shutting the door.

Doc sighed quietly but I shifted off him so he could get out and help. The two of them inspected the drift and had a quick conversation before going behind the truck. George gestured at Dad to go forward.

He gunned it and the two men pushed us through the drift.

"Well, he's strong as hell," Dad muttered, probably not aware he had spoken aloud.

Doc and George hopped on the edges of the truck bed and rode back there until the next drift. They had to push us through several more, but with their help, we were able to make it out to the windbreaks and check the cows. We threw out some more hay, broke ice on the tank, and headed for the horses.

None of the stock were ours, but Dad owned some of the land and most of the cows were Rick's or George's. Dad liked helping out with the stock, and they often used our property to get to the stock since the fields were closest to us.

The horses were easy enough to care for. They all belonged to different people in the town and they paid a little bit to keep them in the field.

Then we headed for the notorious gully. I'd spent more than one afternoon after shitty weather helping to get cows out of it. It was a bad part of what was otherwise a pretty nice pasture and they did put up fencing, but invariably, the cows pushed through the fence during the bad weather.

This storm was no exception. The fence was buried in snow, and the cows had simply walked over it. We parked the truck as close as we could get and followed George and Doc as they broke a trail for us.

Sure enough, about twenty cows had packed themselves into the small gully and couldn't figure out how to turn around and get out. To be fair, the last one was kind of stuck in the narrow opening into the gully. Though the gully entrance was somewhat sheltered from the wind, snow had drifted down and filled the entrance.

Dad sighed and went back to the truck for some ropes.

It took us a half hour to get the first cow out of the gap. Then it took another ten minutes to convince her she didn't want to go back in with her friends.

The cows mooed frantically, and we tried to get a couple more to leave the gully where they would otherwise starve.

Finally, after getting pissed off at cow stupidity, George actually jumped down into the gully on the far side, landing on the back of a cow, and unleashed his wolf just enough to scare the shit out of the cows. Literally, we saw when he followed them out. It coated his legs, but finally, the cows came out of the gully willingly. Now we just needed to get them back to the rest of the herd. The storm would return according to the forecast, and we didn't want to have to dig them out again.

"Help me chase them across the pasture?" George asked.

Doc glanced at me, before nodding. "Sure."

"We'll meet you all back at the house." George waved.

"Be careful," I whispered.

"Yeah." Doc hugged me and headed out after George.

We climbed back into the truck as the wind gusted, kicking up sparkling snow in the late afternoon light. The next wave of storm would be here soon.

The trip back to the house went relatively quickly as we had already broken trail for the truck on the way out. The wind buffeted us, but the heater took the chill out of the air, and I wasn't shivering by the time we made it back. A little surprised I hadn't heard from the demon in a while, I turned my attention inward. She ignored me. I was good with that.

George and Doc made it back about a half hour after we did, and he curled up with me in the armchair with the blanket wrapped around both of us until dinner time. Somehow, he managed to get forgotten and no one noticed that he didn't eat dinner.

The storm kicked back up full force, and the roads were still closed when we finally fell into an exhausted sleep at the end of a long day.

Chapter 27

Ed

"I'm going to puke," Ed groaned out.

Nikolai twisted around and looked at him. "Truly?"

"Oh my god, just watch the road." Ed clutched his seatbelt and squeezed his eyes shut.

"You will survive a crash." Nikolai laughed as he drove Alex's Mustang through the snow, magic acting like a plow in front of them to sort of clear the road.

Allan echoed Ed's groan. "You're insane."

"Perhaps." Nikolai chuckled. "While puke covering Alex's car is amusing, it would smell."

The mage waved his hand, and Ed's nausea instantly eased. He still wanted to puke, but that was all mental now.

"I should have stayed with my car. I'm going to die in a car full of mad men," their other passenger gasped.

Ed glanced over at her and gave her a sympathetic smile. They had seen her car running on the side of the road, stuck in a snowbank, and Nikolai had pulled over. She was tall, had long blond hair and light blue eyes. She had been grateful for the rescue up until she had taken a look at the condition of the car and the mad gleam in Nikolai's eyes. The only reason she had gotten in was because her car was about to run out of gas, and she didn't want to freeze. She said her name was Star.

The speeding Mustang had developed a disturbing shimmy about an hour ago. It had progressed from minor to bone rattling, and Ed was as worried about that as he was the fact that Nikolai didn't actually know how to drive, yet they were speeding over a hundred miles an hour on ice covered closed roads, with him at the wheel.

He had done terrible things to the car before he had even picked up Ed and Allan. He'd crashed it several more times since, even with magic keeping it running. There were several guard rails between Colorado and Nebraska that had saved them from certain death. He'd cackled madly every time, clearly enjoying the shit out of himself.

Somehow, he had magicked the motor, and despite having run out of gas before they had even left the mountains, the car flew along the treacherous roads.

"Are we there yet?" Allan clutched the seatbelt he wore.

"Hopefully," Nikolai answered. "I am not sure how much longer until the wheels fall off."

Their passenger cried, "Wait, what?"

"Are you joking?" Ed asked.

"No."

Ed echoed the young woman's curses.

"If it's any consolation, at least it will be quick?" Ed tried to smile.

Star raised her eyebrows. "Thanks?"

"It is fine. I think this is where we're going." Nikolai slammed on the brakes and skidded sideways through their exit off of I-80.

Star screamed. The only reason Ed didn't was because she beat him to it.

"How do you even know?" Ed finally asked. He had no idea how Nikolai was navigating.

"Um, I can sense Sofia and Doc. You can't?"

"But, I mean…"

"Navigation spell."

"Your spell from the fourteen-hundreds works on our interstates?" Ed momentarily forgot that their passenger was only vaguely aware that they were alive because of magic. Nikolai didn't seem to care one way or the other.

"Yes, of course."

Ed shook his head. "Of course," he muttered.

Star stared at him, screamed again when the Mustang did a full spin, and started muttering some sort of prayer. Ed knew how she felt.

The shudder lessened as Nikolai allowed the car to slow on the way through a small town. He made several random turns, cursed a few times, and finally stopped the car.

Ed finally risked looking out of the car and was relieved to see Doc's pickup sitting parked next to several others.

Allan shoved the door on the Mustang open and leapt out of the passenger seat. Ed and Star were not far behind. All three barely kept from falling to the snow-covered ground.

Nikolai got out a little more slowly and gave the car a sad look. "Too bad."

Ed looked at the poor Mustang and winced. One of the wheels tilted out, and the car settled with a clunk.

"Maybe someday, when you actually know how to drive, you can get another one," Ed managed to say.

"Eh, I will steal another car from Alex. It is fun." Nikolai laughed and headed for the house.

Ed and the others scrambled after him. The snow had lessened, but it was still colder than shit outside, and the wind whipped around them. And he wanted to see Sofia.

Nikolai knocked just as a startled looking Doc opened the door.

"Doc!" Nikolai hugged him enthusiastically.

Ed followed them into the house, saw Sofia, and practically tackled her.

"Ed!" she squealed happily.

Allan and Nikolai both hugged her tightly. Then her eyebrows rose when she saw Star.

"Star?"

"You know these guys? They're insane. I thought I was going to die." She hugged Sofia almost as tightly as Ed had.

"They wouldn't hurt you."

"That one is insane then." She pointed to Nikolai.

Sofia's eyebrows rose higher. "Um, well, probably. What did he do?"

"Drove," Ed grumbled.

"Oh, boy…" Sofia laughed.

"We survived," Nikolai tried to sound offended. He failed.

The reunion had attracted attention. Several other people crowded into the entryway. Ed's hackles rose, and he and Allan both focused on one of the men. He was a werewolf. The werewolf stared at them, but wasn't outwardly hostile.

"I'm certainly happy to see you, but what are you all doing here?"

Ed reclaimed Sofia's hand. He didn't even care that she was only supposed to be dating Doc. He hadn't seen her in forever. They would just have to deal.

He noticed Sofia's dad gave him a hard look, but he pretended he didn't notice.

"Ah, yes. I have answer. We must go. Come on." Nikolai gestured to the door.

Sofia's hand tightened on Ed's, and her breath quickened in excitement.

"You can't leave. The roads are closed. Where would you go?" Beth, Sofia's mom asked. "How did you get here?"

"Uh, we drove." Nikolai glanced at Doc.

Doc shrugged.

"Sofia, would you like to introduce everyone to your friends?" Dan, Sofia's dad, demanded tightly.

"Uh, sure." She did a quick round of introductions. It turned out that Star was her best friend. Star, who was staring very closely at Sofia's eyes. If no one else had noticed the weirdness in Sofia's eyes, her best friend had. The werewolf was George.

"So, where is it you want to go?" Sofia's dad growled.

Nikolai narrowed his eyes at her dad. Ed grabbed the mage's arm to prevent him from whatever he was going to say. He failed.

"Oh, is that the racist?"

Sofia groaned.

Ed saw Doc's lips twitch, but he managed not to smile.

Everyone else's eyebrows went up.

"How exactly are you friends with a fucking communist?" Dan snapped.

Nikolai frowned and glanced at Sofia. "Communist? What is that?"

Everyone who didn't already know Nikolai stared at him, some of them open mouthed.

Sofia burst out laughing.

"It's a form of government, Nikolai. Let's go." She grabbed a coat and stomped into boots.

"Wait. You're Russian?" George walked forward, nostrils flared like he was taking in Nikolai's scent.

"Yes, of course. My accent is obvious."

"How do you not know what a fucking commie is?" George growled.

Nikolai glanced at Sofia, then shrugged. "I suppose it is a Russian thing, since you seem convinced I am one. I assure you, I am not."

"Well, you're not running off with Sofia."

"Stop me." Nikolai glared.

George took a swing at Nikolai before anyone could react. Fortunately, Nikolai was fast and skilled. He grabbed George's hand, twisted, and flipped the werewolf to the ground before landing hard on his chest with his knee.

That took the wind out of George, and he didn't immediately try to fight back.

"Tatar werewolves much tougher than Nebraska werewolves." Nikolai managed to sound disappointed as he stood up and stepped back to Doc's side.

George sprang to his feet and tried again. This time Doc caught his hand, stopping it cold as George tried to punch Nikolai.

The werewolf's nostrils flared, and he growled.

Doc growled back.

"Guys, let's not fight. I'm going with them. We'll come back. It'll be fine."

"Honey, the roads are closed."

"You know, it didn't seem to stop them from getting here. We're fine. There is a spell for that." She smiled, saying the last with a hint of an accent.

Doc still held George's hand in a grip that had to be grinding bones together.

George finally dropped his shoulders and backed off. Doc let go.

"I'm going with you!" Star blurted.

"Yes, yes, that is fine. Let's go. I would like to add that it's entirely possible we were followed. Stealing Alex's car was not subtle." Nikolai opened the door, letting in a blast of cold air.

"Wait, what?" Sofia's mom exclaimed.

"Eh, long story." Nikolai darted outside.

Ed traded a wide-eyed look with Allan, and they both bolted out of the house. Star was not far behind them.

"That one is a mage," Ed heard George say as the door was shutting. "I still don't know what Doc is, but he's definitely lying about being a mage."

Doc swore as the door shut, but there was nothing any of them could do about it.

"Nikolai, my truck hasn't been plugged in. I don't know if it will start."

Nikolai waved his hand dismissively.

"Do not blow up my truck!"

"Of course not. I practiced on the Andersons' vehicles. I will warm it up for you so your overly sensitive diesel engine can start." Nikolai laughed.

Doc sighed.

"I will be careful. I do not want to piss you off."

Doc just shook his head.

Ed's shoulder blades itched, and he looked behind him. George, Rick, and Dan stood just on this side of the door, glaring at everyone.

Shivering, he turned back to the others just in time to see Nikolai slap his hand down on the truck. Blue motes sank into the engine, and Doc groaned, but he climbed into the driver's seat, and the engine cranked right over.

Ed was impressed. Also, he was glad Nikolai hadn't destroyed Doc's truck. He loved that thing almost as much as he loved Sofia.

Everyone else piled into the truck. Allan took the front seat, and he, Nikolai, Sofia, and Star crammed into the back.

Doc whistled. "You really trashed Alex's car."

Nikolai chuckled. "I believe the phrase is 'sorry, not sorry'?"

"Okay, what the hell is going on?" Star blurted once Doc pulled away.

"More urgently, where are we going?" Doc interrupted.

"Someplace we can work spells uninterrupted. I probably need to rest after," Nikolai said.

"Hotel?" Allan offered.

"Yeah, maybe. Find something. Nikolai, please tell me you have a traction spell handy. The roads…"

"Yes, of course. Otherwise, we would have died."

Ed cried a little and clutched Sofia.

"Sofia!"

"Sorry, Star. It's…a long story. Basically, the Andersons got me all possessed by a demon. We're trying to get her out so she can go home and I can have my body back. Nikolai has apparently figured out how to do it, which is why he's here. And, so…they're going to save me before it's too late. It's not too late, is it?" She said the last kind of to herself, and Ed thought she was probably talking to the demon.

"What!" Star yelled.

Sofia, who was basically sprawled between Nikolai's lap and his, shrugged. They both held her tightly, and she sort of melted into them.

"Why didn't you tell me any of this?"

"How, exactly, could I have?"

"Um, I don't know. The words, hey, Star, all these guys—which one of them are you dating by the way? Because that's not as clear as it should be—are trying to protect me from getting turned into a demon. Who does that shit, anyway?"

"The Andersons," Nikolai supplied.

"What does that even mean?"

"Do you want a magical theory lesson? I could give one," Nikolai offered.

"No! I just want to know what's going on."

"We told you, Star." Sofia sighed.

"But it doesn't make any sense!"

"Ah, no!" Sofia bolted upright out of our arms and shuddered. "Humans and their touching. Yuck." She turned her attention to Star, eyes now fully amber.

"What the hell? Your eyes!"

"Yes, Sofia has been sharing space with me for a while now. Neither of us like it, and you're not making it any easier on her by not believing her." Sofia's body sagged, and she collapsed against Nikolai's chest.

Ed took a hold of her hands again, and Nikolai brushed her hair out of her face. After a few moments she blinked her eyes and shivered. "You can fix this, right?"

"Yes. I am as sure as can be without having done this before." Nikolai rested his cheek against her hair.

"I trust you."

Nikolai exhaled. "I know."

Ed squeezed her hand. "We all do," he added.

"Not helping," Nikolai muttered.

"What, our super powerful mage is having self-confidence issues?" Allan laughed, though it sounded forced.

"It is different."

"Nikolai," Doc practically caressed the mage's name with his voice. "You'll do just fine."

Ed thought Doc might have used his vampire powers, because even he felt better about the situation, and the comment hadn't been directed at him.

Nikolai didn't reply, but he had a small smile on his face when Ed glanced at him. Sofia was grinning, too.

Star didn't look convinced, but she stopped trying to get more information out of them.

"There's a hotel about five miles down the interstate."

"That's closed," Star grumbled.

"Traction spell," Nikolai declared and waved his hand around, and dark blue sparkles filled the air. "Also, some degree of invisibility. Don't get hit."

Doc sighed and took the onramp. "At least there isn't anyone else insane enough to be on the roads right now. Let's just hope the hotel has a room left."

Chapter 28

The Demon

She was beginning to enjoy the touching. It was high time to get out of this body. Giving Sofia control, even for the short time she had the last couple of days, was taking everything the demon had as far as self-control went. She wanted to push Sofia out. Instead, they were slowly melding together. Only the mage's promise had kept her from destroying Sofia already.

And now. Soon. She would be free.

She hoped.

The mage's lack of confidence wasn't that concerning. She felt he probably had the answer. She was more worried about being able to leave Sofia's body intact once the bindings were broken.

She would hate to repay the kindness shown by Sofia's men by destroying their woman. She hadn't initially cared. Now she did. Another sign that it was past time to get out of here. She had enjoyed watching Doc and Nikolai handle the werewolf, and it would be interesting to find out what the repercussions would be. That did not mean she was going to stick around and find out.

The demon tried not to enjoy the mage's touch as he caressed Sofia's shoulder and pressed his cheek into her hair. As much as he liked the vampire, he was completely in love with Sofia. Some of it might have been the magic, some of it might have been the connection they had forged, but most of it was simply that he loved her.

The demon worried most about Ed. He would be completely crushed if anything happened to Sofia. He had chosen her, and her death might literally kill him. He loved her as if she were life itself.

Allan was more reserved, but no less in love with her. A deep river with unexplored depths. She could sense the intensity of his emotion every time he looked at her, and it was frightening to the demon, who wasn't used to experiencing those emotions at all. Let alone from several people.

And then there was Doc. Doc who quietly risked everything and calmly tried to take care of everyone. Sometimes he still acted shocked that Sofia wanted him, but he wasn't about to give her up without a fight, even if it meant sacrificing himself instead. The demon hoped it never came to that. Doc was the glue that held that pack together, though Sofia was slowly beginning to fill that role as well.

And what to do about Ash? The other demon believed that Doc and Nikolai would free him. He had spent so much time with her in Sofia's body, that she worried he was starting to fall for Sofia, too. Would the others accept him if he did? What would he do if they didn't? The demon knew Sofia wasn't completely aware she had spent the last month or so sleeping near Ash. They had taken over Doc's bedroom, probably unfairly. Ash had told her he wished to return home, but he had been on this plane for so long, she did not think he would be able to manage it if freed.

The truck slowed, and the demon watched from Sofia's eyes as Doc got out to see if there were any rooms available. The blast of cold air made everyone shiver. No one spoke while Doc was away. His eyes glinted with amusement when he returned.

"Last room." Doc held up a key when he was back in the warm truck. He put it in gear and drove them around to the back side of the hotel. "I wouldn't expect anything fancy, but we will be warm. The clerk was very surprised to see me." He laughed tiredly.

Star groaned. "Why did I go with you all again? I should have stayed with my car."

"You would have frozen," Nikolai replied.

They got out when Doc parked and hurried to the room.

They all wrinkled their noses. The room was probably clean enough, but clearly at one point, it had been a smoking room.

Nikolai muttered and waved his hands. A spray of dark blue sparkles swept the room for a moment, and everyone sighed in relief. "Now it is very clean. You could eat off floor." He looked at the floor. "I wouldn't recommend it, though."

Sofia shuddered in disgust, and the demon echoed that sentiment.

"So, now what?" Star asked uneasily.

The room itself was a standard two bed hotel room with brown carpet, outdated furnishings, and a small bathroom in the back, from what the demon could establish from Sofia's memories.

"Now you sit over there." Nikolai pointed to a chair. "You two keep an eye on things," he pointed at the werewolves, "and I will release a demon." Nikolai rubbed his hands together and managed to look confident and nervous at the same time.

"Seriously?" Star crossed her arms and glared.

Nikolai shook his head and gestured. Sofia's friend yelped as she slid backward into the chair and ropes appeared from nowhere to tie her down. "Just stop distracting me."

The demon noted he also cast a shield around their room, probably to block sound. He claimed he was used to using a lot of magic, but he had likely used a large amount on the way down from Colorado, and she hoped he wasn't wearing himself out before tackling the spell to release her.

"Doc," Nikolai said. "I need access to the demon's magic."

The demon wondered at Sofia's alarm, and a moment later, the memory surfaced of what demon blood had done to the vampire last time he'd tasted it. That also explained why Nikolai was willing to use so much magic. He expected to get a large boost from hers, and he didn't know what her blood would do to Doc.

The vampire didn't hesitate, just held out his hand to Sofia.

She put her hand in his and stepped closer.

"Doc," she whispered.

"Only way," he replied. "I'll be okay."

Sofia tilted her neck back, and the vampire lowered his lips to her neck.

The demon winced as his fangs pierced Sofia's neck, expecting pain. The pleasure that had Sofia moaning and clutching at the vampire nearly caused the demon to forget herself. She almost let herself merge with Sofia, only managing to stop herself at the last minute. The wave of pleasure drowned out Star freaking out in the background.

Sofia staggered back, a smile on her face, breathing heavy, and sat down on the edge of the bed.

Doc's eyes glowed golden, and he quickly removed one of the reservoir bracelets he wore and bit into his own wrist before offering it to Nikolai.

The mage twisted his lips, and the demon got the idea that, while he obviously enjoyed sharing his blood with the vampire, he didn't particularly enjoy drinking it. Even from a vampire.

"Are you okay?" Nikolai asked as he took the vampire's arm.

"Demon blood and I don't get along particularly well," Doc replied through clenched teeth.

"Oh." Nikolai pressed his mouth to Doc's arm. He groaned as her power hit him. She could tell he took as much as he could, but she was powerful, and it wasn't enough to save Doc from the affects.

The vampire collapsed when Nikolai released him.

"Doc!" Nikolai knelt by his friend. Ed and Allan hurried to his side. Star had fallen silent.

"He's not breathing." Ed put his hand on Doc's forehead. "And he's burning up. Sofia saved him last time he did this. I don't think you took enough magic, Nikolai."

"Took as much as I could." Nikolai clutched at the unconscious vampire.

The demon forced Sofia out of the way, taking control of her body "If you hurry, I can help him," she said. It was the least she could do if they set her free. She could feel the vampire's life force being overwhelmed by powers he was never meant to taste.

Nikolai tore himself away from Doc and stood. "Lie down. And stay in control. I need Sofia to bury herself again. Same as before, cling to the pack bond."

Did you get that?

Yes. I hope this works. Sofia tucked herself away, and the demon did the best she could to separate herself from her host's mind.

"We're ready," she said to the mage.

She watched as he wove the spell, her magic and his combining into a golden and blue lightshow, with hints of lavender from Sofia's magic. He muttered in Russian as he skillfully twisted the net of magic into a complicated pattern.

For as difficult as the magic was, Nikolai had the shape completed fairly quickly. He truly was as talented as he claimed, and the demon was impressed.

"Ready?"

She nodded.

Nikolai pushed the spell into the golden cuffs that bound her.

They flared with magic as the spell tried to reject Nikolai's, but his was stronger, and after a moment, they melted away.

The demon winced. That would leave a scar, but better than the alternative.

Freedom tugged at her, and she nearly bolted from this plane, but she had promised to save Doc. Of course, if she did magic in this body, it could destroy Sofia. She couldn't sense the girl at all but also knew that Sofia would choose to help her vampire even with the risk. He would die without her help.

She got off the bed and pulled on her magic. It filled her, burning pathways that had, until recently, barely been used, stretching them, altering them. It felt so good to be reconnected with something that was normally so intrinsically a part of her.

The werewolves had put the vampire on the other bed. She went over to him, put her hands on his chest, and pulled the rest of her magic out of him. His natural healing ability would take over from there. He would have to do this again for Ash. She knew he would, even though it could cost him his life.

"What are you doing?" Nikolai asked. He watched her shape another spell.

"He needs to be able to handle demon blood if he's going to save Ash. I'm making it so that it won't kill him. He will still have an instant hangover from hell, but otherwise, he won't suffer like he does now."

"Quite considerate of you."

"Don't thank me until you get Sofia back. Doing magic in her body may have destroyed her."

"She would have wanted you to save him," Nikolai stated quietly.

"Yes. I know. There. Tell him when he wakes. I'll leave now. Do me one last favor? Make the Andersons pay for this."

"I will," Nikolai replied, his face grim.

In consideration for Sofia's body. She laid down on the bed next to the vampire before she pulled herself out of her host and departed this plane.

Chapter 29

Ed

"Is she gone?"

"The demon is gone. Sofia is not breathing," Nikolai choked out.

Ed and Allan scrambled to Nikolai's side. Ed put his hand on Sofia's throat and couldn't find a pulse. He couldn't hear her heart, either.

"Damn it!" Ed put his hands on Sofia's chest and started pumping, trying to get her heart going again. Tears streamed down his cheeks. He couldn't lose her now. They were so close.

Doc groaned and rolled over, staggering to his feet and leaning against the wall. He clutched his head. "What's wrong?" He managed to get out.

"Sofia's not breathing," Star shrieked from her chair in the corner.

"Shit." Doc staggered over to Sofia's side.

"Nikolai, can you, like, shock her heart or something? See if you can get it started. It's something they do now with a medical tool, but we don't have one of those," Allan demanded while Ed worked.

"Maybe." Nikolai gestured at Ed. "Move."

Ed leaned back, and Nikolai placed his hands over her chest. Magic crackled around his hands and sank into her chest.

Her back arched, but otherwise, her heart stayed silent.

"Doc," Nikolai said desperately. "I might need you."

Doc had already opened his wrist again and poured some of his blood into Sofia's mouth. Ed rubbed her throat to help her swallow and went back to chest compressions.

"Try again," Allan ordered.

Nikolai nodded and sent his power into her chest.

Nothing.

Ed went back to compressions, trying not to press so hard that he broke bones in the process. Tears blurred his vision, but he couldn't wipe them away. She had to come back.

"One more time," Allan ordered.

Ed leaned back, and let Nikolai do his magic.

This time, it worked. Sofia's heart jolted to life, and she gasped, taking a breath. Her eyes snapped open, but even he could tell she wasn't actually conscious. Maybe it was the pack bond telling him that.

Her eyes fluttered shut again, but at least she was breathing.

He stared at Nikolai, willing him to give him good news. The mage simply looked exhausted.

He wilted. "I think it is best we let her rest. See if we can reach her as we did while she was imprisoned. Convince her it's safe to come out of hiding."

"We'll take turns," Ed suggested after a moment. He was emotionally exhausted, but not tired enough to sleep. "Allan and I can keep watch. You two get some rest and see if you can reach Sofia. I can smell how exhausted you are."

Nikolai collapsed into bed next to Sofia, and Doc squeezed in on the other side.

"Hey, mage, before you pass out…I need to pee."

Nikolai glanced at Star, rolled his eyes, and waved his hand. The ropes binding her to the chair vanished. He was asleep before his hand dropped back to his side. Doc was already out.

She got up from the chair, glaring at all of them, and headed to the bathroom.

Ed, not wanting to deal with anything else dramatic for a while, stopped her. "Phone."

"What?"

"Give me your phone."

She glared but handed it over. "Don't trust me?"

"Right now, no."

"Right. Feeling's mutual."

Allan sighed and pulled a chair over in front of the door so he could guard it and keep an eye on everyone in the room.

Ed sank down onto the other bed and prayed to whoever might be listening that Sofia wasn't lost to them.

∞ ∞ ∞

She still hadn't stirred a few hours later when Doc woke. He glanced at the clock. It was the middle of the night.

Nikolai was still out cold, and Ed's eyes drooped. Star had passed out in the other bed. Allan still kept watch at the door.

Doc gestured for Ed to take his place.

"Are you okay?" Ed asked quietly.

Doc nodded. "Heal fast."

Ed lay down next to Sofia and curled up around her. Allan squeezed in on the other side of Nikolai, and though the four of them didn't really fit, they made it work. The mage rolled over in his sleep and rested his head on Allan's chest, his back pressed firmly to Sofia.

He glanced at Allan, who looked surprised, but then shrugged and put his arms around Nikolai.

Ed winked at Allan. Allan blushed.

Sofia still breathed quietly, but otherwise, he really didn't feel like her body was doing anything but existing.

He tightened his arms around her and tried to sink into their pack bond. He'd become quite practiced at it over the last couple of months, but this time, he couldn't get through. It was as if some invisible barrier kept him out. Maybe that was a good thing? Maybe Sofia was protecting herself? Whatever was going on, he knew he needed to reach her.

He could sense Allan and tugged on their connection until he attracted his brother's attention. Allan joined him in whatever nebulous way that made sense in their pack bond.

They pressed up against the barrier and pushed their awareness against it, looking for Sofia.

Nothing.

I think we need everyone, Ed conveyed to Allan.

Allan's presence didn't so much fade as change when he pulled himself back to consciousness. Ed kept himself pressed against Sofia's mind. After a few moments, Nikolai, Allan, and then finally Doc, joined him. Doc's presence was a little more distant, as if he were still conscious but he was with them all the same.

They needed to draw her back like she had for him. If she was there at all.

He shied away from that thought.

Nikolai drew them all together, seeming to know what to do. If anyone would know, it was him.

Ed let himself be guided as Nikolai pressed them all against the barrier and then they took their love for her and used it to try and find their connection to Sofia.

Nothing.

Even semi-conscious like he was right now, Ed's chest constricted. His cheeks were wet. He needed Sofia. They all did. She couldn't leave them. Not like this. If she ever decided to walk away, that would be one thing. It wouldn't feel good, but it wouldn't kill him like this was. She was theirs. She wanted to be theirs. Damn the Andersons for taking her away from him.

They all tried again.

Ed didn't sense anything, but Nikolai perked up through their connection.

Sofia, come back to us, they sent.

Slowly, the barrier that kept them out of her mind softened. After a short time, it faded enough that they were able to slip in. Nikolai held them back for a moment, cautioned that they may not be able to get out if they couldn't actually reach Sofia, and then when all agreed it was worth the risk, pushed through the barrier.

Sofia?

Ed wasn't sure how long it took, but a small eternity later, they got the tiniest bit of a response. All of them followed that response to find Sofia's essence curled into a tight ball, buried in the shambles of her mental image of her magical grove. The trees were next to dead, the ground bare, and Sofia was nearly translucent.

Sofia! Ed raced to her side and put his hands on her shoulders. They sunk in. She wasn't even solid.

Allan joined him, and then the other two, and they poured energy into Sofia. They had to bring her back.

Slowly, she solidified.

Slowly now, Nikolai cautioned. *Don't kill yourself in the process.*

Silently, Ed thought it would be worth it, but he also didn't want Sofia to have to deal with that, either. Still, the energy they did give her was enough. Though she didn't wake, this time, he felt like she would.

Nikolai agreed, because he drew them out of her mind. Fortunately, the barrier recognized them this time, and let them out.

Ed fell back into his own body and drifted off into the first real sleep he'd had in months.

Chapter 30

Sofia

I blinked sand out of my eyes and tried to get them to focus. A heavy weight across my chest restricted my breathing, and I forced my eyes into focus. Ed's arm wrapped tight around me, pressing my back into his chest.

Nikolai lay against my other side. Was this the first time I had woken up with him?

I twined one of my legs around Ed's and took the hand I wasn't laying on and ran it across the mage's back.

Ed's arm tightened around me possessively. "Sofia?"

"In the flesh," I said. "Finally."

He buried his face in my neck. My ribs creaked as he tightened his arm around me. I didn't complain.

Nikolai sucked in a breath and rolled over, crushing me in a hug. I hadn't noticed Allan on the other side of him, but he blinked his eyes open and wrapped his arm around me, squishing Nikolai between us.

"It worked," I finally managed to get out.

"Yeah, you definitely almost died," Star grumbled from somewhere else in the room.

"But I didn't."

The guys reluctantly let me extract myself from their embrace and I sat up, looking for Doc.

Doc sat in a chair he had leaned back on two legs against the door. His lips curled into a tired smile when I met his gaze.

After I checked in with him, I glanced over at Star. She sat in the other bed, arms crossed and an angry scowl on her face. She alternated glaring at Doc, a hint of fear in her eyes, and glaring at me.

Whatever was bothering her, and I could think of a number of things that might be, we would figure it out. I was just so happy to be back in control that I couldn't help the large smile that split my face.

"Demons," she grumbled. "Werewolves, vampires, mages…you just went and found yourself one of everything, didn't you?"

"I, uh…" I glanced back to Doc.

He nodded, so I figured he'd done something that let her know what he was.

"Yeah, I guess."

Star shook her head. "I can't decide if I'm more pissed that you didn't tell me, or that you almost got killed."

"I didn't want to talk to you about it over the phone." I flopped back onto the bed, and the guys curled around me again, Ed pressing into my back and Nikolai pulling me against his chest. Our legs tangled, and Allan reached back around Nikolai and held me, as well. "What time is it, anyway? Or maybe I should ask what day?"

"It's Thanksgiving," Star answered. "And it's still pretty early in the morning. Your parents are probably freaking out. Maybe we could get back and reassure them that you aren't kidnapped and dead?"

I groaned. Dealing with my parents wasn't high on my priority list. I had been in control of my body when Nikolai had shown up with Star and my werewolves, but my memories of the last few days were pretty sketchy. I seemed to recall someone calling him a communist and him throwing George on the ground.

"Do you want to text them?"

"Why don't you text them?"

"I think my phone is back at the house."

"What do you want me to tell them? And you'll have to tell your boyfriends to give me my phone back." She did not sound happy.

Allan sat up and returned her phone. He didn't apologize, and I didn't expect him to. There was enough to worry about without Star making awkward phone calls.

She started texting. "So, you're all right now?"

"Yes." I tried to get up, but Nikolai and Ed refused to let me move, holding me sandwiched between them.

"They want to know when we'll be back."

"Guys?"

"We can head back any time you want," Doc answered. "As long as Nikolai is recovered enough to cast some magic."

"Yes. I should be fine."

"Couple of hours then," Doc answered.

"Great," Star muttered.

"Can that couple of hours include getting some food?" Ed's stomach growled.

I laughed.

"Yes, please," Allan whined plaintively.

"There will be plenty to eat at dinner," Star replied.

"We'll have plenty of room for more," Allan explained. "We eat a lot."

"Why don't we go out and see if we can find anything open. Sofia and Star probably need a minute to catch up." Doc stood and shoved the chair back against the wall.

The guys let go of me this time when I tried to get up, and I scrambled off the bed. Doc caught me in a hug before I could move more than a few steps toward him. I breathed in his clean leather scent and held him tight. After a minute, he released me and herded the others out of the room.

Their absence left me hollow, and I had to reach for the pack bond to avoid running after them. I did not want to be alone, and while I loved Star as a sister, she was not one of my guys. Maybe I should have asked one of them to stay.

"So…" Star prompted.

"What don't you know?"

"Why don't you start with how you're dating a vampire and he hasn't killed you. And then you can start at the beginning and fill me in." She turned to face me.

I sank down onto the edge of the other bed and sighed. "He's like, half vampire."

"Still drinks blood."

"Well, yeah."

"And vampires don't like humans as a general rule, except to eat them. Or so everyone's been told."

"Uh, well, Doc isn't really like that. He doesn't exactly want people to know what he is, if he can avoid it. Nikolai has known quite a few from his time that weren't anything like what people tell us vampires are now."

"No shit? I think you might have some competition from your Russian, though. He seems *very* fond of your fangy boyfriend."

I couldn't read Star's expression, so I shrugged. "Yeah, him and Allan. No competition. I can share with them. I mean, they're sharing me. Seems fair. I kind of like it." I stared at my knees, blushing, not sure what she would think of me after that admission.

When she didn't answer, I looked up and still couldn't read her expression.

"I'm waiting for the rest of your story."

Wow, she really was pissed. I didn't have the energy to respond with any emotion so I just flopped back on the bed and told her as much as I could about the last couple of months.

"Yeah," she said when I was done. "You probably shouldn't have told me that over the phone."

I stared at the ceiling.

"If I had known even half of that, I would have been on an airplane to Denver."

"I wouldn't want you in danger."

"Well, if you don't stay here, you're going to be back in danger pretty quick."

"Actually." I held up my hands and called my magic. The energy burned through me, more powerful than I had ever experienced. "I think it's the Andersons who are in over their head."

Star stared at the swirl of lavender motes that circled my hand.

"The demon, well, she stretched my abilities to the point where I think I can use magic like I've been practicing my whole life now. She also left me with a bunch of knowledge. I don't even know what all I know now."

"She did something to your vampire. Saved him or something."

I thought for a minute and managed to call up the memory. "Doc can't really deal with demon blood. Or, well, he couldn't. I think she fixed that."

"He was willing to die to save you?"

"Yeah, I guess so."

"How do you manage to find four great guys, even if they aren't human, or even from our time, and I can't find anything but a lame ass beach bum."

"You still dating the lame ass?"

"No."

"Well, that's good at least."

She sighed. "Yeah. I guess. So…" Her eyes glinted. "How'd your dad take you dating more than one guy?"

"Oh, I didn't mention that, he totally doesn't know. Well, I mean, he didn't. I'm not sure what they think now. I don't exactly remember everything."

"Well, he really didn't like Nikolai being Russian. Wait, which one does he think you're dating?"

"Doc. Like I told you over the phone."

"Oh, how'd he take that? He's kind of…intolerant, if you had never noticed."

"I hadn't actually noticed until recently." I sighed. "And he freaked out about it a little. I told him off, and he's mostly behaving now. Well, he was anyway."

Star giggled. "Well, they're all hot. And werewolves? What's that like?"

"Big dogs with no sense of personal space. They're great." I heard the diesel engine pull up outside our room, and I glanced toward the door, grinning.

"Back, huh?"

"How could you tell?"

"Your face just lit up like it was Christmas." She smiled.

I got up and peaked out the spy hole in the door before opening it. I knew it was them, but even so, I wasn't about to open the door without checking.

Ed came in first, grabbed me around the waist and spun me around, before sitting on the end of the bed and pulling me onto his lap. I cuddled against him while the others hurried in out of the cold.

"Nothing fancy, but the store was open," Allan said. "We got some toothpaste, too."

Doc sat down next to Ed and put his arm around me so that I was pressed against both of them.

Allan and Nikolai sorted through the bags and got out stuff for sandwiches. "Who's hungry?" Allan glanced at us.

"Everyone." Ed laughed.

Star nodded. I wasn't hungry, but I probably would be once I actually put something in my mouth.

Doc squeezed my shoulder and got up. He headed for the bathroom, pulling off his shirt as he went. Pretty sure my heart skipped a couple of beats, and I didn't hide that I stared.

Of course, Nikolai and Allan stared, too. I caught them looking when I finally wrenched my gaze away. They quickly went back to making sandwiches for everyone, and we all stuffed our faces and took turns in the bathroom. While none of us had clean clothing, showering and brushing my teeth felt amazing.

Once we had all cycled through the shower and the werewolves had stuffed their faces, we piled back into Doc's truck and headed back to my house.

I couldn't hide how nervous I was. I sat on Allan's lap this time, and Nikolai had claimed my legs. Everyone, maybe even Star, could hear my heart thudding in my chest.

We hadn't discussed what to tell anyone, and I didn't know what to do. Facing my parents scared me more than facing the Andersons. At least I knew what to do about them. I rubbed at my wrists. The bindings had left scars around my wrists, except where my magical tattoo had protected my skin. They weren't bad, but the texture threw me off every time I touched it. The guys either hadn't noticed yet or had decided not to say anything until I did.

All too soon, we pulled into the parking area at my parents' house. We all hesitated, partially not wanting to leave the warm truck and partially not wanting to deal with my parents. The storm had calmed, but it was cold enough that breathing the air hurt.

"Well, I guess if it really comes down to it, I can practice my rusty mind control on everyone and make them forget it all happened." Doc sounded resigned.

"Will that work on werewolves?" Nikolai asked.

"Yeah."

"Nikolai, I'm pretty sure you actually know more about vampires than I do, and I am one. Kind of. How could you not know that?"

"Eh, usually we kill the werewolves. There is no need for mind control on dead wolves. I am not sure it ever came up."

"Ah."

"On that completely disturbing note, I'm going in the house." Star got out of the truck, and the rest of us reluctantly followed.

We all piled into the house. Mom surprised me with a tight hug before she surprised me even more by hugging Nikolai.

I glanced at Star. "You told her, didn't you?"

She nodded, not looking at all apologetic. Made my life easier, so I wasn't going to be mad about it.

Nikolai hugged my mom back and held her while she sobbed. He shot a desperate look at Doc, who shrugged, clearly not sure what to do, either. After a minute, she got a hold of herself and hugged Doc.

"Thank you both for saving her," Mom got out around her tears.

Star showed me her phone. The text she had sent stuck with our story that Doc was a mage.

I was grateful that Mom didn't even bother to ask why we hadn't told her.

Dad and the others stared at everyone, a little wide-eyed. Except George, who was glaring at Doc. His expression told me he really wanted to have it out with Doc and find out what he really was. That did not need to happen. I wracked my brain for some idea of what I might be able to do with my new powers should he try and start something. Doc could hold his own, but it would be better if I distracted George from a fight.

I glanced at Doc, who had noticed George's interest. No one else paid any attention to them for the moment, maybe Doc's doing. He straightened his posture, and his eyes darkened. He curled his lip just enough to flash fang and growled almost sub-audibly. The werewolves would be able to hear, and my senses were still tuned up from the demon's presence, so I also heard.

George's eyes widened, and he blanched sheet white. I thought he was going to wet his pants. He dropped his gaze and hunched his shoulders, immediately completely submissive.

I looked back at Doc, who continued to glare at George until the werewolf shifted his stance and bared his throat. I really hoped that was the last of George's issues with Doc. I also really hoped he didn't say anything to my dad.

Doc looked away, completely ignoring George after that. At least outwardly. I doubted he actually took his attention away from the werewolf.

Ed and Allan traded wide-eyed glances with each other. I guessed they probably weren't used to Doc behaving like that.

I had lost track of everyone else, but Bobby ran into the room and threw his arms around Doc's waist, hiding behind him. Matt and Eric followed after, though they slowed when they saw everyone else in the room.

George gauged Doc's reaction to the kid's attention, but all Doc did was put his hand on Bobby's shoulder and ask him what was wrong.

The kid shook his head, though tears streaked his face.

George sighed, grabbed both Matt and Eric by their arms, and dragged them back to their room. He wasn't their parent, but I suspected he was going to have a discussion with them they wouldn't forget any time soon.

"We have enough food for everyone. We hope you'll stay for dinner," Mom babbled, not completely oblivious to George's actions, but ignoring them for now.

Rick and Donna shared a worried look before they apparently decided that the kids deserved whatever George dished out and instead went to rescue Doc from Bobby.

Dad hadn't said much in the chaos, and I hoped it stayed that way.

∞ ∞ ∞

They had enough food for everyone, but for once, they wouldn't have weeks of leftovers.

Nikolai's presence diverted most of the attention from Doc, especially once he finally just told everyone that there was no way he could be this communist thing since it hadn't even been invented when he had been born. He managed to weave a story that somehow made it seem like he had known Doc for quite some time, and also made it clear that he was just catching up on current events.

Then he regaled everyone with war stories for several hours.

I sat in the armchair, in Doc's lap, and listened to him talk. Ed and Allan both sat on the floor, touching my legs with their backs.

"If we're going to leave tonight, we should probably get going," Doc interrupted one of Nikolai's stories.

"Tonight? It's already late," Mom protested.

"We need to get back," Doc said tiredly.

"You sound tired. Are you sure you can drive safely?" Dad asked.

"Yeah, I'll be fine."

"I will keep him awake," Nikolai insisted. "He hasn't heard all of my stories yet."

"Honey, be careful. Those Andersons…"

Nikolai waved his hand dismissively. "Will not know what hit them."

"Be careful, Sofia." Mom hugged me tightly.

"Yeah, I don't think they can hurt me now. I know all sorts of interesting things."

"There are ways to hurt people that don't involve actually hurting you physically. Be careful," she cautioned again.

"Thanks, Mom."

I hugged Dad and then Star.

"You be careful." She shook a finger at me. "Call me."

"I will. You, too. I hope they can get your car out soon."

"Yeah, I need to actually see my parents." She laughed. "The car is a rental, though, so I'm not as worried about it. I didn't drive all the way from Florida. Just from the airport."

I hugged her again. "I'll see you soon."

"Yeah, maybe I'll visit for Christmas."

I beamed. "I'd like that."

We said goodbye to the others and headed out into the cold evening.

"So, did you figure out what he is?" I overheard Dad asking George.

"Yeah…" George hesitated.

I stopped and glanced at Doc. He was listening through the closed door also. Having super hearing was weird, but it didn't seem to be fading.

"Definitely a mage. Not sure why he smells different than the other one, but he's a mage."

We both sighed in relief and headed for the truck. I didn't hear what my dad replied, if anything.

Everyone piled into the truck. Doc driving, as always, and Nikolai in the passenger seat. I crawled into the back with Ed and Allan, and we headed home.

I couldn't wait to get back so we could all snuggle in Doc's large bed. I wanted to see the snow covering the pine trees of my grove, and maybe, just maybe, I would actually get a chance to run with Ed and Allan as a wolf, like they had asked me to a lifetime ago. I had no idea what the future would bring, but with my new knowledge, I felt like I could handle anything the Andersons threw at us.

Above all else, I was glad to be surrounded by my pack. Safe and loved.

Author's Note

Thank you so much for reading my reverse harem tale! More is coming soon! Reviews are so very important, especially to new authors and are greatly appreciated! Even a line or two will do!

About the Author

Dakota has two passions in life: writing and cinnamon tea. Tea so strong she ought to be able to see her future when she drinks it, and the writing? Well she hopes it makes you see stars when you read it. She creates reverse harem romance novels filled with things that go bump in the night. That handsome werewolf walking down the street? The suave vampire you're just dying to get a taste of? You'll find them enraptured by charming, smart ladies ready to make those bad boys work for their affection. When not writing, Dakota can be found on the back of a horse out on the trail or tending the animals on her farm.

Other Works

Mountain Magic Trilogy

Becoming
Demon's Touch
Reckoning- July 2020

Made in the USA
Middletown, DE
05 December 2023